CLOSER THAN CLOSE

Her breath caught in her throat when he moved toward her, and her lips inadvertently parted. Their mouths came together hungrily, his large hand and outstretched fingers cupping her throat, chin, and jaw, for the dual purpose of holding her face in position and concealing the intimacy of their open mouths from the taxi driver's view. She gripped his muscular upper arm and held on, wanting their kiss to go on and on, and she knew she would savor it long after. She couldn't remember the last time she had kissed and been kissed with such fervor, such naked passion. Mitch's kisses told her he was looking for a lover who could also sit with his children when needed; Ray's said he wanted her heart.

When they broke apart she was shocked to see they were just one block from her loft. Kissing Ray had made everything come to a standstill in her mind, but now she saw the world had continued to move around them.

"I've been wanting to do that for a long time," he said quietly. "You could probably tell."

BOOK YOUR PLACE ON OUR WEBSITE AND MAKE THE ARABESQUE ROMANCE CONNECTION!

We've created a customized website just for our very special Arabesque readers, where you can get the inside scoop on everything that's going on with Arabesque romance novels.

When you come online, you'll have the exciting opportunity to:

- View covers of upcoming books

- Learn about our future publishing schedule (listed by publication month and author)

- Find out when your favorite authors will be visiting a city near you

- Search for and order backlist books

- Check out author bios and background information

- Send e-mail to your favorite authors

- Join us in weekly chats with authors, readers and other guests

- Get writing guidelines

- AND MUCH MORE!

Visit our website at
http://www.arabesquebooks.com

CLOSER THAN CLOSE

Bettye Griffin

BET Publications, LLC
http://www.bet.com
http://www.arabesquebooks.com

ARABESQUE BOOKS are published by

BET Publications, LLC
c/o BET BOOKS
One BET Plaza
1900 W Place NE
Washington, DC 20018-1211

All Kensington Titles, Imprints, and Distributed Lines are available at special quantity discounts for bulk purchases for sales promotions, premiums, fund-raising, and educational or institutional use. Special book excerpts or customized printings can also be created to fit specific needs. For details, write or phone the office of the Kensington special sales manager: Kensington Publishing Corp., 850 Third Avenue, New York, NY 10022, attn: Special Sales Department, Phone: 1-800-221-2647.

First Printing: January 2003
10 9 8 7 6 5 4 3 2 1

Printed in the United States of America

For Chester E. Morris, Sr.

ACKNOWLEDGMENTS

My sincere appreciation to The Bard Group; aNN Brown ("Sis"); Eugenia McDaniel Brown; Cheryl McFadden Charles; Cheryl Ferguson; Felice Franklin; Jackie Hamilton; Sharon McDaniel Hollis; Maureen King; Marcia King-Gamble; Beverly Griffin Love; Toni Bonita Robinson; Elaine Thomas of the Delta Sigma Theta Sorority, Palm Coast/Flagler County Alumni Chapter; Kimberly Rowe-Van Allen; and Cynthia White.

A special thank-you to Dawn Henderson Stewart for long-term friendship and invaluable assistance.

And, as always, to my husband, Bernard Underwood, who never complains when I'm sitting in front of the computer instead of cooking dinner; and to Mom, Mrs. Eva Mae "Bettye" Griffin, who in her own special way tells me how proud she is while simultaneously cautioning me to make sure people don't think it's *she* who's writing these books!

And to my brother Gordon, I know you actually left us in 1986, not in 2001, an error I unfortunately did not catch before publication of my last book, FROM THIS DAY FORWARD. I can just hear you saying, "You peasant!" but hey, it's the thought that counts.

Prologue

"Reports of My Demise Have Been Greatly Exaggerated"

Ivy Smith stood at the oversize windows in her living room. The view of West Twenty-eighth Street from her third-floor loft was a colorless tableau of beige and gray. The winter solstice had slipped in while everyone was busy getting ready for Christmas. The gaiety of the holiday season helped conceal the fact that there weren't any leaves on the trees, that the sky was shrouded in darkness more than half the day, and that it was frigid out. But now, three weeks into the new year, all the decorations and bright lights had been taken down, leaving the ugliness of winter in New York unadorned. The dismal scene made her wish she could throw some shorts and swimsuits in a bag, flag down a cab, and get on the first plane headed for Florida or the Caribbean. Unfortunately, her work didn't allow for impulse travel, even if her budget did.

She turned away and stretched her whole body, even parting her fingers and bare toes. She felt restless, not wanting to do a doggone thing, and she didn't have to, for there wasn't a lot that needed doing. January was traditionally a slow period in her line of work, and the loft was clean. The hardwood floors in the living room and dining area had become rather dull and scuffed from dozens of walking and dancing feet at her annual New Year's Day open house, but tackling that job was more than she cared to do at the moment.

Ivy sat at her desk and turned on her computer. Surfing the Net was more in line with what she had in mind. It took little effort to rotate a trackball, even less than it took to steer a traditional mouse.

When the welcome screen came on it featured an ad for a Web site that allowed its visitors to catch up with high school classmates. Ivy wrinkled her nose. Last June marked twenty years since she'd graduated, and she hadn't seen anyone from school in all that time, nor had she thought of any of them.

Still, it might be fun to see if anyone she knew had posted. She clicked on the link and eventually was forwarded to her old school in Lakewood, New Jersey. Less than half of those from her graduating class had found the site, but there were dozens of posts to read. She went into each folder and read them all, and in the process learned that a surprising number of her fellow graduates still lived in different areas of the state. Her class was holding a reunion in March, a formal affair at the Hilton in New York.

But the twentieth anniversary of graduation was *last* year. Ivy looked askance at the screen. People were supposed to send money to someone who couldn't get the right sum when adding twenty? Hmph. Not her.

Then, reading the details, she learned the function had originally been planned for the previous Thanksgiving weekend, but the organizer's son was struck by a car, and he put the plans aside. According to the update, the little boy had made a full recovery. Thank heaven for that, but now she felt guilty for her earlier thought. Perhaps all the years living in New York had made her jaded.

Hmmm, maybe she'd go after all. It might be fun to learn what her former classmates had been up to, and how they had fared.

She scanned the screen. People had posted update information, as well as reminiscences about favorite teachers, the big football game, and the prom. But it was another section that caught Ivy's eye.

She held her breath as she entered the folder called Classmates Who've Passed On. It was unlikely that twenty years could pass without at least one member of a graduating class meeting an early death, but the thought of it made her nervous. She knew Evette Smith was dead; she remembered her mother telling her about the crash on the Garden State Parkway. Maybe she'd be the only one.

But she wasn't. Liza Giacomo was also listed. But Liza had been diagnosed with leukemia while still in high school, so that wasn't really a surprise. Billy Howard was there, too. The story was that he was run over in Atlantic City while fleeing the scene of a robbery. Ivy rolled her eyes. That wasn't a surprise, either; Billy had been left back so many times that he sported a beard by ninth grade. He was hardly a candidate for greatness.

Still, three out of their class wasn't bad. She glimpsed at Evette's name, and when her eyes focused on the letters her mouth dropped open in disbelief. It didn't say *Evette* Smith, it said *Ivy* Smith. That was crazy. *She* was Ivy Smith, and she was alive, well, and living in Manhattan. Quickly she clicked to read the postings.

Cecily Thomas had made the first post. *That figures. I never could stand that hairy little witch.* "Ivy Smith was killed in a high-speed crash on the Garden State five or six years ago," Cecily had written.

Oh, fine. Cecily had gotten her confused with Evette. That was spooky, but maybe somebody had corrected her in a subsequent posting. All through school people always got Ivy and Evette confused because their names were so similar.

But what followed was a list of tributes from class-mates. It was like being the proverbial fly on the wall at her own home-going services. "That's really bad news. I always liked Ivy." "Oh, I'm so sorry to hear that." "She was such a nice girl."

She held her fingers poised over the keyboard, ready to declare that they'd all made a terrible mistake, but her fingers immobilized in position as she had second thoughts. Maybe it would be better if she kept quiet. The reunion was less than two months away. She'd attend and freak everybody out. With the social slump she was in, returning from the dead might be the most fun she'd have all year.

As it was she'd probably have to have her fun by herself. Not only was she not seeing anyone, she hadn't even met anyone lately, not even at her annual open house. Each year she combined resources with her good friend Bethany Willis and a few others to host the event, and they all invited the most interesting people they knew to guarantee new faces. Usually a casual conversa-tion with a new man would lead to an exchange of telephone numbers and a few dates, but as the degree of her business success sank in most of the men began to feel inadequate and stopped calling.

Not that it mattered much. The newness of her rela-tionships usually faded by mid-February, and the reunion was a month after that. It would be better if she could bring a date, but she'd go alone. Men were never around when she needed one, but she was used to it.

She was tired of it, too. Her lower lip poked out in defiance. She was going to show up at that reunion not only looking fabulous herself, but with a to-die-for escort.

Even if she had to kidnap or rent one.

Chapter 1
Number, Please

Ivy thanked the mailman after they did a trade: She gave him her outgoing mail, and he handed her the day's delivery. Jubilee, Inc., the business she founded eight years ago, had grown to five full-time employees, including herself. They operated from her loft, and because her personal mail was delivered along with the business mail, she preferred to collect it herself.

From the very beginning it was apparent that she needed a staff to handle the restaurant consulting and employee training that had been Jubilee's original focus. After two years she began event planning. It was the latter that really made them a major player in the busy New York social scene, creating parties ranging from the simple to the lavish for some of the best-known companies and biggest names in the city.

She scanned the mail. The distinct heavy block letters of the Internal Revenue Service stood out among the other white envelopes. Ivy drew in her breath. She hoped she wasn't being audited. While she dutifully reported every cent of her income, the CPA she used for her major accounting needs was in the midst of getting a divorce and no doubt would be too busy hiding his assets from his soon to be ex-wife to be of much assistance to her.

The letter was addressed to her personally, so Jubilee was safe. She tore it open while riding the elevator and quickly read it. Her lips shaped into a smile when understanding set in. An itemized deduction she'd taken had been disallowed, with the result being that she owed them the piddling sum of sixty-five dollars. She clutched the letter to her chest and took a few deep breaths of relief before stepping into the hall.

The office hummed with activity, phones ringing and keyboards clicking. When she hired her first two employees she rented a tiny office in midtown, then moved to a roomier space when the billing justified. When the event planning began to take off she decided to move to a property that could serve as both home and office. Her kitchen was in the front of the loft, opposite a large storage closet and powder room. She'd had a sliding door installed at the entrance to the hall that led to the bedrooms. Everyone said the loft was too large for just one person, but when she began renting it she still had hopes of getting married and having children. Now, at thirty-eight, having children was an unlikely possibility, but she still had hopes of finding her soul mate.

Ivy handed the mail to Reneé Walker, her bookkeeper. "There's a couple of checks in there, probably from all those Christmas parties we did. Let me know how much the total is, eh?"

"Sure." Reneé's sharp eyes, aided by bifocals perched low on her nose, caught sight of the envelope still in Ivy's hand. "Internal Revenue Service? Are we in trouble?"

"No, it's for me. The IRS looked at my return and

decided that instead of a refund, I'm sixty-five dollars short. I'll get a check out to them Friday."

"Send them a money order."

"A money order? Why would I go through all that trouble when I can just send a check?"

"To keep the IRS out of your business."

Ivy shrugged. "I don't have anything to hide from the IRS."

"I don't mean to insinuate you do," Reneé said quickly. "It's just that I believe in caution, especially where the IRS is concerned. Not that anything will stop them once they decide they want to attach someone's bank account, but why make it easy for them to find it?"

"They already know where I have my bank account."

"No, they don't, unless you've made major changes since I did your tax return last year. The only 1099s you got were from your mutual funds. Remember, I asked you about it. You said you generally just deposit enough in your checking account to pay bills, and it didn't earn any interest. I told you then it's always nice to have a bank account the IRS doesn't know about, in case you need to move funds in a hurry."

"I remember now. I'll give some thought to paying by money order." But Ivy was just being polite. She dismissed Reneé's caution regarding the IRS as mere paranoia, then turned her attention to the work at hand and promptly forgot all about it.

" 'Night, Ivy," Reneé said.

"See you tomorrow." Ivy latched the door and turned to what was once again her living room. The open workstations with their computers, telephones, built-in shelves, and note-laden corkboards were now closed up into handsome armoires spaced throughout the large

room. Rolling file cabinets and office chairs had been
returned to the storage closet. The only giveaway that
work was being done was a gooseneck chair Ivy had
taken from one of the two seating areas and positioned
in front of her own desk. It wasn't unusual for her to
continue to work well into the evening, but not tonight.
It wasn't even five-thirty, and everyone was gone for the
evening. Reneé was the only one who hadn't left the
office early. Randy was overseeing a publishing house's
cocktail party celebrating the new release by one of their
top authors, Diane was supervising an executive's dinner
party in Riverdale, and John was conducting training
for wait staff in midtown. January was a slow month for
Jubilee, but it followed their most hectic time, October
through December. Checks were coming in from a very
profitable fourth quarter. She'd more than earned a
relaxing evening at home, and she'd start taking it easy
as soon as she straightened her desk.

She picked up the bill from the IRS. Her thoughts
went back to what Reneé said earlier, and she suddenly
remembered various horror stories she'd seen depicted
on *60 Minutes* and other TV newsmagazine programs
about taxpayers who became embroiled in disputes with
the agency over the amount due, to the point of having
all of their assets seized, often in error, none of them
thinking such a nightmare could ever happen to them.
Maybe Reneé had a point. The post office was only a
few blocks away, on Thirty-second Street. It wouldn't
hurt to get that money order after all.

Ivy frowned at the long line of people in front of her.
She rarely came to the post office. They used a postage
scale and a Pitney Bowes postage dispenser in the office,
which Randy or John brought in for refills because of
its heavy weight. She leaned sideways to see the counter

ahead. Only two clerks were on duty, one male and one female. Her gaze passed over, then quickly returned to the man. He had wavy black hair, a moustache, and a neat goatee. His complexion was rather fair; she couldn't tell if he was Hispanic, black, or both, but he was certainly one of the better-looking men she'd seen lately. A broad, beefy frame suggested he was past his youth, which she could appreciate, being past her own.

As the line advanced and Ivy moved closer, her eyes kept settling on the handsome postal clerk. She found herself holding her breath when she was at the head of the line, waiting to see which clerk would be finished with their customer first and hoping it would be the man. She stepped forward eagerly when he called out, "Next, please."

Her eyes went to the nameplate identifying him as Raymond Jones. "Hello, Mr. Jones," she said with a smile. "My name's Smith."

He returned the smile. "Hello, Ms. Smith. What can I do for you today?"

"I need to get a money order for sixty-five dollars, please." Her request was pleasant but businesslike. She didn't know what made her flirt with him in the first place. Perhaps as she approached forty and remained unmarried she was feeling less confident about her own attractiveness.

Now that she stood opposite him she could see the graying at his temples and other areas of his neatly cut dark hair. Even his moustache and trim beard contained a few light strands. With all the millions of people who worked in Manhattan every day, the odds were favorable that a good percentage of them would be good-looking, but still, good-looking, eligible—the clerk wore no wedding band—fortyish men were hard to find.

"Will you be needing any stamps today?" he asked as he tore off the post office's copy of the money order.

"No, that'll do it." She handed him seventy dollars, and he gave her change and a receipt.

"Thank you, Ms. Smith."

"Thank *you*, Mr. Jones." Doggone it, she was doing it again. No, she decided. She was merely responding to his courteousness. Sometimes she'd forgotten how much more pleasant life could be with a little smile here or there.

Her inner voice didn't let her get away with feeding herself that line. *A smile's one thing, but you tilted your head just so and grinned like Jimmy Carter.*

She decided it didn't matter that she'd overdone it. The encounter made her feel good, and doggone it, she wasn't going to hide it.

Still smiling, she went to a counter opposite the mail slots to write out the money order. Her eyes met the disgruntled stare of a woman clearly unhappy about having to wait in the long line, which made Ivy's smile dissolve. The woman continued to stare at her. *She probably thinks I'm a candidate for the psychiatric ward at Bellevue.* Ivy looked away, filling in her return address on the outer envelope before turning her attention to the money order and writing her social security number and the tax year and form number in the memo section. She tore off the stub to keep for her records and was about to place it in the envelope when she noticed it was for three figures, not two. Six hundred and sixty-five dollars. The clerk must have hit the six twice.

She blocked out her social security number, grabbed the envelope and walked to the front of the line, ignoring the hostile stares of the waiting patrons. She owed them no explanation; it really wasn't any of their business.

She waited a few feet behind and to the right of the gentleman Raymond Jones was presently serving. She held up the money order as she moved into his place opposite the counter. "I'm afraid you've made a terrible mistake. You gave me a money order ten times the amount I paid for."

"I sure did, didn't I?" he said as he accepted it from her. "I'm terribly sorry about that. I'll have your replacement made up in just a minute. And I want to thank you for your honesty."

"Oh, you're welcome. I certainly wouldn't want to profit from someone else's grief."

"Well, Ms. Smith, I guess what the world needs is more people who think the way you do. My guess is that nine out of ten people would've made this out to cash, cashed it at a post office uptown or in Brooklyn someplace, and pocketed the difference. I'm real glad you're the tenth person." He looked at the new money order carefully before handing it to her. "This one's the right amount. And thanks again."

Ivy thought about the incident as she walked home. Somehow she doubted the federal government would forgive a six-hundred-dollar error made by a postal clerk, or a six-cent one, for that matter. If a clerk's drawer was short at the end of the day, the difference would probably come from his or her paycheck. She was glad she'd been able to prevent that from happening.

Raymond Jones was one good-looking man. If he had done more with himself career-wise he'd be a real catch.

Ray had one more request for a money order before he was done for the day. He checked the amount carefully before handing it to the customer, as he should have done with the one he'd made for that nice Smith woman. His carelessness could have cost him six hundred dollars. While it wouldn't have caused him undue hardship, he couldn't overlook the principle. If each careless mistake had a price tag of six hundred dollars, eventually he would have nothing left. The financial settlement he'd recently received guaranteed his daughters' future. Safeguarding and increasing it was his responsibility. He'd better start paying more attention to what he was doing.

He knew he wasn't as alert as usual because of worry about Maya, his three year old. She was suffering from a cold, and when he had left for work that morning she'd had a fever. When he talked to his mother a few hours ago, Maya still had a fever, although just a slight one. He was anxious to get home to her. She'd looked so unhappy when he left, crying helplessly as clear-colored mucus poured from her nostrils. Funny. The child whose arrival had stunned he and Dolores thirteen years after the birth of their first daughter, Yolanda, was a tremendous comfort to him now that Dolores was gone. Ironically, it was the proceeds from the lawsuit he filed after Dolores's horrible death that assured all their futures, but it was up to him alone to make sure Yolanda and Maya remained healthy and well cared for.

Again he thought of the lovely Ms. Smith and the honesty she displayed. He found himself noticing women a lot more these days than he had in the months immediately following Dolores's loss. Ms. Smith had been blessed with good looks to match her sunny smile. Well, New York had no shortage of pretty women—they came in the post office every day—but it was especially refreshing to see one who acted as pretty as she looked.

Chapter 2
Lonely at the Top

Ivy shut down her computer. She felt pretty good about the in-depth consultation she'd done for a new restaurant in the East Village. Writing came easier to her when she had complete quiet. She'd been so engrossed in it she didn't realize how much time it took. The living room clock read nine-forty P.M., and everyone had left hours ago. She'd give it one last read-through with fresh eyes first thing in the morning before printing it out and sending it.

As she turned off the monitor, her personal telephone line began to ring. She carried the gooseneck chair a few steps, gently placing it down on the edge of the Oriental rug that defined the seating area, and picked up the extension on an end table. "Hello."

"Hi Ivy, it's Stephanie. We've got a problem."

She blew out her breath and spoke with a deliberate edge. "Hello to you, too, Stephanie."

"Oh, I'm sorry. It's just that I only have a few minutes.

Remember, you may be at home relaxing, but I'm at work."

Ivy rolled her eyes. Her sister never tired of harping on how difficult it was to work a twelve-hour night shift, the insinuation being that Ivy merely sat on her behind all day and collected huge fees from her clients. Ivy didn't bother to point out that she'd been working since eight that morning, nearly fourteen hours ago. "Forget it. What's the problem?"

"It's Otto."

"I might have known. What did he do now?"

"He's really driving Mom and Dad crazy, Ivy."

"Why don't they just throw him out? They're not required to take care of him anymore; he's a grown man."

"You and I both know they'll never do that."

"Well, sometimes only tough love works. It's not going to get any easier, and they're not getting any younger."

"Well, that's easy for you to say, Ivy. You don't have kids."

Ivy's eyes narrowed at the dig, but she decided not to give Stephanie the satisfaction of getting a reaction. "What exactly did Otto do?"

"He borrowed Mom's car. Said he'd be back by a certain time. She accepted a nursing assignment, but she wasn't able to keep it. She was real upset, and I can't blame her. Canceling at the last minute is just so tacky. But it's not like she could take a cab all the way to Englishtown."

"Well, that's too bad. I just don't see what I can do. I've always urged them not to do so much for him, that it was going to make him not want to do anything for himself."

"I didn't think you'd be any help."

"I don't know what you expect *me* to do. I mean, if

you're so anxious to help, why don't you invite Otto to come live with you?"

"I have a tiny three-bedroom house that's home to my family of five. I'm not living all by myself in a huge loft."

"Oh, I get it. I'm supposed to ask him to come live with *me*."

"I have to get back to work, Ivy. I'll talk to you another time. Good-bye."

Ivy slammed the receiver down. She should have known there was an ulterior motive behind Stephanie's call. She couldn't remember the last time anyone in her family had called just to say hello or to see how she was doing. They only called when they wanted her to do something for them, and it hurt more than she dared admit, not to them and not to herself.

"You don't know how lucky you are to be an only child, Bethany," Ivy said after the waiter set their plates before them.

Her friend nodded as she lifted her fork. "You mean, I've been spared getting calls from siblings asking for loans they have no intention of ever paying back, or having my parents call me and ask me to help out brother and his wife, or sister and her husband, or the grandchildren. A guy I dated used to complain about his family treating him like a human ATM machine. He called it the curse of the overachievers. Is it happening to you, too?"

"I'm just tired of only being contacted when somebody wants help with their dirty work, which usually involves Otto." She shook her head. "Thirty-one years old and totally useless. But it's my parents' fault."

"That's not really fair, is it, Ivy?"

"I'm no Dr. Spock, but I do believe you have to train

your children to be independent if you expect them to one day be on their own. But my parents insisted on doing everything for Otto. That's why he's still living with them. That's why he doesn't have a profession and earns seven or eight dollars an hour at best. And now—surprise!—they're getting tired of it."

"I don't get it, Ivy. You and your sister are both self-sufficient, so why isn't he?"

"We were just girls, while he was the son they had dreamed of having. I was seven when Otto was born, and Stephanie was five. It's not like my parents left us to our own devices or anything like that, but Otto was clearly their favorite. My good grades got me some recognition, but poor Stephanie was just an average student. I think she got the worst of it, being the middle child along with not having any special talent. I try to be patient with her because of that, but sometimes it's awfully hard." She felt her mood darkening. Even her fried shrimp sandwich, usually one of her favorites, met with little response from her taste buds. If she didn't change the subject soon she'd be thinking about the problem with her brother long after she and Bethany returned to their respective offices.

She smiled at her friend. "I like your hair auburn," she said. "Are you going to keep it that way?"

Bethany patted her newly tinted tresses. "Thanks. I think I will. The lighter color makes me look younger than I do with my hair its natural shade, and that means I can get away with wearing it long like this without looking like a hag."

"You could easily pass for thirty-five, Bethany."

"Yeah, well tell that to my scalp; it keeps sprouting gray hairs. You won't have this problem; your hair is brown, not almost black like mine. Are you still planning to go to your high school reunion?"

"I'm going shopping for a dress this weekend. All I

need now is someone to escort me. You wouldn't happen to know anyone who'd make a good impression as my date, do you?"

"If I did I'd be going out with him myself. I was so desperate the other week I almost called Charles."

"Charles? It's been months since you two broke up. What happened?"

"I came to my senses before I made a fool of myself. Face it, Ivy. It's lonely at the top. We aren't secretaries; we *have* secretaries."

Ivy studied her friend. Bethany Willis was a few years older, in her early forties. Like herself, Bethany had never been married, but she had done magnificently in her career. Her hard work and sharp mind resulted in her being appointed CEO of a struggling Internet corporation she was now slowly guiding toward profitability, picking up millions of dollars' worth of stock along the way. They'd met at a meeting of an organization for professional black women about four years before and had become fast friends. About a dozen women from that organization spun off into their own social group, getting together every four or five weeks to discuss careers, love, and life.

"Bethany, have you ever thought of dating a man who made less money than you do?"

"*Everybody* I date makes less than I do, Ivy. Except maybe Bryant Gumbel and Samuel L. Jackson, but they're taken. The men at the top usually are, and if they're getting divorced they've already got the next missus picked out. Half the time they announce their engagement before the divorce papers are signed." She shrugged. "Just because a man is wealthy doesn't mean he has good taste."

"Those are men at the top. But what about someone . . ."

"An average Joe? Sure! I'm no snob, Ivy. I've gone

out with all types of fellows, black guys, white guys, blue-collar workers, and professionals. I'll keep right on doing it as long as they treat me well. I'm not saying I'd go out with someone from the unskilled labor pool, because I probably wouldn't, but I see nothing wrong with dating a man who gets his hands dirty. Plenty of women tease me because I date plumbers and electricians and airplane mechanics. Hmph. I tell them if they don't think a plumber performs a viable function, then try living without running water for a day."

"I hate to even think about it." Ivy shuddered.

"But one thing is certain. It doesn't matter how they make their living, sooner or later it becomes apparent that they can't deal with it."

"Deal with what?" But even as Ivy asked the question she knew the answer.

"My success. Eventually they all start to feel like my money threatens their masculinity or something."

"You'd think that feeling would be present from the beginning."

"I've figured that out, too, or at least I think I have. They probably get the same ribbing I do. Their friends and families give them a hard time about dating a woman who makes so much more than they do, and they start to resent my success. I can't think of any other reason why two people can be getting along fine and then all of a sudden the man becomes sullen and disagreeable. But I've accepted that I'll never get married. The way men feel about this sort of thing runs too deep." Bethany raised a skillfully arched eyebrow. "Why are you asking me about this, anyway? Have you met someone?"

"No," she said quickly. "I was just curious." But as Ivy ate the rest of her lunch she kept thinking about Raymond Jones, the handsome post office clerk who sold her the money order.

* * *

Ivy had never understood women who loved to shop.
She hated it, whether it was for food, clothing, or personal items, but of course there was no way around
it; cupboards grew bare, stockings got runs, and soap
disintegrated. She tried to complete it as quickly as
possible. Her routine was to put on her gym shoes every
Saturday morning and get everything she needed in
one trip, from toiletries to groceries, along with quite
a bit of exercise.

She saw the midnight blue velvet dress in the window
of a boutique on Madison Avenue. When she tried it
and saw how well it fit she knew she'd bring it home.
A sexy variation of a classic sailor suit decorated with
double breasted white satin buttons, it fell to just above
her knees, and just above her breasts the velvet was sewn
into a shirred white satin stand-up collar that left her
shoulders and collarbone bare. Just how much skin she
wanted to show was up to her, for the fabric folded
down or up to accommodate both modesty or daring.
The dark blue had the touch of drama she wanted, and
the white gave it a touch of brightness. The influx of
black in women's formal wear had become overpower-
ing. It was by far the most popular color, even, incredibly, for guests at weddings. Ivy felt it was extremely
bad taste to show up to celebrate someone's marriage
wearing black just because it was slimming.

All she had to do now was find a matching shoe,
preferably in suede, with a comfortably high heel . . .
but she'd do that another time.

She stopped at the Kmart near Herald Square to pick
up some personal and household items. She piled a few
impulse purchases—a paperback novel, a new pouf to

use with liquid soap, a pretty button-down handknit sweater—as well as heavy items like bleach, detergent, and mouthwash. By the time she got to the checkout, she knew she'd have to get a taxi to get her packages home.

The cashier was ringing up her purchases when she held up the pouf, searching for a price tag they both soon realized wasn't there.

"There must have been a thousand of those in the bin. Leave it to me to pick the one without a price tag," Ivy remarked as the cashier, a pretty teenage girl, called for a price check.

"It'll only be a minute. I'm sorry."

"It's not your fault. The people behind me might not be too happy, though," she added in a low voice. Collective groans could be heard behind them when the cashier turned on a blinking red light to indicate a problem, and eventually they all defected to other registers. Ivy thumbed through an *In Style* magazine as she waited for the price to be confirmed. It was probably hypocritical of her, but if she was a celebrity she would never consent to have her home photographed for all America to see yet she had no problem studying the furnishings of Will and Jada's living room or Melanie and Antonio's bedroom.

She was putting the magazine back with a bored sigh when she noticed a man approaching them, a toddler perched on his shoulders. A plastic bag was looped through his right arm.

"Yo-lan-da," the little girl called out from her high stance.

The cashier turned. "Hi!"

"We brought you some lunch," the man said.

Ivy tried not to stare, but she couldn't help it. Of all places to run into that handsome Raymond Jones from the post office. Were these girls his daughters? He hadn't worn a wedding ring that day, but perhaps he was married after all.

"Oh, thanks! I'm going to ask if I can take a break." The cashier turned to the approaching manager, who held a different colored pouf in her hand. "Jean, can I take a break now? My dad brought me lunch, and no one's on my line."

"Sure, go ahead," the manager replied. She handed the cashier the pouf, then pulled a metal chain across the aisle to indicate the line was closing. "Turn off your light."

The cashier complied. She scanned the replacement pouf and put the correct one in Ivy's bag, then hit the Total key.

"Something smells awfully good," Ivy said as she handed over a bill. "Just a second, I think I've got three cents."

"It's a gyro. My favorite," the cashier said.

"Mmm." As Ivy handed the cashier the pennies she noticed Raymond staring at her. She smiled at him and the little girl who still sat on his shoulders. "Hello."

He looked embarrassed. "I'm sorry for staring. I know you from someplace, but I can't remember where."

"I'll give you a hint. 'Hello, Mr. Jones. My name's Smith. I'd like a money order.' "

He snapped his fingers. "You're the honest lady who gave back that money order when I made a mistake on it the other week."

"I recognized you right off."

"Daddy, can we have pizza now?" the little girl asked.

"In a minute, Maya." He smiled apologetically at Ivy. "My daughters. This is Yolanda," he said, indicating the cashier. "And this one on my shoulders is Maya. Girls, this is Ms. Smith."

"Please call me Ivy." He probably had more children

at home, since there was easily a dozen years between these two.

The girls greeted her politely.

"And I'm Ray," he said.

"Nice to meet you, Ray."

"I'm going to take my lunch break now, Daddy. Thanks a lot for my gyro. See you, Maya," Yolanda said.

"All right, honey. See you at home," Ray said as Maya waved good-bye.

"Bye, Miss Ivy," Yolanda added.

"Good-bye, Yolanda. Enjoy your lunch."

"Daddy, pizza," Maya said impatiently.

"All right, Maya. We'll get our lunch now." Ray paused, turning to Ivy. "Why don't you join us? It's the least I can do after you saved me all that money."

She hesitated, but quickly decided an informal pizza lunch in the presence of his daughter was harmless. But there was something else to consider. "Are you going very far? One of my bags is kind of heavy. I was going to get a cab home."

"We were just headed a few doors down. Here, let me get them for you." He reached up and scooped Maya by her waist and put her on the ground.

"Oh, I can carry this one; it's light," she said quickly, taking the bag with her sweater, book, and pouf.

Ray easily carried the heavy items, cradling the double plastic bag against his chest. With his free hand he held onto Maya, and Ivy instinctively took the child's other hand.

The pizzeria was moderately crowded, but most customers were content to either eat at the stand-up counter or munch while they walked outside. Only half of the few tables in the back were taken. They settled at a table first, and then Ray asked Ivy what she wanted.

She entertained Maya while Ray placed the order. He

returned with a regular slice for Maya, slices with extra cheese for himself and for Ivy, and drinks.

"There's nothing like a slice of New York pizza with extra cheese," Ivy said as she took a bite. The cheese stringed as she pulled the slice away, and after some difficulty she managed to break it with her fingers, much to Maya's delight.

"What a nice coincidence, running into you at Kmart," Ray said as Maya blew on her pizza trying to cool it. "Yolanda worked there during the Christmas season, and they kept her on afterward. It's her first job."

"How old is she?"

"Sixteen."

"You have other kids between her and Maya?"

"You'd think so, wouldn't you? But it's just the two of them. My wife and I tried for years to have another child, but nothing happened until Maya came along when we were both pushing forty. It was a wonderful surprise. I'm grateful for a second chance to be a dad, now that Yolanda is almost grown."

"Just because she's a big girl doesn't mean she still won't need her daddy for advice."

"Yeah, I guess."

"And it's so sweet of you to take Maya out and give her mom a break."

"Actually, my wife was killed when Maya was a year old."

Ivy wished she could take the words back. She'd been fishing for information, but this was the last thing she expected to hear and she was genuinely distressed. "Oh, no! I'm sorry. I didn't know."

"It was a freak accident. She was walking down East Thirty-ninth Street when she was struck by a window air conditioner that fell from a ninth-floor office. The doctors said she never knew what hit her."

She winced. "Oh, how awful! I hope you sued."

"I did. We didn't go to court, though; we reached a settlement with the insurance company. The lawyer took a third as his fee, but we still did very well. Both my girls will get first-rate educations. We always had Yolanda in parochial school anyway, but now neither of them will have to worry about anything for the rest of their lives, at least nothing within reason. As it is, Yolanda expected me to hand her hundred-dollar bills every time she saw something she wanted."

"That's pretty typical for a teenager."

"Having this little job is good for her. I'm teaching her how to manage the few dollars she makes. I don't want her to make any foolish mistakes in case something should happen to me and she inherits what will seem to her like a windfall. Our family paid a very high price for her and her sister to be able to live worry-free lives, and I won't have it thrown away."

"Yes, you did. I think it's wise to give her guidance. But don't you worry about her coming home after dark?"

"Right now she only works weekends. Anything more than that would interfere with school. When she worked during Christmas I came to walk her home every night. We don't live far from here, Thirty-seventh between Ninth and Tenth."

She nodded. "Hell's Kitchen."

"Yes. It's not as bad as it was years ago, when there was a grisly murder every other week. My parents live in the next building—actually, it's two connected buildings—and they help out with the girls a lot." He paused to bite into his pizza. "Now it's your turn," he said after he swallowed. "Tell me about Ivy Smith. All I know is that you've got principles."

"Some people would be surprised to learn I'm still alive." She laughed at his obvious confusion, then explained about the postings she saw on the Internet, including her plan to attend the reunion.

"You're going to cause quite a sensation."

"It'll be a night to remember, I'm sure."

"What kind of work do you do, Ivy?"

She told him, then waited for his reaction.

"What are you, like a caterer?" he asked.

She smiled. That was the usual response, and she understood perfectly. It wasn't like she practiced law or medicine; her unusual occupation always required additional explanation. "No, but we work with caterers, match them with clients, and hire wait staff as well. We put together entire affairs, from the people who greet guests at the door to the people who play the music. All the client has to do is tell us what they want, tell us how much they want to spend, and then show up to accept all the compliments from their guests on how nicely everything was done."

"You make it sound simple, but I'm sure it isn't."

"No, it's not."

"Where's your office, midtown?"

"It's in Chelsea, Twenty-eighth Street between Sixth and Seventh. I have a loft in a building zoned for commercial and residential use."

They talked some more, mostly about her work, and then the pizza was gone and Maya let out a loud burp. Her subsequent quick glance at Ray, all wide-eyed and palm covering her mouth, made Ivy smile. Ray wiped her face while he instructed her to say "excuse me," then steered her little arms back into her jacket.

"You really take good care of her," Ivy said as he replaced the child's knit cap on her head. "I admire you for it. I know it can't be easy."

"Like I said, I'm grateful for the second chance, especially now that—" He broke off, but she knew he was thinking of his wife's untimely death. "Maya will be with me well after Yolanda goes off on her own."

In other words, Ivy thought, he wouldn't be lonely.

Outside in the February cold she thanked him, and he helped her into the cab she hailed. She felt an odd sensation of emptiness as the cab drove down Thirty-third Street. He was movie-star handsome and quite nice, and once she recovered from the shock of learning he was a widower she had hoped he would ask to see her again. Maybe he felt the gap in their lifestyles was much wider than the nine blocks separating them geographically. She could hardly fault him for that; she had initially felt that way herself. Not only was there the matter of their professions being at different levels, but another glaring difference as well, one he may not even have noticed. When he talked it was mostly about his children and his late wife, while when she talked it was mostly about her work. The only family life she knew began to disintegrate the day her parents brought Otto home from the hospital.

For years she told herself it would be different when she had her own children, that she'd never show favoritism, but that was pretty much a moot point. She wasn't an idealistic young girl anymore; she was a woman in her late thirties without any romantic prospects. Just like Bethany accepted the unlikelihood of ever marrying, she had to accept that she'd probably never be a mother.

Ivy had gone out with various men over the years. Her work had been instrumental in offering opportunities to meet eligible, successful bachelors, businessmen as well as actors, directors, and professional athletes, but nothing had clicked. As for men she met on her own at social functions, they stopped calling once the depth of her success became apparent to them. Bethany was right, most men simply couldn't cope with her tax bracket. The exclamations of surprise and comments about how much rent she must be paying from guests at her annual New Year's Day open house made her so uncomfortable that she took to concealing her success from people she didn't know well, claiming to be apartment sitting while the real tenant was on an extended European work assignment. Prosperity was nothing to be ashamed of, but she couldn't deny that it changed the way people looked at her.

She wondered if Bethany was right. Did making it in the business world really mean she had to be lonely?

Chapter 3
Come with Me to the Casbah

The time had come to send in her check for the reunion, which was two-and-a-half weeks away, but Ivy still didn't have a date. Sometimes men could be like toilet tissue; you didn't pay much attention until you needed it and it wasn't there. Any other time she would have met someone new by now, but because she was so anxious to find someone to bring to the reunion, every man she came in contact with socially either wore a wedding ring or was over fifty, and sometimes both. She was so desperate she even considered dressing her brother Otto in a tuxedo and passing him off as her date; there was enough of an age gap where he wouldn't be known as her brother to anyone she went to school with, but he wasn't so young where people would think she was cradle snatching. But that wouldn't work. Otto was simply too unreliable. He'd think nothing of going off if he had a last-minute invitation and leave her literally holding his tux.

Her brother-in-law Jerome Overton couldn't help

her, either. He graduated the year before she did from the same school, and she doubted it was a secret around Lakewood that he had married Stephanie. Even if Jerome wasn't known to her former classmates, asking him to escort her was out of the question. Stephanie already took every opportunity to flaunt her marriage and children in Ivy's face. The last thing Ivy wanted was for her sister to learn of her difficulty finding a date.

As she pulled out her checkbook she hoped the organizer wouldn't be too upset with her for not sending in a deposit earlier, as had been requested. Her tardiness shouldn't cause too much of a problem; the organizer would have her full payment by the time he had to provide a final head count to the hotel's catering department.

She had dated her personal check and was about to make it payable to the organizer of the reunion when she realized that sending in a check would spoil the surprise she planned. She'd have to pay by money order, anonymously. She could put in a note saying she would bring in the other half of her money order as proof, or merely tell them that Graduate X and guest were coming and would identify themselves as such at the door.

As for going alone, she was sure she wouldn't be the only female attending unescorted, formal event or not. If she felt truly uncomfortable she could always leave early.

She left the office at three-forty-five and walked to the post office. She wanted to allow plenty of time to get up to Sutton Place. A senior vice president of one of her corporate clients and his wife were hosting a dinner party for a visiting executive from Chicago. This was the first function Jubilee had organized for him personally, and she wanted to make sure it went off without incident so it wouldn't be the last. Of course, she probably could have gotten a money order from the corner store, but Ray Jones didn't work at the corner store.

This wasn't the first time she'd gone to the post office with hopes of seeing him. For years she'd used the office postage machine to send her personal mail, but last week she suffered a convenient attack of righteousness, telling herself it was wrong to use company supplies for personal use. Ray wasn't at the window, and she feared he'd been sent to work at another branch. That prospect disturbed her more than she expected, making her realize just how badly she wanted to see him again. She didn't understand why. He'd had an opportunity to ask her out but didn't. Ivy's clinical side identified three possible reasons for this: One, he didn't find her particularly attractive. Two, he decided she was too rich for his blood. Three, he was still mourning the loss of his wife.

She couldn't make herself believe the first possibility. She might not be the prettiest flower in the bouquet, but she was reasonably attractive, and heads often turned for a double take when she passed. Her skin was free of blemishes, her teeth were straight, she had a standing weekly salon appointment to keep her hair, nails, and eyebrows maintained; and her weight had never been a problem, probably because of all the walking she did.

But Ivy felt less certain about the likelihood of the other two. At lunch she was pleased by his seemingly genuine interest in her work without sounding overly impressed, but maybe he figured she was one of those women who had preset rules against dating men who weren't considered professionals. He wouldn't be entirely wrong, for unlike Bethany, Ivy had never dated anyone who didn't wear a jacket and tie to work. Dating was hard enough in her position; going out with someone who drove a truck for a living would only hasten the inevitable. She knew from her friends that she was hardly alone in feeling the way she did, but of course that didn't make it right. That enjoyable lunch with Ray made her reconsider. One more encounter might be all the opportunity she needed to subtly get across that she'd welcome the opportunity to see him socially.

As for the third possibility, there wasn't a doggone thing she could do about that, but in her mind two years was certainly long enough to adjust to the fact that his wife wasn't coming back. His single parent status might keep him busy, but he was still a man.

Only two people waited in line in front of her. Better than that, Ray was working a window. She thought he might have smiled at her briefly when he looked up, but it was so quick she couldn't be certain.

Any doubts she had about his recognizing her dissolved when the other clerk called her forward. Ivy hesitated, and Ray said something to his coworker, who shrugged and turned his attention to something else. Ray motioned to Ivy that he'd be with her shortly, and she nodded and waited, her eyes not leaving his face. He really was marvelous looking. It would feel so good to go to her reunion with someone who looked as good as he did.

While Ivy had friends through high school, her lasting friendships were those she made in college or after. She was content to let her friendships from high school fade. Ivy didn't have particularly fond memories of her high school years; by that time she was eagerly anticipating leaving home to continue her education. Her parents' blatant favoritism of Otto had become unbearable, and Otto was difficult because he was now old enough to recognize how their parents felt about him. Her eagerness to leave the past behind contributed to her surprise at the fond tributes people posted on the Internet message board when they thought she was dead. Still, she wanted to avoid having her classmates whisper that her success meant she had no love life. Showing up with someone who looked like Ray would make her the envy of every woman present, and even the men would have to admit she had it all.

Ray finished up with his customer, and when the woman left, Ivy stepped forward. "Hi, Ray."

His smile was genuine. "Good to see you, Ivy. You're looking well."

"Thanks. You, too. I came to get another money order." At that precise moment a crazy idea came to her. Why not, she reasoned. He'd told his coworker he would take care of her. Surely that meant something. She did a quick calculation and named an amount double the original figure.

"How've you been?" he asked as he ran it through the printer.

"I'm well, thanks." *Now. Do it now, before you lose your nerve.* She gulped, her Eve's apple sounding like a cannon to her ears, and her palms suddenly felt damp as she grasped the straps of her handbag. "Ray . . . I wanted to ask you something. Do you think you can call me at home later?"

"Sure."

As she expected, he looked curious, but didn't ask for more information. She scribbled her home number on the back of a business card. "I've got to go uptown now, but I'll be back home by nine."

He raised an eyebrow. "Everything all right?"

That depends on you. "Oh, yes. I'm just overseeing an event, but it won't be late."

"No, I mean . . . is everything all right?"

"Oh! Nothing's wrong. I just think you might be able to help me with something."

Ivy checked her watch. Eight-fifteen. The evening was dragging by. She generally didn't linger long at events this small—just twelve guests—but these were first-time clients who entertained often, and she wanted to impress them so they would call Jubilee the next time they had company. She had removed her navy blazer and placed a full apron over her blue chambray tailored blouse with "Jubilee" embroidered on the breast pocket. She never worked with food, but she knew the caterer always appreciated an extra hand wiping down messy counters and stovetops, and it wasn't like she was doing anything else but standing around watching everyone else work.

She was pleased by the professionalism of the two waiters she'd engaged to serve the group. The moment one returned after passing a tray, the other would carry out a different item, or merely go out and empty ashtrays or see to the needs of the guests. They worked well in tandem together, like a figure skating team doing complicated jumps in perfect symmetry. Jubilee kept several hundred waiters and waitresses on call, all of whom were required to attend an extensive training session. Many were students or housewives looking for part-time work. Others already belonged to the work-force and were eager to make a few extra dollars.

In another ten minutes the caterer had the kitchen restored to the way it looked when they arrived. One waiter was clearing dinner plates and loading the dishwasher, the other was serving coffee. Ivy decided it wasn't necessary to stick around while dessert was served. She left the standard evaluation form and embossed pencil with a business card on the counter, bid the caterer and wait staff good night, then slipped out the service entrance.

Downstairs, the doorman hailed her a cab. The subway was faster, but it meant a walk of several long blocks in the dark. Sutton Place, one of Manhattan's most exclusive neighborhoods, was largely residential, with most pedestrian traffic consisting of nannies pushing prams in the daytime hours and residents walking Dalmatians, Boxers, and other expensive breeds of dogs in the evening.

She checked her watch when she got back to her loft. Eight-fifty-one. She hung up her coat, then plopped on one of the couches and pulled off her boots. She leaned back into the couch and reached for the remote control for the TV. In the few seconds it took for the television screen to light up she did a visual inspection of the room. Reneé was in charge of closing the office when she wasn't there, and everything looked as it should when business hours were over.

Ivy wasn't much for television, but she found an interesting documentary on the Discovery Channel about skyscraper construction. They had broken for a commercial when the phone began to ring. She peered at the caller ID rectangle on the back of the receiver. "Unknown caller," it read. She let it ring a second time before answering. "Hello."

"Ivy Smith, please. Ray Jones calling."

"Hi, Ray; it's Ivy. Thanks for calling me."

"Sure. This is actually a good time for me, after I get Maya in bed." He paused. "You said you had something to ask me. What's up?"

She took a deep breath. "Do you remember that day when we had lunch and I was telling you about my high school reunion?"

"Oh, yeah. Your classmates got you mixed up with someone else who died."

"Well, the reunion is two weeks from Saturday, and, um, my boyfriend and I broke up recently." It was a lie, of course, but at least this way she wouldn't sound too pathetic. "I really hate to go alone. It's . . . well, it's kind of embarrassing. A lot of women will have their husbands with them and will be showing pictures of their kids. I was hoping you could help me out.''

"You want to borrow some pictures of my kids?''

In spite of her nervousness, Ivy laughed. She found herself feeling more relaxed. Ray seemed to have a knack for averting a potentially uncomfortable situation, as he had done when telling her of his wife's untimely death. "No. What I mean is it can be a little difficult when the people you went to school with have half-grown kids and you've never even been married.''

"You don't have anything to be ashamed of, Ivy. From what I understood, you've done very well for yourself.''

"It's more than doing well for myself. You know how people can be. They'll snicker that I'm still single because I'm too busy making money or something. I was . . . I was hoping you might agree to escort me to my reunion. I'd pay all expenses, of course, your tux, the transportation, and the tickets. The tickets include a buffet and open bar," she added.

Silence.

She waited for what seemed like a very long time but was probably just a few seconds. When she could bear it no longer she prodded, "Ray? You still there?''

"Oh, I'm sorry. I was just thinking.''

"Why don't you take some more time to think about it?" she suggested quickly. "You can call me tomorrow with your answer, or if there's anything else you need to know." She read his hesitation as a pending refusal. Maybe if he thought about it, he'd realize it was harmless. She hoped.

"That's a good idea. Why don't I get back to you tomorrow?''

"Sure.''

*   *   *

Ray frowned as he hung up. All afternoon and evening he'd been curious about what Ivy wanted to ask him. He couldn't imagine what he could possibly help her with.

He'd thought of her often since their impromptu lunch together. He found her fresh-faced natural beauty refreshing, and he liked the way she gravitated toward Maya, automatically taking her other hand as they walked on the crowded downtown street, and talking to her at the pizzeria while he placed their order at the counter. But instead of asking to see her again like he wanted to, he ended up merely waving with Maya when Ivy's cab pulled off. It had been so long since he'd asked a woman for a date, and he'd also been a tiny bit afraid that she would turn him down. He felt disheartened as she rode away, certain that his hesitation would prevent him from ever seeing her again. At the post office he spent as much time working behind the scenes as he did on the window, so if she happened to come in the odds were that he wouldn't see her. But not only had he seen her again, now he had the opportunity to take her out.

Or sort of, and that was why he was frowning.

He wasn't sure he understood Ivy's motives. Was she hoping to pass him off as her husband or something, and say that Yolanda and Maya were *their* children, just for the sake of saving face for some people she hadn't seen in twenty years and would probably never see again? Talk about a bane to his ego, as if the nagging suspicion that asking him was her last resort wasn't bad enough.

Ray had no illusions about his station in life. He worked at the post office, sorting mail and selling stamps. It provided a reasonably comfortable living for his family, which in turn gave him a sense of satisfaction. But he was just another working stiff next to a woman like Ivy. She probably wouldn't have looked at him twice if she hadn't desperately needed a date. And that part about her paying all expenses for the evening stuck in his throat like dry bread. It was all right for her to buy the tickets, but he found the idea of a woman picking up the tab for his tuxedo rental and paying for drinks at the bar unsettling.

Then he remembered her saying there would be an open bar. That was okay, but still, he wasn't going to let her dress him like he was a gigolo or something.

His mouth set in a hard line. Ivy Smith might want her former classmates to feel she had achieved success both professionally and personally, but he wasn't about to try to pretend to be something he wasn't. If she wanted him to escort her to her reunion, it would have to be on *his* terms.

Chapter 4
Function at the Junction

"Ooh, Daddy, you look so handsome," Yolanda said. "Like a movie star."

"Well, thank you." Ray adjusted the collar of his rented tuxedo. "I guess I don't look half bad for an old guy of forty-two."

His mother, working in the kitchen, snorted. "Old guy, my foot! You look wonderful, son."

"Thanks, Mom, but I know I can easily stand to lose twenty pounds."

She announced that the bowl she'd used to blend the brownie mix was ready, prompting both Maya and Yolanda to rush to the kitchen. Both girls knew that the sooner they poured the batter into the pan the sooner they would be able to eat the drippings that clung to the bowl. Ray smiled at his daughters' eagerness. His mother knew just what to do to keep them occupied. They probably wouldn't even miss him.

He was glad Ivy agreed to his insistence on paying for his own formal wear. She did say she didn't feel he should have to incur any expense in doing her a favor, but he held firm and she relented. She said she would pick him up at seven-fifteen, which meant she'd be here any minute.

Ivy smoothed her sheer navy hose. She enjoyed formal occasions, getting all gussied up with jewelry and makeup, but in truth she was more likely to organize this type of affair than be a guest.

She remembered how surprised she'd been when Ray asked her if she wanted them to pretend to know each other better than they did. "No, of course not," she'd said. Then he wanted to know how she would feel if someone asked him what he did for a living. That time she tried humor, his own preferred method, to ease the tension. "You think I'd prefer you to say you take numbers or something?" she'd said. As he laughed, she added, "You make an honest living, Ray, and I'm sure a good one as well." Not until that moment did she realize his questions were for screening purposes and that her responses would have a direct bearing on his decision.

She was thrilled when he accepted; all the tension and worry she'd been carrying around for weeks was gone in an instant. She made a sincere attempt to pay for his tux rental, but she wasn't surprised when he insisted on doing it himself. It was male pride, she knew, the same emotion that made Bethany so certain no man would ever accept her out-earning him.

In a gesture she often performed when she was deep in thought, Ivy attempted to twist a lock of her short hair around her index finger. The strands felt unnaturally hard because of the hair spray the stylist applied, so she lowered her hand and drummed freshly tipped nails on the armrest. She wanted to do something to thank Ray, preferably in a manner that would scoff at traditional male/female roles. She'd come up with something eventually.

She moved her face close to the window as the driver pulled over in front of a four-story apartment building with two entrances. She had always been rather nearsighted, a condition only exacerbated by years of long hours in front of a computer. When the limousine driver opened the front door to ring the apartment bell, she glimpsed a tiny, dimly lit vestibule. Ray only lived nine blocks north of her, but in all her years in the city she had never had any reason to visit Hell's Kitchen. The name alone made her think of a seedy district full of drifters hanging around the Port Authority Bus Terminal, and she had feared she would see graffiti-covered tenements and junky bodegas, but it was actually a quiet block of mostly well-kept low-rise apartment buildings and brownstones that looked no worse than any other part of residential Manhattan. Ray's building could probably use a good steam cleaning, but weathered-looking brick in New York was hardly an oddity.

She sat back when the driver emerged and took his place poised to open the door, eager to get a first look at Ray in formal wear but not wanting to look like she was ready to pounce on him. The windows of the Lincoln were tinted, but one never knew how much someone on the outside could see.

Ray emerged, and the surprised look in his eyes as he took in the long black limousine made her tense up. Did he really think she was going to show up behind the wheel of the Jubilee van? No, that wasn't fair. He probably thought she would be in a cab.

She quickly slid to the left so he wouldn't have to climb over her.

"Good evening," he said cheerfully as he got in. "This is a surprise. I was expecting a taxi."

"I wanted the evening to be special. Actually, I requested a standard car, not a stretch, but those were all booked. At least they didn't give me one in white."

"Not a problem. It's not like I have anything against riding in limos. Hey, nice coat," he said, fingering the reddish brown fox fur.

"Thanks. You're looking pretty sharp yourself." He wore a gray coat over his tuxedo. From what she could see he'd gone with the traditional style, and he wore it well.

"Thanks."

Traffic was favorable, and the chauffeur soon was pulling into the crescent-shaped, greenery-filled driveway of the New York Hilton. The driver opened the door on Ivy's side and offered her his hand as she gracefully arose. Ray got out and stood beside her. "We'll be ready to leave at about midnight," Ivy told the chauffeur.

"Yes, ma'am."

"Shall we?" Ray said, offering his arm.

She took it, and they entered the hotel. Ivy enjoyed the pleasant glances of the people they passed on their way to the escalator. Smiles from complete strangers in New York were rare. She and Ray must look exceptionally good together to elicit such reactions. Even the unoccupied clerks at the front desk were beaming at them.

After checking their coats, they entered the banquet room. The cocktail hour was in progress, with pockets of people standing around talking against a background of jazz music. Ivy enjoyed the not-so-subtle elbowing, heads turning her way, and abruptly stopping conversation as people noticed her standing at the entryway. The scene was straight out of one of those old E. F. Hutton commercials.

"Ivy?" the organizer, Bobby Knight, asked haltingly.

"Yes. I'm the mystery guest who sent a money order. You did get it, didn't you?"

"Yes, but . . . A lot of people said you were dead. We were just talking about it a few minutes ago."

"They made a mistake. It was *Evette* Smith who died in a car crash."

She was surrounded by former classmates in a scene reminiscent of the moments following the crowning of a new beauty queen. As she accepted their good wishes, Ivy made rapid, repeated explanations that someone had apparently gotten her confused with Evette. Now that the confusion was over she didn't want it ever to crop up again.

In the commotion she lost Ray, and she looked around in panic, immediately relaxing when she spotted him smiling at her. She began moving toward him, but stopped with a delighted gasp when she saw Leslie Solomon, who had sat directly behind her in alphabetized classes. The two women hugged like excited children, and the moment they stopped Ivy became aware of the heated gaze of a tall man with a shaved head standing nearby. He didn't look familiar. Was he with Leslie? If so, why was he looking at *her* like she was a pork chop and he hadn't eaten in three days?

"I remember when Evette got killed," Leslie said. "If I'd known people thought it was you, I would have straightened it out right away. But I haven't gone to the school Web site."

"I knew you would have set things straight. Unfortunately, all it takes is one confused person to start a rumor." Relaxed now that the moment of truth was over, she gestured to Ray to join her. "I want to introduce you to one of my good friends from high school. Leslie Solomon, Ray Jones."

After acknowledgments, Leslie reached for the arm

of the man who kept staring at Ivy. "This is my cousin, Mitchell Crews."

"Call me Mitch," he said as he shook Ivy's hand, then Ray's.

"Why don't we find a table?" Leslie suggested. She fell into step with Ivy and said in a low voice, "Your date is some handsome."

"Thanks. I think so, too."

"You two serious?"

"No. We just met a few weeks ago, actually." Ivy knew she wasn't being completely honest, but pride wouldn't allow her to admit the truth. "What about you?"

"I never got married. It's more than a cliché, a good man really *is* hard to find. I'm not even seeing anyone right now, and I really didn't want to come by myself to a black-tie affair, so I asked Mitch to come with me," Leslie confided. "Keep it on the Q.T. that we're cousins, okay? He's easy on the eyes, and everybody doesn't have to know I couldn't get a date."

"I know exactly what you mean." Ivy knew this was the time to tell Leslie the truth about Ray, but she couldn't bring herself to do it.

"Four of the girls did get together to spend a weekend here. They got in yesterday, had lunch, went shopping, and after the party they're having a pajama party in one of the rooms."

"Sounds like fun. Do you have a room here, too?"

"No, I'm staying at Mitch's. He lives here in the city."

The four of them found seats at an unoccupied round table set for eight, Ivy and Leslie sitting next to each other on the inside so they could giggle about old times and share observations, some flattering and others less so, about classmates they recognized. Bobby Knight came over with name tags for Ivy and Ray. Unlike the others, which had been computer generated in advance, their names were handwritten. "It's almost eight, so we're going to start," he told them before heading for the dance floor, when he took the mike from the deejay and made opening remarks. Moments later the jazz was replaced by dance music from their high school years, and the chafing dishes of the buffet were uncovered.

"Looks like a nice party," Mitch commented.

"I'm glad you don't regret coming," Leslie said with a smile.

"Oh, come on, cuz, you knew I'd come through for you."

"Yeah, right." Leslie turned to Ivy and Ray. "Funny how ninety-nine percent of the time his live-in house-keeper is off when I ask him to go someplace with me."

Mitch shrugged, an embarrassed look on his face. "Even housekeepers get to have personal lives, Leslie."

"You probably should think about lining up an alternate. Not just so you can take out your poor dateless cousin when she needs an escort, but to keep yourself covered. You're the custodial parent now, and their mother isn't exactly across town."

"I manage all right. The neighbor's daughter usually helps me out when Charlene is off."

"Yeah, but she's got a heavy schedule, between college classes in the daytime and going out most nights."

"Does your ex live outside the city, Mitch?" Ray asked.

"I'll say. She lives in San Juan."

"Puerto Rico?" Ivy said in surprise.

"She was promoted last summer to managing director. She's with Ernst & Young, but accepting meant relocating to their San Juan office. The kids spent the summer there and enjoyed it, but they decided they wanted to stay in their old school here in New York."

"Being a single parent can be tough," Ray said. "I have a three-year-old and a sixteen-year-old."

"And you have custody?" Leslie asked.

"Yes."

Ivy was glad that he left it at that, for the tragic death of a young mother simply wasn't the type of conversation appropriate for a party.

Leslie jumped out of her chair. "They're playing the 'Electric Slide.' I don't want to miss this. Excuse me."

Mitch smiled as he watched her race toward the dance floor. "I'm afraid I'm not much for dancing," he said sheepishly. "But Leslie loves it."

"Ivy Smith! I'd know you anywhere."

She broke into a smile when she recognized Gregory Palmer, then stood to embrace him. "It's so good to see you again!"

"You, too. You look fabulous."

"Thank you. And you haven't changed a bit."

He patted his belly. "Just more of me these days." Gregory had always been husky.

Ivy placed a palm on Ray's shoulder. "Gregory, this is Ray Jones . . ." She paused while the two shook hands. "And this is Mitchell Crews. Leslie Solomon is sitting with us, too, but she's dancing right now."

"I just saw Leslie. She told me where y'all were sitting," Gregory said as he shook Mitch's hand. "My wife is dancing, too. I married Cecily Thomas. You remember her. Long, silky hair."

She's the one who started that rumor about me. Ivy managed to conceal her surprise, except for an uncontrollable reflexive action of a raised eyebrow. "Of course," she said, nodding. "But I had no idea you two were even seeing each other, much less married."

"Twelve years now."

After chatting for a few minutes, Gregory prepared to move on as the music faded. "Cecily'll be wondering where I am. But we'll catch up with you later, Ivy."

"Okay."

Ray moved in close after he left. "Do you really remember his wife? You had kind of a funny look on your face when you said you did. I suspect a lot of folks at high school reunions say they remember people when they don't.''

''I'll never forget Cecily. She was the one who started the rumor about me being dead. I didn't really care for her much. She acted like she thought she was cute.''

''Why, because she had long, silky hair?''

''Hmph. Too bad it was all on her legs.''

Ray laughed heartily.

''And on her upper lip,'' Ivy continued, giggling.

They managed to confine their laughter to soft snickers, but when they overheard Gregory saying to the people at the next table, ''I married Cecily Thomas. You remember her. She had long, silky hair,'' they just about lost it.

''Come on,'' she said, impulsively grabbing his hand. ''I think it's time we made the rounds.''

She was having so much fun she didn't notice Mitch's eyes following her.

Ivy exchanged a few words with everyone she recognized, but she found she had to look at a surprising number of name tags. Men were losing their hair; women formerly brunette were now blond; and except for a lucky few, just about everyone was heavier in varying degrees than they had been twenty years before. Ivy and Ray posed for pictures, one that would be used in a special edition yearbook, and another that was developed right away, which Ray purchased for her.

They stopped at the buffet to fix plates, and when they returned to the table they were soon joined by Gregory and Cecily Thomas-Parker, who sat on Ray's other side. Leslie was off mingling, and as Ivy and Ray chatted with the newcomers Ivy tried to look everywhere but at the dark shadow on Cecily's upper lip.

Ivy was startled by a sense of movement on her left. She smiled at Mitch, who had moved into Leslie's vacant chair and now sat directly next to her. She felt a lot more comfortable about his open admiration of her now that she knew he and Leslie were cousins, but still, he was awfully bold. After all, she was here with Ray.

"Leslie seems to have abandoned you," she said pleasantly.

"She always does. I'm used to it."

"It sounds like you often go out together."

"She's been a real sport about coming along when I need a date for business functions, now that I'm single again. Do you live here in the city, Ivy?"

"Yes, in Chelsea. What about you?"

"Murray Hill."

"Well, that's certainly convenient. Can you walk to work?"

"It'd be an awfully long walk. I'm in the financial district."

She laughed. "You're right about that."

"Do you work in midtown?"

"No, actually, I work in my loft." She explained her service and was pleased when he understood what she did right off.

"Hey, that's all right. I've always had a dream of working for myself, but it can be a risky move once you get established, starting from scratch with nothing."

"Oh, I agree completely. I was very fortunate that everything fell into place so quickly, but I did have an advantage. No one was providing the service I was, and you'd still be hard pressed to find someone to train wait staff, even though event planners are plentiful. Still, it wasn't a decision I made lightly. I sank every dime I had into Jubilee. Ultimately, I decided I was still young enough to start over if it didn't work out, and of course the tax laws are very favorable for entrepreneurs. But it did. The very first week I was in business I grossed six hundred dollars. It wasn't much, but I was thrilled with the potential."

"Do you have a card on you? I have cause to do some entertaining every now and again. We might be able to work together."

"I never leave home without one." She reached for her purse.

"I see we're playing musical chairs," Leslie said, appearing with a plate from the buffet. "Just kidding," she said as Mitch started to move back to his own chair. "I'll sit here."

"Leslie, how about a dance?" Ray asked.

Ivy stiffened. Ray hadn't asked *her* to dance all night. Why didn't he ask her now instead of asking Leslie?

Leslie promptly put down her plate. "Sure! I can eat later. Come on."

Ivy handed Mitch her card. As he studied it, she watched Ray follow Leslie to the dance floor. She didn't know why their dancing together bothered her, but it did. Then she leaned back in her seat and smiled at Mitch. The interest in his eyes shone like sea water sparkling in the sun. She found it flattering.

A full ten minutes had passed before Ray and Leslie returned. Ivy struggled to conceal her annoyance as she made conversation with Mitch, Gregory, and Cecily. Why had they been gone so long?

Ray tried to dance his way out of his foul mood. He noticed Mitch staring at Ivy all evening, and he wasn't surprised to see him move in on her while Leslie was out of her seat. Ray continued calmly talking with the Parkers, but his lower lip suddenly felt rigid and unnaturally thick. Overhearing Mitch asking for Ivy's business card was more than he could bear, so he asked Leslie to dance. Cecily got up at the same time, perhaps to go to the ladies room, and even the sight of the long black hairs visible through her sheer hose failed to make him smile.

Of course Ivy was free to talk with anyone she wished, and he certainly couldn't say she was flirting outright with Mitch or otherwise behaving inappropriately. He knew little about Mitchell Crews other than the man was divorced, had custody of his children, and had a live-in housekeeper. The fact that he could afford household help meant he was a large wage earner, just the type of man most suitable for Ivy.

That was what bothered him.

The deejay announced the last dance of the evening. Ray reached for Ivy's hand, and she smiled at him before pushing her chair back and rising. The Thomases also prepared to dance, and a uniformed Marine, distinguished and straight postured in his dress blues and a big hit with the unescorted women, came for Leslie.

He and Ivy did a two-step to the selection, which, in a change of pace from the R&B music played for most of the evening, was a medley of standards. Ninety percent of the attendees were on the floor, but the intense crowd only made the setting more intimate. "Don't step on my blue suede shoes," Ivy joked as their space diminished more and more.

Ray welcomed the close quarters. Ivy was lovely enough to be featured in a fashion and beauty magazine. Her short brown hair had been styled with a higher crown than he'd seen previously, with spiky bangs. Her face was flawless, with waxed brown eyebrows accenting her luminous eyes, and her cheeks were just touched with bronze. Her neck and shoulders looked luscious sheathed in the white satin of her collar. The hem of her dress ended just above her knees, revealing shapely but sturdy-looking legs, like those of a professional ice skater. He closed his eyes and allowed himself the indulgence of imagining the satin collar was a sheet, there for him to remove at his discretion. He visualized himself reaching for it to pull it away when he inadvertently pulled her closer.

She raised her head. "You okay?"

"Yeah," he said, suddenly embarrassed.

But after just a few cautious turns he forgot all about it and closed his eyes again.

Chapter 5
The Party's Over

The group spilled out into the hall when the music stopped. Most of the attendees headed for elevators to go up to their rooms. A few, Ivy and Ray included, stopped at the coat check room.

Ray fished in his pocket for the tickets to reclaim their coats. "Your wife's fur is beautiful," the girl working the coat closet said as she handed it to him.

"Thanks," he said cheerfully, enjoying her presumption. He laid a bill in the tip bowl and helped Ivy into her coat before shrugging into his. They rode the escalator down to the lobby directly behind Leslie and Mitch.

"The nice part of attending a hotel function is that there's never a problem getting a cab," Mitch said.

"We'd be happy to drop you guys off," Ivy offered. "We've got a car waiting."

Ray felt his body go tense. He appreciated Ivy's including him in her reference to "we," but nothing would please him more than to say good night to Leslie and

Mitch at the front door. He fervently wished Ivy had been able to secure the simple sedan she'd wanted, for there was no way four adults could fit in the backseat of a standard Continental.

Leslie squealed when she saw the stretch limousine. "I like this, Ivy. You believe in traveling in style, don't you?"

Ivy seemed embarrassed. "Only on rare occasions, believe me."

When they were seated, he and Ivy sitting opposite Leslie and Mitch, Ivy instructed the driver, "We're going to Murray Hill," then looked at Mitch for more information. He stated an address on a street Ray had never even heard of, and he'd lived in New York all his life. Sniffen Court? Where the devil was that?

It was off East Thirty-sixth Street. Ray felt physically ill as he watched Ivy's already bright eyes light up at the sight of the five-story town house. Much to his consternation, Mitch Crews had just become the man of her dreams. Ray chastised himself for allowing her to get away from him that day they had lunch. He didn't want her to slip away again, but he knew Mitch was ready to stake a claim. No way could Ray compete with the moneyed, sophisticated lifestyle Mitch obviously led.

He bid Mitch and Leslie good night, with only a dim sense of their getting out of the limo and disappearing inside. Not until he heard Ivy give the driver his home address did he come out of his daze.

"You can't drop me first, Ivy. It's my responsibility to see that you get home safely."

Her smile shone in the dark interior. "How sweet. All right." She depressed a button, and the partition between the front and back seats slid open. "Change in plans. You're going to drop me first, then Mr. Jones."

The driver acknowledged her request, and she closed

the partition. "I'm so grateful to you for coming with me tonight, Ray. I hope you had a nice time."

"I did. It was a wonderful evening. Good people, good music, and I escorted the prettiest girl in the class."

"You're too kind. What did you think about the food?"

He wrinkled his nose. "I ate the pasta. That meat was too rare for my taste."

"They always cook it rare in the better restaurants and hotels. If you request it well done they often give you a cheaper cut."

At least that he understood. He was still trying to figure out what was wrong with a white limousine. "That's unfortunate. I never gave much thought to where beef comes from, but one bite of that meat and I could hear the cow screaming."

When they arrived at Ivy's building she covered his hand with hers. "I want to thank you again, Ray. Because of you I was the envy of every unmarried woman there, and even some of the married ones, I suspect. And I want you to promise you'll call if there's anything I can do to return the favor."

"You almost sound like you're saying good night to me right here."

She shrugged. "I am."

"Oh, no. Never in my life have I let a woman enter a building alone after dark, and I'm certainly not going to start now. Come on, I'm going to see you to your door." When they got out he tapped on the driver's window. "I'm going to bring Miss Smith upstairs. I'll be back in just a moment."

"Yes, sir."

*   *   *

"I see there are a lot of business offices in this building," Ray remarked as they walked down the hall of the third floor.

"It's zoned for either. A lot of people have the same type of setup as I do, a combined office and apartment." She stopped in front of the door marked 306. "This is it."

"Yes. Ah . . . I just wanted to make sure you got in safely. I guess I shouldn't keep the driver waiting."

"I understand. Well—" She extended her hand.

He stared at it for a long second, then took it, but instead of shaking it he raised it to his lips. "My pleasure." He kissed the back of her palm and held it, not taking his eyes away from hers, and not caring that the desire he felt for her could be clearly seen in their depths. Even after he lowered her hand, he didn't let it go right away.

Finally he gently broke away. "Good night, Ivy."

Ivy removed her shoes and carried them into her bedroom. She walked slowly and tentatively. With each step she took she felt Ray Jones's soft lips making contact with the back of her hand.

In her bedroom she put away her shoes and hung up her dress. She stared at her hand as her palm rested on the padded hanger, half expecting to see it glowing where Ray had kissed it. Her skin bore no visible marks. All she had was a delicious, warm, tingly feeling at the site.

After she removed her makeup she slipped into a comfortable lace-trimmed flannel nightgown and slid between the cool sheets. The sheets generally felt cold against her skin when she first got into bed, but tonight all she had to do was close her eyes and remember that look in Ray's eyes as he kissed her hand, and the warmth spread from the small spot on her hand to her fingers, up her arm, and beyond.

She was asleep within minutes.

"Call for you on one, Ivy."

"Thanks, Reneé." Ivy depressed the line and picked up the receiver. "Ivy Smith."

"Ivy, Mitch Crews."

She removed her glasses and leaned back comfortably in her chair, the way she usually did when she took a personal call. "Hello, Mitch. How nice to hear from you."

"I was wondering if you were free for lunch today."

"I should be able to get away for an hour or so, yes. What'd you have in mind?"

"There's a great place called Brewbaker's on John Street, one block north of Maiden Lane. Are you familiar with the financial district?"

"It won't be a problem. I'll take a cab. How's one o'clock?"

"That'll work. See you then."

Ivy cut her huge hamburger in two, knowing it would still require two hands to pick up. She had learned Mitch was a vice president at Morgan Stanley, and he was talking about the rapid influx of African Americans in the field of finance.

"What's it been, maybe thirty-five years since the corporate white-collar sector opened to black people? Accounting and finance weren't popular choices for a long time, but I'm happy to say now that it's as much an option as anything else."

"So you're not the only black VP?"

"No, but we're talking investment firm. We have as many VPs as a bank does."

She nodded, but she felt they had talked about his work long enough. A man in his position was attractive to women everywhere, whether they were the receptionist at the front desk or up in the executive suite with their name on the door, and he probably knew it. She was impressed, yes, but he didn't have to know that. Besides, it wouldn't hurt for him to talk a little about his personal life.

"Tell me," she said, "how does it feel to be a single parent?"

"I think I'm managing all right. The kids really miss their mother, though. I'm sorry about that. First they had to deal with the separation, then the divorce, and now their mother is so far away."

"I gather she lived nearby before she accepted the promotion."

"Not really. She lived with her parents in Westchester. It was a temporary for her while she looked for a place in the city. But then she was offered the promotion in San Juan, and next thing we knew she was packing her bags."

"A change of scenery is probably a good thing after a divorce."

"Maybe. I'm just glad I was able to keep the house. That was the main reason my ex agreed that the kids stay with me, even though she saw them all the time, taking them out to dinner or the movies after work and up to Westchester on the weekends. We both wanted them to have as little upheaval as possible. The baby-sitter wasn't too happy when I moved her to the top floor of the house, but I needed the rental income."

"Didn't she have some kind of contract or something guaranteeing her separate living space?"

"Yes, but I inserted a clause that gave me the right

to move her into the house if I so desired, so there was nothing she could do.''

''That was smart. I'm glad your divorce was so amicable.''

''There really wasn't any need to be nasty. We were already positive there was no chance for reconciliation, and giving each other a hard time would only upset the kids.''

Ivy involuntarily raised her eyebrows as she sipped her root beer. She knew he was telling her this to assure her that he and his former wife weren't about to kiss and make up.

She couldn't say she was sorry to hear it.

''I was thinking you'd forgotten about us,'' Reneé said when Ivy returned home. ''I've got a bunch of checks for you to sign. Creditors wanting their ounce of flesh.''

''Pound of flesh, Reneé.'' Her bookkeeper was brilliant at the dual responsibilities of running the office and controlling the funds on hand, but the Bronx native had a tendency to confuse her proverbs. ''I forgot to tell you I might be late. I had a date.''

''Ooh, a date! Tell me all about it.''

''Well, I ordered the bacon cheeseburger, medium rare. . . .''

''That's not what I meant, Ivy. Hey, he didn't take you to Mickey D's, did he?''

''Of course not. A lot of places serve bacon cheeseburgers. You know I don't eat McDonald's unless I'm grabbing some breakfast.''

''And how does a postal worker get all that time off for lunch, anyway?''

''For your information, I had lunch with a corporate

VP. You're thinking of Ray, the fellow from the post office."

"Yes, that good-looking guy I've seen at the window, the one who went with you to your high school reunion. So where'd this new guy come from?"

"I met him at the reunion. He was escorting his cousin, a friend of mine."

"You were out with one guy and met another. That reminds me of how I met my second husband."

Ivy playfully rolled her eyes. "Please, not another story about your husbands." Reneé was the only person Ivy knew who had been married three times, and Reneé's résumé included three divorces as well.

"I'll spare you the details. But what I want to know is, what's going to happen to the guy from the post office?"

"Uh, Reneé, didn't you say you had some checks for me to sign?"

"Yeah, I know, quit gabbing and cut the cake."

Business was beginning to pick up now that springtime was approaching. Jubilee had become a popular choice among consumers to organize weddings. All three of her event planners were busy with last-minute arrangements for spring nuptials, and Ivy was ecstatic when a movie actress called to request a meeting to discuss a function she declined to identify over the phone.

The potential client was free that afternoon, and Ivy agreed to be at her apartment at four P.M. Reneé immediately began to contemplate that the actress, who was involved with a much older actor and was rumored to be pregnant, was planning a wedding. Ivy only half listened. Her mind kept going back to Reneé's earlier statement about what was going to happen with Ray

Jones. Somehow it didn't seem right for their budding friendship to end after having such a good time at the reunion . . . especially after he kissed her hand the way he had, with his eyes boring into her soul. Just thinking about it made her upper body shiver.

"I'm leaving," she said, reaching for her handbag.

"So soon? It's not quite three yet. You're only going to Central Park West."

"I have to make a stop."

"All right. Now remember, I want to hear all about her apartment."

"I doubt she'll take me on a tour, Reneé." Ivy smiled. Many of Jubilee's clients were wealthy, but only a few were also famous. Going to already swank Manhattan penthouses and townhouses, beach houses in the Hamptons, or country estates in Westchester or Connecticut became that much more exciting when a celebrity lived there.

Ivy walked to the neighborhood florist. "I'd like to have a plant sent," she said. "Actually, a dish garden with blooms is what I had in mind."

"Certainly, ma'am," the man behind the counter replied in an eager tone that suggested all the profits from those hundred-and-fifty-dollar Valentine's Day roses had been spent.

She wrote the card while the florist worked. "Ray— You're a real sweetheart. Please call if I can return the favor, or any time. Ivy." She sealed it inside an envelope, gave the florist Ray's home address, paid for the arrangement and the delivery, and then headed for the uptown subway.

She still didn't have an answer to Reneé's question. She could still feel the heat of Ray's gaze, not focusing on her body, but on her face, like he wanted to know all about her, what made her happy, what made her sad, what made her passionate. In her heart she knew she wanted to see him again, wanted him to get the answer to his burning questions. Her pride wouldn't allow her to chase after him—women had pride, too—but at least she'd let him know that she'd welcome hearing from him. What happened after that would have to be up to him.

Chapter 6
Thanks for the Memory

Ray could tell from the I-know-something-you-don't know smirk on Yolanda's face when he let himself in his apartment that something was up. He ignored it at first and asked about Maya's whereabouts. After he determined that his youngest had walked to the store with his mother, he asked, "All right, what's going on?"

"A surprise came for you this afternoon."

"Oh, yeah? What is it?"

"Daddy! I said it's a surprise. Why do people always ask what it is when they've already been told it's a surprise?"

"All right, I'll rephrase. *Where* is it?"

"On the table."

He felt her following close behind him as he walked toward the dining alcove. He saw the blooming plant right away; generally the oblong pinewood table only held a napkin holder and matching salt-and-pepper shakers.

"Who could be sending me a plant?" he mused.

"There's a card."

"I see it, I see it." He hooked his thumbnail under the edge of the seal and tore it open. He smiled as he read it. How thoughtful of Ivy. He should have known.

"So who's it from? And why'd they send it?"

"It's from Ivy, the lady I went out with last week. She wanted to express her appreciation."

"A lady sent you flowers? Cool!"

Yolanda's words barely registered as Ray reread what Ivy had written in a cursive script neat enough to be on a schoolroom blackboard. "Please call if I can return the favor, or any time." His eyes kept focusing on the last three words. Was he imagining things, or was really she inviting him to call her? Would she accept if he asked her to dinner?

You're being stupid, he told himself, annoyed at his gullibility. He'd seen Ivy reach in her evening bag to hand Mitch a business card, seen the impressed look on her face when she saw his town house. Maybe Mitch was the type who flirted but didn't follow through, and she was turning to him to soothe hurt pride. Or maybe she was just trying to be nice, but really didn't mean it.

But what if she did?

He handled the card roughly, shoving it back into the envelope. He was stuffing it into his pocket when his mother returned with Maya, who ran to him with her arms outstretched, inviting him to pick her up. He wondered if losing the mother she didn't remember had anything to do with her always being so happy to see him.

"Pretty plant," his mother said.

Ray knew she wouldn't come right out and inquire who had sent it; that wasn't her style. But he knew she would have plenty to say after she learned it was from Ivy.

"It's from Ivy, the lady I met at Kmart. She's the one Daddy took out Saturday night," Yolanda said.

"Oh, yes. The one who's married to her career."

Ray didn't like the contempt in her voice. "Come on, Mom."

"Come on, what? She's so busy making money that she can't find a date. Isn't that why she asked you to take her to her school reunion, to fool people?"

"We weren't trying to put anything over on anybody. Women generally don't go to black tie events solo. And it wasn't like she was going around telling people how well she's done. A few people exchanged personal information, including their occupation, but what people do for a living won't become general knowledge to all until they publish the book they're putting together. It's like an updated yearbook. They took individual pictures of all the class members at the reunion plus a group picture for it, and they were all asked to write a few sentences for the organizer about what they're doing now."

"And when people see she owns her own company they'll say, 'But at least she's got a handsome boyfriend to keep her warm at night.' If you weren't with her they'd think the same thing I do, that she's married to her career."

"I don't think you're being fair, Mom"—Ray said as he put Maya down—"but it doesn't really matter. It was a one-time event, and it's over and done with. I'm going to start the chili." He went into the kitchen and removed a Dutch oven from a lower cabinet.

"Imagine sending flowers to a man. I never heard of such a thing. A bread-and-butter note would be plenty sufficient to express gratitude. But I suppose she likes to flaunt the fact that she's got money."

Ray shook his head in annoyance, knowing he was safely hidden from view by the open refrigerator door. He loved his mother, but sometimes the combination of her strong opinions and tendency to stay on a subject ad infinitum could grate on his last nerve, and his reserve nerve as well.

"I need to check on my roast. You know your father won't get up out of that La-Z-Boy, even if there's smoke pouring out of the oven. I'll see you tomorrow."

Ray halted his dinner preparations for a few seconds while he walked her to the door. When he returned to the kitchen he sliced an onion into rings and cut the rings into large chunks right over the pot as the ground beef browned. The sound of cartoons filtered in from the living room television. Funny. One minute Yolanda was insisting she was old enough to stay out until two A.M., and the next minute she was watching *Top Cat* with her baby sister.

After dinner he gave Maya a bath while Yolanda did the dishes. He tucked Maya in bed in the room she shared with her much-older sister. Much as Yolanda loved Maya, she longed for her own room. Unfortunately, three-bedroom apartments were at a premium in a city populated largely by singles, roommates, and childless couples. For years people tended to move to the suburbs after they started families, so the majority of apartments in the city were studios, efficiencies, and one or two bedrooms. A safer, more child-friendly Manhattan in recent years helped reverse this long-standing trend, but demand surpassed what was available, and what was available came with astronomical rents.

Maya slept in his and Dolores's bedroom until she was nearly a year old, and he and Dolores had begun looking for a larger place when they moved Maya to Yolanda's room. When it appeared their search would be unsuccessful—they simply couldn't afford a large increase in rent—Dolores took steps to provide both girls with privacy, getting Ray's father to install a drapery rod in the middle of the ceiling and hanging curtains in a nonsheer fabric that could be pulled forward or backward at will. Ray remembered affectionately teasing her that it gave the girls' room the appearance of a semiprivate hospital suite, but it actually was quite effective.

He briefly considered buying a house after receiving the settlement for Dolores's death, but everything available in desirable areas was out of his price range. He talked to Yolanda about it, and she absolutely hated the idea of living on Long Island or in New Jersey or Westchester, of having to change schools with less than two years until graduation and leaving all her longtime friends. It pained Ray to see his sixty-eight-year-old father, a retired butcher, do the work of a live-in superintendent to supplement his pension. He dreamed of being able to afford to buy a place large enough for all of them. In the end the best he could do was buy his parents some badly needed new furniture and take them along when he took the kids on vacation, like the cruise he booked for them in July.

Alone in his bedroom, he pulled Ivy's card out of his pocket and read it a third time. He'd never forget how lovely she looked that night, the coppery skin of her bare shoulders against white satin, navy velvet molding to her hips, her shapely legs encased in sheer navy hose and seemingly lengthened by sexy high heels, with the bright eyes and radiant smile that had caught his attention in the first place that day at the post office. And he had to admit he thought he looked pretty spiffy in his tux.

He hadn't worn one since his wedding, and except for the absence of that ruffled shirt that had been the fashion of the day, little had changed. The people at the tux rental place had shown him more modern styles, all of which he vetoed. He liked the ethnicity of a kente cloth vest and bowtie, but he felt the odds were high

that the bright gold, orange, and green would clash
with Ivy's dress. Nor did he feel he had the right build
for those new longer coat styles, like the one Mitch
Crews had worn. Ray stood five feet, ten inches and had
become a bit stocky in recent years. A long coat would
make him look dumpy. Tall, slim dudes like Mitch or
actors Samuel L. Jackson or Will Smith were the ones
who could carry off that look. Still, he felt he and Ivy
made an attractive couple, like they had been a pair for
years rather than two people who barely knew each
other.

He'd thought of her often in the days since the
reunion. When he closed his eyes at night he could
practically smell her musky perfume.

Ray had been involved with only one woman since
Dolores was killed, a coworker who sent signals that
eventually became too obvious to ignore. It couldn't
really even be called an involvement: A few movies, an
occasional dinner, but mostly take-out pizza or Chinese,
followed by hitting the sheets. It had been comfortable,
a good fit that prevented both of them from being too
lonely, but then she met someone she was wild about
and suddenly it was over.

He showered and changed into his standard winter-
time sleep outfit of a crew-necked undershirt and sweat
pants, then set the automatic timer on the TV. He closed
his eyes to the sound of a movie he'd seen many times
before, and immediately he saw himself holding Ivy in
his arms and kissing her passionately.

Mitch raised his wineglass. "Here's to getting to know
an exciting, interesting woman."

"And here's to the exciting, interesting man making
the toast," Ivy replied.

They were sitting at a table for two at B. B. King's

blues club in midtown, enjoying dinner before Dr. John took the stage.

"How's your catfish?" he asked.

"Just perfect."

He yawned. "Excuse me," he said quickly. "I had a busy day today. The kids and I went skating. Normally we do that on Sundays, but they're participating in a special program at church tomorrow."

"Are you generally so busy on the weekends?"

"Well, we don't get to church every weekend. After the program tomorrow we'll go home and chill out, get some Chinese food or something. It's our routine."

"How old are your kids?"

"Casey is eleven and Elgin is eight."

"Would you say they're adjusting well?"

"They're doing fine. Having a steady routine is good for them, and their mom gets to New York about once a month or so, so it's not like they go for months without seeing her. But it's hard."

They chatted amiably in the cab back to her place, but Ivy's smile hid her nervousness. She always felt this way in the closing moments of a first date. Of course, they'd had lunch, but afterward they'd returned to their respective offices, so that wasn't really a date. She used to think she'd outgrow the good night–kiss jitters, but if she still found herself feeling this way at her age she probably never would.

The cab eased to a stop in front of her building, and they both got out. To Ivy, riding in a cab wasn't the same as a private vehicle or a limo, where she would wait for the door to be opened for her. She watched as Mitch slipped the driver some money and asked him to wait a few minutes. The gesture made her relax. She'd gone out with one or two men who dismissed the cab, and soon made it clear that they planned to spend the night with her. She presumed they'd taken the subway home after she informed them that she had other plans.

"I enjoyed tonight, Ivy. Can we do it again sometime soon?" Mitch said as they walked toward the elevator.

"I'd like that."

It was over quickly. He put his arm around her as they walked from the elevator to her door, and as soon as they were inside he pulled her close to his well-toned body and kissed her, briefly but satisfyingly. He bade her good night, and she closed the apartment door behind him.

Ivy gently rubbed cold cream onto her face. She liked Mitch; he was charming, handsome, successful, and he even liked blues music, her favorite. He was the kind of man women dreamed of. She wondered if he could be the one she'd been waiting for.

Would you listen to me? I just met the man, for crying out loud, have gone out with him one time. Next thing you know I'll be practicing writing "Ivy Crews" so I can see how it looks.

In an unintentional response to her foolish thoughts she began wiping her face with more force than she should have. She quickly lightened her touch and recalled the pleasant evening. Funny. People said everything happens for a reason.

Could it be that Mitch Crews was the reason she hadn't heard from Ray?

Chapter 7

You Can Pick Your Friends, but You're Stuck with Your Relatives

"Here's an interesting article," Bethany said, holding up the Money and Business section of the *Times*. "It's all about a celebrity couple and how they handle their money."

Ivy was frowning at the Sunday Jumble in the Arts and Leisure section. She was hung up on two of the six words. "Anybody I know?" she asked absently.

Bethany named the prominent couple. "This says they maintain their own homes, pay to take care of their own children—the ones they had with other people before they got together—and when they go on vacation, he sends his bills to his accountants, and she sends her bills to hers."

"Sounds awful. Where's the romance?"

"Apparently, both of them went through financial battles with their former spouses. You know what they say, 'Once burned, twice shy' . . . something along those lines. I forget exactly how it goes."

"You sound like Reneé," Ivy said. She grinned triumphantly as she realized the fifth word unscrambled to spell 'cruise.' All those vowels threw her. One more to go, then she could solve the riddle.

"I guess the rich really are different."

Ivy abruptly decided the last jumbled word could wait and put down the newspaper and pen. "Do you realize how absurd that sounds, Bethany? You sit here in your duplex apartment, with double digit millions, and you're calling somebody else rich?"

"All right, so that sounds silly. But I'll tell you something—no way would I want to live like these two do. I think an ironclad prenuptial agreement is sufficient if one or both parties are wealthy. But if I married a man with children, no way would I let them go to CCNY if there was enough money to send them to NYU. The way I see it his children would be my children, too."

"I agree. I guess those two must have had really bad experiences with their exes."

"Too bad they didn't base their finances on percentages. X percent of what they bring home goes for household expenses, x percent for leisure activities, and x percent for savings and investments. Whatever's left should be theirs to do whatever they want with. That way, if the marriage doesn't work, their joint holdings get divvied up the way it was put in, whether it was one-third/two-thirds, or ninety/ten, that's what they get out of it."

"Sounds fair, but still lacking somehow."

"It's not the most romantic thing in the world, but sometimes you've got to be practical. But naturally," Bethany said loftily, "if you marry that guy you went out with last night you won't have to worry about it."

"Yeah, right." Ivy took the last bite of her ham, egg, and cheese sesame seed bagel, then rolled up the wax paper, napkin, and paper bag in one big ball. "The bagels at that deli taste better every week."

"I like their breakfast pizza, myself." Bethany burped loudly. "As you can tell. I felt that coming. Sorry. Hey, are you sure you don't want to join Janice and me at the play this afternoon? She really needs cheering up, and two witty friends are better than one."

"Why does she need to be cheered up?"

"Her husband just moved out. I say she's well rid of him, myself. He hasn't been acting right since she started going to law school years ago, always complaining about how she's behind on her housework, stuff like that."

"Making her feel guilty."

"You think if he was so concerned *he'd* pick up a broom. He's really made her life miserable," Bethany said. "From what she's told me I think he's been fooling around. Now that she's finishing law school and been offered a promotion he walks out. It was all right while she was supervising the paralegals, but now that she's going to be an associate he feels like she's taking the upper hand."

"It's silly, isn't it," Ivy said. "Marriage is supposed to be a partnership, not a competition."

"Janice is only thinking of making a good future for them and their kids. You'd think her husband would do the same and concentrate on taking the sergeant's exam, or whatever rank comes after detective, instead of trying to goad her into giving up her dreams. If you ask me it's emotional abuse."

"That's too bad," Ivy said. "I wish I could help out, but I've been summoned to Lakewood. My parents have requested to see all of us this afternoon. Apparently they have something they want to tell us. Tell Janice hello and that I'll see her at our next get-together."

* * *

Ivy disliked traveling on bridges and tunnels, but there was no way off Manhattan Island without utilizing one or the other. She wasn't sure which one she dreaded the most, for she reacted the same way. After the first few minutes of driving through the Holland Tunnel she found herself breathing in shallow gasps and grasping the steering wheel of her car with increasingly damp palms. Just when she thought she could stand the dim lights and enclosed rounded space no longer and was ready to scream, the light of New Jersey became visible. Still, her breathing didn't return to normal until her car had completely emerged.

It sure would be nice to go somewhere for once that doesn't have a toll, she thought wearily as she paid the six-dollar fee for the tunnel and then headed for the first of the two toll roads she would take to her parents' home.

Less than an hour later she eased her car into one of the spaces reserved for visitors at the development of attached town homes where she had grown up. She recognized Stephanie and Jerome's minivan; her parents' cars sitting in their assigned spaces told her Otto hadn't gone off somewhere with one of them. Everyone being there already meant she shouldn't have to stay long, and she was glad. It was the blustery type of winter day where it felt good to just lie at home and devour the newspapers.

Her nieces and nephew, ranging in age from eight to fifteen, greeted her with more enthusiasm than anyone else. Stephanie had a gloomy look on her face. Ivy felt a sudden rush of panic. Had one of her parents become ill? Had her mother confided in Stephanie privately before filling in herself and Otto?

Ivy greeted her family affectionately. Her mother and father were sixty-two and sixty-five, respectively, but they looked small and shrunken, old for their ages. They were both healthy, but Ivy suspected the situation with Otto had made them unhappy.

"I hope I didn't keep everyone waiting, but now that I'm here I've got to tell you I'm very curious about why you wanted all of us to come over," she said.

"Let's all sit down," her mother suggested.

They all went to the living room, even the children. Ivy watched as her mother nodded to her father.

"We wanted to tell all of you at the same time," he began. "We met with a realtor last week. We're putting the house up for sale."

"What?" Otto said. "Where are we going to live?"

"Your mother and I are going to move to North Carolina. We have friends who've retired to the Asheville area, and we've been to visit them. We've decided it's time to stop working, even though your mother might continue with her private duty nursing."

"What about me?" Otto demanded.

"You're old enough to take care of yourself, Otto."

His face twisted in fury. "This is all because I was late getting back with the car that time. You're willing to go through all this to punish me. I told you I was sorry."

"Oh, Otto, grow up," Stephanie said. "Stop thinking everything is all about you. It's plenty time for Mom and Dad to retire."

"Yeah, I should've guessed you'd say something like that."

Ivy decided she didn't want to get involved in the disagreement between her brother and sister, and addressed her parents instead. "You're obviously very happy about your decision. I'm sure you'll love it down there."

"Thank you, dear," her mother said. "We're looking forward to it. We're going to get a place that's all on one floor, since the stairs here are getting a bit difficult for us. But we'll have extra rooms, so the kids can spend part of their summers with us."

Stephanie's younger daughter perked up. "Will there be other kids there, Grandma, or just old people?"

Ivy's mother laughed. "Oh, there'll be kids there for you to play with, I'm sure. Grandpa and I have no intention of moving to a retirement village. You'll love visiting us."

Otto shot out of his seat and walked over to the window, hands stuffed in his jeans pockets. "I'm glad everybody's so happy, but what about me? Where am I supposed to go when you sell the house out from under me? I don't want to go to Asheville. Not that I heard anybody saying there'll be a room for *me* in the new house."

Ivy watched her parents exchanged worried glances.

"You know, Otto, this house won't go for much. Maybe you can buy it," Jerome suggested.

"Buy it? With what?"

Ivy didn't know if her brother-in-law was trying to be funny or not. Otto had managed to hold on to his present job for several months, but he didn't even own a car.

"Well, I know Stephanie and Jerome don't have space for another person," her mother said. "Maybe Ivy can put you up until you get on your feet."

Ivy felt her features harden. She should have known this was coming.

Her brother responded before she could. "New York's almost an hour away from here, Mom, you know that."

"Otto, there are plenty of jobs in New York."

Ivy held up a hand, palm out. "Whoa! Did somebody put Windex in with my orange juice this morning? You guys talk like I'm invisible. Don't you think someone should talk to me before Otto starts packing his bags?"

Otto pointed an accusatory finger at her and opened his mouth to say something, but their father silenced him with a calming gesture.

"There's no need to rush into anything, Ivy," he said. "We're just getting the house listed. It'll probably take some time to sell. We just wanted to alert all of you that we'll be leaving the area."

"I had a feeling it was something like that," Stephanie said. "I know you'll like it there, but I'm going to miss you so much." Her voice broke, and Jerome put a comforting arm around her shoulders.

Otto muttered a contemptuous "Shhhhh" before storming out with long, bold strides. They all heard the front door being opened and then slamming shut.

"Well, I might have expected as much from him," Stephanie said. "He'll be back when he's hungry, I guess. I'll check on the ham." She got up.

Ivy and their mother followed her to the kitchen.

"Mom, I didn't know you were making dinner," Ivy remarked.

"Stephanie and Jerome brought a ham, plus greens and macaroni and cheese. Wasn't that sweet? They said they didn't want me having to cook if the whole family was over. They even brought rolls. But I did make a chocolate cake for dessert."

Ivy immediately felt a pang of guilt. She should have thought to do something. If Stephanie told her what she was planning she would have been happy to contribute. But that was just like Stephanie, to do it all herself, all the while complaining about how useless her siblings were. Well, fine. Let her reign triumphant because she'd brought the dinner she would have made for her family anyway to their parents' house.

"That was thoughtful," Ivy said. "But I hope you won't be upset if I don't stay. I'd like to get home and be lazy. A busy week starts tomorrow. We've got a lot going on this week at Jubilee."

"You can bring a plate with you, Ivy. No need to feel guilty," Stephanie said.

She spoke calmly, refusing to be baited. "I have nothing to feel guilty about, Stephanie. I'm just anxious to get home. I spent the morning having breakfast at a friend's, and I haven't had much time to enjoy my solitude."

"I know what that means. You're saying you don't want Otto to live with you because you enjoy your solitude."

"No. I don't want Otto living with me because he's a leech," she replied matter of factly. "He'll be asking to borrow my car, asking me to loan him money he has no intention of paying back, and it won't take long for him to start acting like it's *his* place. As for it being just until he's settled, we all know how long that'll be. I don't think so. I don't feel I have to make excuses."

"But he's your brother, dear," her mother said. "And you have so much, and he has nothing."

"And is that supposed to be my fault? Nobody handed me my company. I started it from scratch. I worked fourteen-hour days—I still do sometimes—and did everything myself in the beginning. Otto is a grown man, Mom. He shouldn't be looking to crash on anybody's couch; he should have his own. You and Dad gave him fair warning that it's time for him to get himself together. If he starts taking steps right away he'll be fine. If he can't afford an apartment he can always rent a room at the Y."

Stephanie withdrew her breath. "You'd rather have him live there with all those transients? That's cold, Ivy."

She turned to her sister defiantly. "Then *you* take him in."

Ivy fumed all the way home. Every time she saw her family she always left with the same feeling of unhappiness and frustration. She never felt loved or appreciated just for herself, only when she did something for someone. She could just imagine her parents' reactions if she had agreed that Otto could stay with her. They loved her in their own way, she knew, but not the way parents were supposed to love their children. That was reserved for Otto, but she and Stephanie only received affection when they did something special for their parents. It had rendered Stephanie almost pathetic in her competitive quest for approval.

Ivy could still see the stricken expression on her sister's face when Ivy presented their parents with tickets for a five-day cruise to Key West and Mexico for their fortieth anniversary, or hear the sharp tone in her voice as she ordered her children not to nag Auntie Ivy with requests to ride in her PT Cruiser, saying a car was a car.

Ivy felt comforted as the Manhattan skyline came into view. In just a few minutes she'd descend into the tunnel again, drive deep under the depths of the Hudson River, and emerge in the city that had become her home. She'd park at the garage and retreat to the comfort of her loft, where she would put on some music as she drew up her schedule for the week.

Working would keep her mind off the unpleasant subjects of the day, like Janice's husband leaving her, or wondering how it would feel to be loved freely and unconditionally, without those ever-present strings attached.

* * *

Ray tapped on Yolanda's closed bedroom door. "I'm going to pick up Maya. We'll have dinner when I get back. I need you to set the table."

"I'll have it done by the time you come back."

She spoke in a dull monotone, telling him it was no coincidence that he found her in her bedroom alone instead of at his parents' apartment, where she usually went to do her homework after coming home from school. "You all right, Yolanda?"

"Yes. It's just that I've got a lot of homework to do. I asked Nana to keep Maya until you got home."

Ray didn't know what had Yolanda so down, but he knew his mother would. He ran down the flight of stairs, went out the front door and into the building next door. He let himself into his parents' building with the key they gave him, but when he stood opposite their ground-floor apartment door he rang the bell, as was his custom. "It's Ray," he called when he heard footsteps inside.

Maya ran to greet him as his mother opened the door. He picked up his daughter and kissed her hello, then asked her to watch television for a few more minutes while he talked to Nana.

They stood in the vestibule, near the rack holding the tenants' keys. "Mom, do you have any idea what's wrong with Yolanda? She's been behind closed doors ever since I came home. She insists she's fine, but I can hear it in her voice that she's not."

His mother sighed heavily. "She called and asked if I would keep Maya until you came home. She sounded like she'd been crying. I asked her what was wrong. She said something about a new holiday, Take Our Daughters to Work or something like that. Apparently it's existed for several years, but this is the first time her school is allowing the girls to participate."

"Except she can't participate. Not this year, not ever." Ray sounded defeated.

She put a comforting hand on his upper arm. "I thought of suggesting that maybe she could go along with one of her friends, but now I'm thinking that a lot of offices might not want to have too many young people around. That can be disruptive for a place of business. I'd take her around with me, but it won't be too exciting for her to watch me clean out the laundry room or place new grout around the bathtub in 2-B."

"All right," he said quickly, not wanting to hear any more of her sarcasm. He knew his mother hadn't had an easy life. His younger brother's sudden death from an internal obstruction at the age of eight had robbed her of her enthusiasm, and in its place was a cynicism bordering on bitterness. "At least I know what the problem is. I'll talk to her about it after dinner."

"Ray, it seems to me that you should ask that girl you took out the other week to help you. She owns her own company, so she can invite anyone she wants to the office. Besides, it's the least she can do, after you spent all that money on a tuxedo so you could save her face."

"Mom, like I told you before, Ivy offered to pay for my tux. I insisted on taking care of it myself."

"I don't know why. She's got plenty of money."

"So do I, remember?"

She snorted. "Yeah, but she's got lots more where that came from. Yours is a one-shot deal. And she doesn't have children to educate, like you do. You try to live that high life, and Maya will end up going to public school."

"That's enough, Mom," he said, a warning in his tone. He called to Maya to get ready to go, then turned to his mother again. "Where's Dad?"

"He's repairing the lock on the window in 4-C. He'll be back soon."

* * *

Ray wasn't surprised when Yolanda only picked at her pork chops. "I talked to Nana about you today," he said. "We'll talk about it later, after I get Maya to bed. I just want to tell you not to worry about it. We'll work something out, all right?"

"All right."

Ray treated Maya to a bubble bath after dinner. She was clapping the bubbles away when she suddenly asked, "Daddy, where's my mommy?"

He physically felt his heart leap, but quickly recovered. He knew this would happen sooner or later. Maya was at the stage where she was beginning to wonder why other children had mothers and she didn't. He shifted his hip on the hard edge of the bathtub as he thought about what to say. "We actually talked about this once before. You don't remember that, do you?"

"When I was little?"

He smiled. "Well, I guess you were littler than you are now. Your mommy loved you very much. She was taken away from us when you were just one year old. She had an accident and went to Heaven."

"When is she coming back?"

"Well, that's just it. When people go to Heaven they don't get to come back. We won't see them again until we get to Heaven ourselves, and that won't be for a long time. But Mommy left you with me, and Yolanda, and Nana and Granddad."

"Is Yolanda sad because she misses Mommy?"

And he thought he was being discreet. It was awfully difficult to hide anything from children, even three year olds. "I'm afraid so. You have to remember that Yolanda is older than you, and she remembers Mommy very well. We have some movies of Mommy with us. Would you like to see them?"

"Yes."

"All right. It'll be time for you to go to bed soon, but I promise that I'll show them to you tomorrow, okay?"

"Okay."

As much as Ray hated to admit it, his mother might have had a point when she suggested he ask Ivy for help. A small business like hers—he imagined she only had a few employees, since she worked out of her home—was the ideal setting. Besides, it would give him the opportunity to see her again. It had only been two weeks, but he was still thinking about her more often than he should. The memory dimming he kept telling himself would come with time simply hadn't occurred, he could recall every detail of being with her like it was just the night before.

Then he remembered the promise he had made to Yolanda and realized he had no choice. He *had* to call Ivy.

Chapter 8
A Friend in Need

Ivy nodded, even though she was talking on the phone and no one could see her. "That's right. It's not necessary to spend good money on other desserts when you have a wedding cake. After all, you're going to be spending a lot of money for the cake. You don't want it overshadowed by a double chocolate chip cookie, do you? That's right. It'll be fine. There are plenty of other ways to save money without having to sacrifice quality. All right, go let him in. I'll speak with you tomorrow. Good night."

She sighed when she hung up. Good thing her client's fiancé had shown up at the door, or she never would have gotten off the phone. Traditionally at the end of March, event planners were busy with the early stages of fall nuptials and the late stages of those scheduled for the spring. It made for late nights, as most brides-to-be called her in the evening, but it was part of the job. Weddings brought in big money for Jubilee, both from the fees they were able to command and from the referrals that always came out of them.

She added the page of notes she had just made to the client's file. Her eye caught sight of another pending file, the one for the actress who had secured Jubilee's services to organize her wedding. The affair was being put together both quickly and on the quiet, but it would attract plenty of attention, with one weekly magazine having been guaranteed the first photo rights. Jubilee's role was certain to be mentioned, and perhaps she'd even see her own name in the cover story. Few bonuses compared to free publicity. Ivy knew human nature well enough to know that people loved to be stylish and "in," and once word got out that Jubilee had overseen all the wedding arrangements for these celebrities, both of whom were currently hot, plenty of others would want them to plan theirs as well.

Ivy was just about to reach for the file when her home phone rang. She picked up the extension on her desk.

"Hi, Ivy. It's Ray Jones."

She immediately broke into a smile. "Hello, Ray. How nice to hear from you."

"I got the plant you sent. That was sweet of you. You'll be glad to know it's thriving. Yolanda picked up a beautiful ceramic flowerpot at Kmart with her employee discount and replanted it."

"Oh, good." She could feel her pulse racing. If he wanted to tell her how well the plant was doing he would have told her as soon as he received it. Why had he called? Did he want to see her?

"I have the card you sent with it," Ray said. "I kept it. At the time I didn't think it would be necessary for you to return the favor, but I find myself in a bit of a jam, and I think you can help."

"How can I help you, Ray?"

He felt buoyed by both the swiftness of her answer

as well as the genuine concern in her voice. He could imagine the sincere concern in her expressive brown eyes. Ivy's realness and genuine interest in everyone she met was one of her most endearing traits. "Have you ever heard of Take Our Daughters to Work Day?"

"Oh, yes! Girls spend a few hours with their mothers at their workplaces. I think it's a wonderful idea. It gets girls thinking at an early age about what type of career they'd like to pursue."

"Well, this year Yolanda's school is allowing the girls to take part of the day off so they can spend it with their mothers at work. The ones who go have to submit a report of what their mothers do."

"Oooohhhh."

She managed to inflect enough compassion in that one syllable so that he knew further explanation of his dilemma was unnecessary.

"I think the point of the holiday is for young girls to see women at work," Ivy said. "The obvious person for them to go with would be their mothers, but it can really be any working woman. I'd love to have Yolanda spend the afternoon with me here at Jubilee, if you'd like. Granted, what I do isn't as beneficial to society as the more traditional occupations like teaching or nursing, but I'm sure her teacher and classmates will appreciate that it's certainly different."

He closed his eyes momentarily in relief. "You're pretty special, you know that? Here I was, worried that you wouldn't want a teenage girl underfoot at your place of business, and you offer to let her come down without my even having to ask."

"Well, I don't know how special I am, but I'm glad I can help. Who knows, Yolanda might take to the business. Not that I'd try to steer her toward event management if you'd like to see her get into something else," she added quickly.

He laughed. "I'm not one of those parents who map out their children's whole lives for them. I've told Yolanda that whatever she decides to do is okay with me. My only requirement is that she get at least a bachelor's degree."

"Good advice. What type of work did her mother do?"

"She was a paralegal."

"Oh, that's very interesting work."

"I remember the firm she worked for being a little stuffy. If they allow daughters in at all they'd probably insist on limiting their observations to a half hour or so."

"When's the date?"

He snapped his fingers. "I forgot to make note of the date, and just before I called you I was in Yolanda's room getting all the details. All I remember was that it's the twenty-something of April. The notice she showed me said it's on a Wednesday, but I can get back with you and confirm that."

"That'll be fine. How've you been, Ray?"

"I'm . . . I'm good. Yourself?"

"I've been well, thanks."

"Have you gotten your reunion book yet?"

"No, I think it'll probably be another couple of weeks."

Her voice sounded wonderful with its distinct flawless diction. It had been foolish of him to ask about the updated yearbook. Of course they couldn't have gotten it printed up and mailed this soon. Reluctantly he realized the time had come to end the conversation.

After he thanked her for helping Yolanda, he told her he'd be in touch. He hung up feeling satisfied. Yolanda's problem was solved, and he'd gotten to speak with Ivy for a few minutes. He would talk with her again when he called to confirm the date. Maybe he'd even go to pick Yolanda up after Ivy showed her how her company operated. He was often off on Wednesdays when he worked the previous Saturday. He could take them all to dinner. Who knew what it could lead to?

He whistled as he headed toward Yolanda's room to give her the good news.

Ivy and Mitch applauded heartily as the cast of the play joined hands and took a joint bow. "That was wonderful," she said to him.

"You really enjoyed it, huh?" he asked as he guided her toward the exit.

"I loved it. But I could have done without the couple next to me."

"Did I hear the husband repeating a lot of the dialogue for her?"

"If he wasn't doing that he was explaining the characters' actions or intents, because she apparently didn't get it." She shook her head. "They really were a cute old couple, but I've got to tell you they were driving me nuts. I felt like I was sitting next to Helen Keller."

Outside the theater, they slipped into one of the many cabs that waited at the curb, hoping to get a fare. As had become habit, Mitch came upstairs with her. The dinner they'd had before the theater had worn off, so she kicked off her shoes and put some bread in the toaster and made sandwiches out of the leftover Honey-baked ham in her refrigerator. It felt a little awkward to be spreading mayonnaise and mustard and slicing tomatoes in her good black velvet suit, but she feared Mitch might interpret a change to loungewear as an invitation for him to stay the night. Best to keep things simple, with no room for confusion.

She carried two sandwiches on plates into the dining area, then went back for glasses of limeade, her long skirt folded over at the waist to prevent it from dragging on the floor.

"This hit the spot," Mitch said after he swallowed his first bite. "Thanks, Ivy. I always sleep better with something in my stomach. Hey, did I tell you my kids are going to Puerto Rico for their spring break? I'm putting them on a plane the day after Easter, and they'll be back the following Sunday."

"So you're getting a little break."

"I need it. But I'd really like for you to meet them. Are you doing anything Easter?"

"Not really. My sister's making Easter dinner, but we're kind of on the outs right now. I'm afraid that if I went it would only be uncomfortable for everyone."

"I'm sorry to hear that. My parents are going down to Maryland to spend the holiday with my sister and her family, so it'll just be the kids and me. We'd love to have you join us."

"I'd like that. Thanks."

Thirty minutes later she walked him to the door, his arm around her shoulder and hers around his waist. "It was a lovely evening, Mitch. I always have such a nice time with you."

"And I with you." They faced each other, and he kissed her lips lightly, then pulled back and gazed at her a few seconds before kissing her more intensely. Her arms went around his neck, and she balanced her body on tiptoes to accommodate his height and her bare feet.

"You know," he said softly afterward, "I like kissing you good night, but one day soon we're really going to have to see how it feels to kiss good morning."

She leaned on the door after she closed it behind him, smiling dreamily. She and Mitch had been dating for several weeks now, and they always had a good time together. She wondered if he had introduced his children to any other women. It didn't take a trained psychologist to figure out that it probably wasn't good for children to be exposed to a parade of their daddy's lady friends.

She had a real good feeling about Mitch. And to think if she hadn't gone to the reunion she would have missed out on meeting him. She had Ray Jones to thank for that.

So why did she keep thinking about Ray and wonder what he was doing?

Chapter 9
Sense and Nonsense

"This is weird, Bethany," Ivy said. "I've been brought to meet men's parents before, but never their children. I'm as scared as a turkey in November. Is it silly for me to be so nervous about meeting an eight year old and an eleven year old?"

"Listen, my experience was that sometimes the kids can be worse than the parents. I've had kids be outright hostile to me, like they blame me for their parents not being married anymore."

"Ouch. Bethany, did you ever think about having kids of your own, or even adopting?"

"I would have been a great mother. To tell the truth, I'm good at anything I put my mind to. But I won't be having any kids. I don't even think about it anymore. I'm going to be forty-two, Ivy. My thoughts have gone from cute, cuddly babies to making sure I don't outlive my money and taking steps to prevent osteoporosis."

"Well, do you have any advice for me at all?"

"Don't do anything special. Be yourself. If they don't

like you, that means there's something wrong with them."

Outside the church in her hometown, Ivy gathered with her family members.

"It was a lovely service, wasn't it?" her mother was saying.

"It didn't seem as long as it usually is. Not that I'm complaining," her father replied.

"Aunt Ivy, I want to ride home with you in the Cruiser," Cheri, Stephanie's oldest daughter, said. Her wish was quickly echoed by her younger siblings.

"I'm sorry, kids, but I'm not having dinner with you today. I accepted an invitation in the city."

"But you always have Easter dinner with us, Aunt Ivy."

"And I'm sure I will next year." She hoped not, but surely a little fib couldn't hurt. "Please don't be disappointed. After all, Uncle Otto didn't come to church, but you'll see him at dinner." She put her arms around the two younger kids. "Next time I'll take you for a ride. I promise."

"It's just a car, kids," Stephanie said, somewhat testily. "No need to be disappointed. It's not like we have to walk home."

Ivy's father rested a palm on her shoulder. "I'm sorry you won't be joining us for dinner. I understand Stephanie is making a leg of lamb. At least she put it in the oven. Jerome is doing the rest."

"Nice way for him to get out of going to church. I'm sure it'll be delicious, but I promised my friend I'd have dinner with him. I thought it would all work out if I came to church with you guys."

"We're glad we at least got to see you."

"You could have brought your friend with you," her mother said. "We would love to meet him."

"It's a little more complicated than that, Mom." She didn't feel this was the place to discuss Mitch's status as a custodial parent. "I'll tell you about it another time."

"Sounds like it might be serious between you two."

"No, we've only been seeing each other about a month. We're having fun. I like him."

"What does he do?"

Ivy smiled; her mother always asked this type of question. She always went "tsk, tsk," when Ivy identified typical professions like teachers, bank managers, or computer programmers, but this time she was in for a surprise. "He's a vice president at a Wall Street investment firm."

"That's wonderful, Ivy! I'm glad you found somebody who's more your equal."

Stephanie crossed her arms in front of her in a hostile gesture. "I guess you'd be embarrassed if he sees that Jerome and I don't have a huge country house and live like millionaires, huh?"

"Oh, Stephanie, give it a rest."

"Girls," their father cautioned. "It's Easter. Can you put aside the bickering for one day?"

"It's all right, Daddy. I'm leaving, anyway." Ivy hugged her parents, nephew, and nieces. "Good-bye, Stephanie," she said pointedly over her shoulder as she left, not waiting for a response.

It was going on two-thirty when she emerged from the Holland Tunnel. She decided to garage her car. After a quick freshen-up at home, she'd walk to Mitch's. The sun was shining, and the temperature was in the low sixties.

She set out at a leisurely pace, walking north on Fifth Avenue, then headed east when she reached Thirty-sixth Street. Mitch's town house was even more attractive in daylight. It was five stories high, constructed of a light red brick, and a black wrought iron fence surrounded it.

She rang the doorbell, which was quickly answered by Mitch, who wore faded, starched jeans, a tailored white shirt with its sleeves rolled up to midforearm, and a big smile. "Welcome! Come in."

He glimpsed around quickly before kissing her hello while they stood in the spacious foyer, an action she found irritating. What was shameful about a quick kiss between consenting adults who were free to show affection?

"Am I too early?"

"No, you're right on time. We've been home over an hour. I was just about to light the grill."

"You're barbecuing?"

"It's a little cool yet, but since it's hot over the fire it kind of balances out." His gaze swept over her appreciatively. "You're looking lovely, as usual."

"Thanks. I went to church with my parents and sister in New Jersey. It never occurred to me to change clothes," she said, eyeing his casual attire. Even fully clothed, it was clear how perfectly he was built. Mitch was forty-three years old, and she knew at that point in life a flat stomach didn't happen all by itself. He probably worked out at least a couple of days a week.

"You're completely appropriate for dinner. It wasn't like I was planning to ask you to watch the meat. Come on outside."

He led her down a hall to the back door. They stepped into a fenced-in garden featuring cobblestoned grounds with a patio set consisting of an oblong ceramic and wrought iron table with umbrella and six comfortably cushioned chairs, as well as a gas grill with a side burner with a bistro table and chairs for two just a few feet away.

"How lovely!" she exclaimed.

"I had the kids bring up the cushions from the basement." He yelled, and a boy and girl appeared from the corner of the yard, where they had been romping with a German shepherd. "Kids, this is Miss Smith. Ivy, this is Casey and Elgin."

"Hello, Miss Smith," they said in unison.

"Hi, kids. Why don't you tell me your dog's name, since your daddy didn't introduce us."

"This is Timmy," Elgin said.

"He looks like a friendly dog, unlike most German shepherds I know."

"He won't hurt you," Casey said.

Ivy reached out and tentatively rubbed the dog behind his ears. He laid down at her feet. "I think he likes me."

"Have a seat, Ivy, and keep me company while I cook." Mitch pulled out a chair at the bistro set.

"So what's on the menu?" she asked as she sat down.

"Stuffed flank steaks, baked potatoes, and corn." He lit the grill, then placed four foil-covered ears of corn over the flames. "I'll give these a head start. It won't take long for the meat to cook."

"Good. I didn't eat lunch."

The children eventually made their way toward the grill. Elgin stared openly at Ivy. "You're pretty," he said.

"Why, thank you, Elgin."

"Are you my daddy's girlfriend?"

"Your daddy and I are just friends."

"Elgin, I want you to go to the kitchen and get me that squeeze bottle with no label on it. That's where I put my special moisturizing sauce," Mitch said.

Ivy wrinkled her nose. "Moisturizing? That makes me think of lotion."

"No, it's just some water flavored with vinegar and spices. It helps keep the meat from drying out."

Elgin was out of breath when he returned.

"You shouldn't have run all the way, Sport," Mitch told him, affectionately rubbing his back. "But thanks a lot."

"I understand you kids are going to Puerto Rico for your spring break," Ivy said chattily.

"Our mother lives there," Casey said. "She's a financial analyst, and she's in charge of her company's office in San Juan."

Ivy found the girl's obvious pride amusing, but she supposed eleven was old enough to know that all children didn't live in five-story East Side town houses, attend private schools, and fly to Puerto Rico for their vacations unless somebody was making big bucks.

"What do *you* do?" Casey asked.

"I run my own company. I plan business functions and social events all over the metropolitan area."

"What's the name of your company?"

"Jubilee, Incorporated."

"Is it here in the city?"

"Yes."

"Where?"

She was beginning to feel like she was on the witness stand and looked to Mitch for help, but he didn't seem at all perturbed by his daughter's curiosity. "In Chelsea," she answered, hoping that would be an end to the rapid fire questions.

Casey nodded thoughtfully.

"Daddy, can I have some more candy?" Elgin asked.

"Not until after dinner." Mitch caught Ivy's eye. "Elgin gave up candy for Lent. Now he's ready to eat his weight in jelly beans."

"But Casey's chewing gum. She's been chewing it all day."

"I've been chewing the same piece for hours, Elgin. Don't go bringing me into it," his sister said sharply.

"I said not until after dinner, Elgin," Mitch repeated.

Elgin's face puckered, like he was about to cry, but that soon dissolved in favor of his poking out his lower lip. He headed for the back door.

"If you're going in, run the microwave for seven minutes. The potatoes are already inside," Mitch said.

Elgin turned around instantly. "I'm gonna stay here," he said.

Ivy suppressed a smile. Any fool could tell Elgin had intended to go inside until his father asked him to do something. She was going to enjoy seeing him get his comeuppance. She waited for Mitch to order him to go turn on the microwave—and to wipe that smirk off his face.

But instead, Mitch turned to his daughter. "Casey, go upstairs and start the microwave. Seven minutes. We'll be up in a bit."

Ivy raised an eyebrow. No one had gotten away with sulking like that in the Smith household, not even Otto.

A few minutes later Mitch moved the meat and corn to a glass dish. He turned off the flame and shut off the gas. "I think we're ready to go in now."

"I can carry something," Ivy said, getting to her feet.

"No, we've got it. Elgin, c'mere and grab the rest of the stuff."

Elgin didn't move.

"Elgin! Move it, huh?"

"I don't want to eat, Daddy."

"Did I ask you if you want to eat? I said take those things inside."

Elgin sullenly picked up the spice containers, the plastic bottle, and the long-handled cooking utensils.

Inside, Ivy was surprised to see a small elevator parallel to the back door. She'd thought the windowless wood-toned door was a closet or something. "An elevator! I'm impressed."

"An earlier owner had it added on. It's really a necessity in a house with five floors and a basement. There are five floors because it's so narrow, just sixteen feet wide. We've got to go up to the third floor just to eat." Elgin had taken the stairs, so just Ivy and Mitch got in, and Mitch hit a button.

"A lot of town homes on the Upper East Side don't even have elevators."

"I wouldn't know about that. There wasn't anything up there listed that we could afford, so we skipped looking there, right along with Tribeca and Grammercy. For some reason real estate is less expensive here in Murray Hill. We jumped on this as soon as it was listed."

"What floor do you and the kids stay on?"

"My bedroom is on the fourth floor. The kids are on the fifth. The housekeeper was up there, too, after I moved her from the ground-floor apartment, but then she quit. Now I just have someone come in during the day so someone will be here when the kids get home from school. It works pretty well, except when I have to travel for work."

The elevator stopped, and she followed him to a kitchen with oak cabinets and cranberry-tiled countertops. "Your home is really beautiful, Mitch."

"Thanks. We've been here six years, so it really feels like home."

They fixed their plates in the kitchen, then sat down at the brown mahogany table in the dining room.

"That's a pretty suit, Miss Smith," Casey said after Mitch said grace.

"Thank you. I wore it to church today." She half expected the curious child to ask which church she attended, but Casey was silent.

"I meant to ask you, how was traffic?" Mitch asked.

"It moved very nicely. No delays at all. And it was a beautiful day for a ride."

"You have a car?" Casey asked.

"Yes, I have a PT Cruiser."

"I like those," Elgin said. Then he made a face and said, "We don't have a car anymore."

Mitch looked a little embarrassed. "When my wife and I separated, she took the car up to Westchester. She needed it up there to get around. Then when she accepted the promotion, she sold it before she relocated. It didn't make sense for it to sit at her parents' collecting dust, and by then I didn't want it back. The kids might make out like we're poverty stricken because we don't have a car anymore, but the truth is we do fine without it. The kids' school sends a bus for them, and I take the subway to work. I usually take cabs at night, and when we go out of town I rent a car. All in all, it's a lot cheaper than the cost of maintaining and garaging a car every month."

Ivy nodded. "I didn't always have a car. When Jubilee really started to take off, I decided to purchase a vehicle that could be used for business as well. The backseat of the Cruiser folds down, and it can be loaded with supplies. Sometimes during our busy season the two vans we have aren't enough."

"Do you put together a lot of events outside of the city?"

"Oh, yes. We go to New Jersey, Connecticut, Westchester, and Long Island." She chuckled. "The absolutely worst experience I've ever had with Jubilee was at a party we organized at a country estate in Northern New Jersey. An art collector was showing off his newest acquisition to about sixty of his closest friends. It was really a nondescript little piece of art, as I recall, a vase with some flowers."

"Who painted it?" Casey asked.

"I think it may have been a Van Gogh. I'm not really sure. Art isn't something I know a lot about. I just remember thinking it seemed terribly overpriced. It was no bigger than eleven by fourteen inches, and it sold for over a million dollars.

"Anyway," she continued, "when it came time to get the hors d'oeuvres in the oven, it wouldn't light. The caterer was near hysterical. By the time we packed everything up and loaded it in the van and drove 'next door,' "—she held fingers up as quote marks—"which was nearly fifteen minutes away—"

"Why did it take so long to drive next door?"

Casey again. She should have known. "Because we were in the country, where people have fifty- and hundred-acre estates so they can ride their horses for miles and still stay on their own property."

"Casey, you've traveled enough to know that everybody doesn't live on top of each other like they do here in the city," Mitch said.

Ivy continued her story. "By the time they got them cooked and packed up again, we were running an hour late. To top it all off, on the way back a police car comes out of nowhere and pulls me over for speeding." She laughed.

"How fast were you going?"

Ivy stopped laughing. Casey's relentless questions were starting to get on her nerves. She had to struggle to keep her voice from sounding short. "I honestly don't remember, Casey. It was a long time ago. Besides, it really isn't important. What's important was that I was pulled over and had to wait while the policeman ran my license for outstanding warrants and then asked me all kinds of insulting questions." She realized the moment the words were out that she was courting another question.

Casey didn't disappoint. "What type of insulting questions?"

Ivy glanced at Mitch. It was definitely time for him to step in and tell his daughter she was asking too many questions, but all Mitch did was cut another piece of meat and pop it in his mouth. Who was running things here anyway, him or his children?

"Casey, I'm sure your father will tell you all about how police tend to act when they pull you over once you start driving. Anyway . . . it was a disaster," she concluded lamely. The anecdote simply didn't seem as amusing anymore, thanks to Casey's constantly interrupting her to ask for unnecessary information.

"Will you take me for a ride in your car, Miss Smith?" Elgin asked.

"I'm sure we can do that."

"Today?"

"Well, not today, Elgin."

"Oh, maaaaaaan!"

There he went with that lip again. She wanted to smack him.

The children asked to be excused. Mitch gave permission after a cursory inspection of their plates. "For somebody who didn't want to eat, E, you really cleaned your plate," he remarked.

"Can I have candy now, Daddy?"

"All right, go ahead. And Casey, you can have more gum."

Elgin and Casey scurried toward the kitchen, plates in hand.

Mitch shrugged. "Well, those are my kids. I hope you didn't find them too unbearable."

Certainly a loaded question, but no way was she going to walk into that one. "Oh, they're just typical kids, I suppose," she said airily.

"I probably let them get away with too much, but I'm

trying to be easy on them. It's been hard for them, my ex and I not getting along, then the separation, then the divorce, and now their mother living so far away.''

Ivy quickly took a sip of wine so she could merely nod her head without having to make a verbal reply. In her opinion Mitch was way too lenient with those kids. Elgin never should have been allowed to sulk the way he had, and Casey's nosiness was outrageous. But of course how he raised his children wasn't any of her business.

She kept him company while he loaded the dishwasher. When he turned to her after starting the cycle, she pointedly glanced at her watch. "I guess I'd better be getting home. Work tomorrow, you know.''

"Like you aren't going to do any work tonight?''

"All right, I've been found out. I'll probably look over a few files and make some notes on my to-do list for tomorrow. This was a slow weekend because of the holiday, but I think we've got six weddings next week, between Thursday and Sunday.''

"I know self-employed people generally work harder than anyone. Come on, I'll get you in a cab. We'll walk to the corner. It'll be easier to flag one down on Third Avenue.''

He called the children downstairs so they could say good night to her. Ivy got a kick out of their obvious anxiousness to get back to what they were doing.

She and Mitch took the elevator downstairs. The moment the doors closed he pulled her to him. "My kids are enjoying gum and candy after going without them for six weeks, but did I tell you what *I* gave up for Lent?''

Chapter 10
Company

"It's hard, isn't it, Ivy?" Bethany said.

"What's hard?" Ivy said, after swallowing a bite of roasted chicken tenders and lettuce.

"The question of whether or not to continue dating a man when you can't stand his kids."

"I never said I couldn't stand them, Bethany." Her friend's knowing look prevented her from saying anything else. "All right. So they didn't leave a good impression on me."

"And?"

Ivy took a deep breath. "So maybe Mitch doesn't seem quite as appealing as he did before. This is a potentially serious situation. Dates come and go, but children are forever. I don't want to sound like I'm jumping the gun or anything. We really haven't been seeing each other very long, but I don't think I can deal with it. Those kids made me want to run like pantyhose."

"I hope you don't give up on Mitch because of his

kids' bad behavior." Bethany signaled for the waitress. "Another cup of ranch dressing, please."

Ivy shrugged. While she felt that putting a halt to seeing Mitch Crews was too drastic an action, she couldn't deny that meeting his kids had ebbed her enthusiasm about being involved with him. She knew he was ready to move their relationship to another level from his comment about wanting to kiss her good morning that night after the theater, and he couldn't have been more blunt than when he told her he had given up sex for Lent. She knew that Casey and Elgin would be in Puerto Rico until Sunday. It didn't take a Ph.D. to know he was expecting big things from her, things she wasn't ready for. Fortunately, his children's vacation coincided with an exceptionally busy weekend for Jubilee. She would be overseeing weddings both Friday and Saturday and couldn't even spare enough time to get away for a movie.

But she did look forward to seeing Ray's daughter on Wednesday.

When the bell rang at three minutes to one, Ivy was sure it was Yolanda Jones. "I'll get it," she called.

She opened the door to see the nervous-looking teenager standing on the other side. "Hello, Yolanda. Welcome."

"Thank you, Miss Ivy." Yolanda stepped inside, and her eyes sparkled as she took in the large room. "Wow. This is huge!"

"Have you ever been inside a loft before?"

"No, but I've heard about them. And you live here, too?"

"I know it's hard to believe now, but when the others leave you'll see the transformation my living room goes

through every night. I'll introduce you to everyone. Did
you want to call your father?"

"He made me promise I'd let him know I got here
all right."

John, Randy, and Diane were all either on the phone
or hard at work and merely exchanged friendly hellos.
Reneé was filing and had a little bit more time for
pleasantries. "Oh, aren't you pretty!" she exclaimed.
"You remind me of my first husband's little sister, or
at least the way she looked twenty-five years ago."

"Thank you," Yolanda said shyly.

"Reneé, please let Yolanda use your phone."

"Sure. It's right there, dear. Sit down and help yourself."

Yolanda sat at Reneé's desk. "Is it difficult to get hold
of your dad at work, or do you call him on a cell phone?"
Ivy asked.

"Actually, he's home today. He gets a lot of Wednesdays off because he works a lot of Saturdays. He generally
takes my little sister to the Y, but by now he's home
because it's time for her nap. He said he was going to
come pick me up."

Ray was coming! Ivy hadn't expected that and was
surprised at how excited she felt at the prospect of
seeing him again. She immediately did a quick assessment of how she looked. Fortunately, she believed in
getting dressed and at least putting on lipstick before
sitting down at her desk, saving the bathrobe, T-shirts,
and sweatpants for days when she was alone. She ran a
hand through her short hair. It still looked good from
the wash and set she'd gotten on Saturday. At the time
she'd been unhappy with the long wait on the busy day
before Easter, but now it all seemed worth it. She was
going to see Ray . . . She was going to see Ray. . . .

"I've got a chair for you here, Yolanda," she said

when the teen hung up the phone. "Let me explain to you what Jubilee does . . ."

The afternoon flew by, and soon it was approaching five o'clock. Reneé, the only Jubilee employee who didn't organize events, was often the last to leave, but today she had no reason to linger past quitting time. She'd been working hard in earlier weeks, completing the corporate tax return, as well as the entire staff's personal tax returns, in time for the April 15 deadline, but those were all finished. Invoices for the previous week's events had been printed and would be dropped in the corner mailbox on her way home. Ivy suspected she was hanging around deliberately, hoping for a glance at Ray.

"Reneé, what are you still doing here?" she asked innocently.

"Oh, just finishing up a few things." She paused a beat. "Yolanda, did you say your father's coming for you?"

"Yes. He should be here any minute. You know, we only live nine blocks from here, and it's broad daylight. Sometimes I think he's overprotective."

"Well, sometimes we just don't know people's reasons for doing the things they do," Reneé said with a meaningful glance Ivy's way.

"I think I'm going to call it a day," Ivy said, anxious to change the subject. "This wedding season always wears me out. Between following up on all the last minute details for the ones happening this weekend and the planning sessions for the ones to be held in the fall, I barely know my own name."

"I think your work is exciting, Miss Ivy," Yolanda said.

"Well, it helps a lot that I really do love the business." The doorbell rang. "Oh, that must be your father. I'll get it."

"Who is it?" she called through the closed door.

"My name's Jones."

She opened the door. Ray, casually dressed in earth colors, pullover sweater, khaki pants, and Oxfords, looked even better than she remembered. "My name's Smith," she said with a smile.

"Hi!" Maya said in her squeaky child's voice.

"Well, hello Maya. I'm so happy you came to see me today." She met Ray's eyes. "Not that she has the slightest idea of who I am, of course. Good to see you, Ray."

"Likewise."

"Come in, please."

"I hope Yolanda didn't get in your way this afternoon."

"She was a joy," Ivy said simply.

"Nice place," he said, looking around casually.

"Thanks."

Maya had left them to run to her big sister, and now Ivy and Ray crossed the large room.

Ray smiled at his elder daughter. "You're looking awfully idle for someone who's supposed to be working."

"No, not really. Come closer, and I'll show you what I mean." When Ray stood beside her in front of Ivy's desk she said, "I was on the computer. See, the monitor's underneath, but when you're sitting down you can see it through this glass panel. The keyboard pulls out here"—she demonstrated as she spoke—"and the CPU is in here"—another pause as she snapped open a vertical cabinet on the left—"and the printer is behind that door way on the left. Here on the right are built-in file drawers. Miss Ivy has an entire office right at her fingertips, and it's all hidden. Have you ever seen anything like that?"

"No, never. Pretty nifty."

"I've always hated clutter," Ivy remarked. It always made her uncomfortable when people fussed over anything she owned. "Besides, with this also being my home, I've been known to cover the top of it with a cloth and set it up as a buffet table when I entertain, and no one's the wiser. I just wish there was enough room so everyone could have one, but they're awfully wide." She didn't say that the desk had also been quite expensive, which was an equal hindrance to buying more of them.

"In the meantime we poor working stiffs have to make do with these assemble-it-yourself numbers from Office Depot," Reneé said, laughing. She held out her hand to Ray. "I'm Reneé Walker, the bookkeeper here. Your daughter is charming."

He shook her hand. "Thank you, Reneé. I'm Ray Jones."

Reneé pushed her chair back and closed her armoire.

Ivy watched Ray glance around the room and knew he was counting the four armoires neatly spaced on the right and left walls.

Reneé stood. "I'm out of here. Good night, all." She rested her handbag on top of a rolling file cabinet and dragged both the cabinet and her chair toward the storage closet.

Ray jumped to his feet. "Let me help you with that."

"Oh, how chivalrous," Reneé said, demonstrating the charm that had gotten her three husbands. Ivy half expected her employee to bat her eyelashes.

"Okay," Ray said to Yolanda after Reneé left, "tell me what you did today besides acquaint yourself with the workings of Ivy's desk."

"I made some inquiries and some follow-up calls about this party Jubilee is setting up in East Hampton next month. The people giving it are gonna have that guy we watch on TV Saturday mornings do the cooking, but because the kitchen in their summer house is tiny, Miss Ivy is setting up a kitchen in their garage just for this event. Can you imagine? Stove, refrigerator, work space, the whole ten yards, just for one party."

"Yolanda, it's actually the whole *nine* yards."

Her face wrinkled. "That's funny. I was just repeating what Miss Reneé said. I could have sworn she said it was ten yards."

"I'm sure that's exactly what she said," Ivy said. "Reneé hasn't gotten a proverb right yet."

"So you're booking events with celebrity chefs, huh?" Ray said to Ivy.

"Yes. They seem to be all the rage now. This particular party presents a whole new logistical challenge, though."

"I'm glad you had a productive afternoon," Ray said, then added, "both of you."

"My report will probably get an A, Daddy."

"Good. I'll bet you felt a little suffocated when I told you I'd be down to pick you up, didn't you?"

Yolanda hedged. "Well . . ."

"Yeah, I know. I thought I'd surprise you by taking all of you out to dinner, my way of saying thank you to Ivy for taking time to show you how her business works."

"Oh, how sweet. But you don't have to. We can eat right here," Ivy said.

"And have you cook for three extra people? No way."

"Why don't we get some take-out or something and eat here? It'll be more comfortable than a restaurant." She liked the idea of having company for dinner. Too many times the loft seemed like a ghost town after business hours, and she couldn't think of anyone she'd rather have join her than Ray and his daughters. It would almost be like she had a family of her own.

"Can we, Daddy?" Yolanda said. "I like it here."

Ray shrugged. "All right. What'll it be, pizza or Chinese?"

"Pizza!" Maya cried.

"Chinese!" Yolanda said simultaneously.

Ivy laughed. "I'm partial to Chinese myself. But there's a pizza place on the next block. We can get some for Maya while we're waiting for the Chinese to be delivered."

"Sounds good," Ray said.

Yolanda offered to go get the pizza, and Maya insisted on going along. Ivy felt a tingling of excitement as Ray handed Yolanda a bill. It would just be the two of them alone for the brief time it would take the girls to walk a block and back.

She put on the early news and sat near him in one of the seating areas in the large living area as he called in the order, confirming her address and apartment number for him when he gestured to her.

"They'll be here in forty-five minutes," he said as he hung up. "It's five-forty. I guess we ordered just in time to keep from starving."

"I rarely eat before seven anyway. At least Maya won't have to wait that long."

"That's good. I try to get her in bed by eight, and I like her to digest her food before that so she won't have nightmares." He glanced around the room. "I've always liked hardwood floors. Aren't they high maintenance?"

She masked her disappointment. The last thing she wanted to talk about was the maintenance of hardwood floors, but she felt she should follow his lead rather than try to turn the conversation more personal.

They spent a few minutes discussing the floors, and then he asked, "Did you have to put a lot into decorating?"

"No. I just signed a lease and moved in."

He looked startled. "Oh. I thought you owned this."

"No, I rent. A good portion of it is tax deductible. Maybe one day I'll get around to buying a place, but for now this meets my needs perfectly. I'll take you through it when the girls get back." Maybe he had a reason for making impersonal small talk. He might have met someone since the reunion. A man as good-looking as Ray wouldn't lack for female attention, and after all, she was seeing Mitch.

But she never got this excited when she saw Mitch, not even the very first time they went out. Ray's coming by wasn't even a date, but when she learned he was coming she'd behaved like a child about to open her birthday presents.

Yolanda and Maya returned, and Ivy set up Maya on a floor pillow with a folded towel as an oversize place mat. When Maya was done, she brought her to the powder room and helped her wash her hands and face, both of which were oily from the pizza.

"What's back there?" Maya asked when they were returning to the living room.

"That's the rest of my apartment. Want to see?"

Maya nodded, and Yolanda jumped up. "I want to see, too. Can I, Miss Ivy?"

"Of course. You too, Ray."

Yolanda was clearly impressed with the large master bedroom and two smaller rooms, one of which was set up as a guest room and another as an exercise room with treadmill and stationary bicycle. "Your loft is tight, Miss Ivy. I just love all these windows," she said. "And I can't imagine having all this space. I share my room with Maya."

"I shared a room with my sister, too. It wasn't one of my fondest memories. But of course Maya is a lot sweeter than my sister." Ivy impulsively picked up the toddler. She usually scoffed at people who carried children who were able to walk, but there was something irresistible about Maya. Yolanda was a sweetheart, too, all youthful exuberance and questions. She felt genuine fondness for Ray's daughters, a fondness she suspected she could never feel for Casey and Elgin Crews.

The ringing of the doorbell announced the arrival of their dinner. "Time to eat," Ivy said.

"But I already ate," Maya said.

"Yes, but the rest of us are still hungry, Missy." Good heavens, where had *that* term come from? She had a faint recollection of her own mother calling her by that affectionate nickname. That was unsettling, but one glance at Ray beaming at her made her forget everything else. She could barely remember the way to the front door. He clearly enjoyed the sight of her interacting with his daughter. She wondered if his being a parent had interfered with any other relationships he may have had since his wife's death. As lovable as his girls were, single parenthood could easily clash with dating.

Ivy put Maya down, and she and Yolanda unpacked the white cartons onto the dining table and identified them while Ray paid the deliveryman.

"I wanna watch cartoons," Maya said.

"Well, let's see what's on. I guess it would be silly for you to sit at the table and watch the rest of us eat," Ivy said. "Yolanda, you can eat in the living room too, if you want."

"I think she should eat at the table, in case something gets knocked over," Ray said as he joined them.

"Oh, Daddy, you'd think I was no older than Maya."

"Let me show you guys something." Ivy walked over to the conversation area directly opposite the large television set. She sat on one of the sofas and in one motion pulled the coffee table in front of it into a higher position, the same level as that of a desk or dining table. "Voila!"

"Hey, that's tight work!" Yolanda exclaimed.

"Don't tell anyone, but I'm secretly a couch potato. I usually have my meals here when I'm home alone."

Yolanda turned to Ray. "Is it okay, Daddy?"

"Sure. I didn't know that table converted. But be careful."

Yolanda fixed her plate and brought it over to the repositioned coffee table. "I'm going to get something to drink, Maya," she said, "and then we'll find something to watch."

Ivy and Ray settled in the dining room among opened cardboard cartons of food. "This is good," Ray said. "You know, the one thing I like about living in Hell's Kitchen—"

"They call it Clinton now, don't they?"

"Only people who don't live there. The good thing about it is that I can take my family out to dinner without spending a fortune. There's a great German place on West Forty-ninth Street. Every time I eat there I imagine I'm back in Frankfurt."

"Oh, were you in Germany?"

"I did two tours in the army. Yolanda was born there."

"I don't think I've ever had German food."

"You had a chance tonight. That was where I planned to take you guys."

The words came out before she could analyze them. "Can I get a rain check?" She could tell from his surprised expression that she'd caught him off guard, but he recovered quickly.

"Of course."

After dinner Ray helped her clean up, disposing of the cartons and wiping down the table while she filled the sink with hot, soapy water. "Thanks, Ray. I love seeing men in the kitchen, but I can take it from here," she said.

The girls made the expected mild protests when he told them it was time to go, but Ray held firm. "You know you've got school tomorrow, and I've got to go to work. And so does Ivy. So let's go."

"I really like your loft, Miss Ivy," Yolanda said. "I'd be real comfortable living here."

"I don't think Ivy is looking for a roommate," Ray remarked.

"What a great place to have a birthday party."

"When's your birthday, Yolanda?" Ivy asked.

"August sixteenth. I'll be seventeen."

"Did you have a sweet sixteen party last year?"

"No. Our apartment is too small."

Ivy put an arm around the teenager. "It'd be fine with me if you wanted to have a party here, as long as you didn't invite too many people."

"Really?"

"Really." Ivy smiled as a grateful Yolanda hugged her. "Now, you be sure and let me know how you do with your school paper about your experience here today."

"I will."

"And call if there's anything else I can possibly help you with. I'll tell you a secret." She lowered her voice to a loud whisper that concealed nothing from Ray and Maya. "I was sixteen once myself."

They all laughed, and Maya approached, waving. " 'Bye, Miss Ivy."

"Good-bye, Maya. I hope you'll come back and see me again."

Maya looked to Ray for confirmation, and when he nodded she said, "I'll be back."

Ivy removed her arm from Yolanda's shoulder and stooped. "Good. Do I get a kiss?"

The child obliged, pressing her lips to Ivy's cheek.

"I can't thank you enough," Ray said to her as the girls walked down the hall toward the elevator. "Yolanda hardly seems like the same girl who was so upset over not having any way to spend Daughters Day just a few weeks ago. You have no idea how good that makes me feel as a parent.''

"No, I guess I don't, since I'm not a parent. But I'm glad I could help.''

"Daddy! Elevator," Yolanda called.

"All right. G'night, Ivy. I'll be in touch.''

Ivy usually stood in the doorway until her guests disappeared inside the elevator, but instinct told her it would be unbearably difficult to watch Ray and the girls leave, so she closed the door right away.

Never before had her loft seemed so empty.

Ray had already given Maya a bath before they went to Ivy's, so when they got home he put her to bed right away. The walk between Ivy's loft and his apartment was nothing for adult-size legs like his and Yolanda's, but it was enough to wear Maya out. He carried her from Thirty-fourth Street on, and when they reached their apartment she was already half asleep.

He turned on the night light and closed the door softly as he left. He could hear Yolanda talking to someone on the phone. Listening for a few moments revealed she was bragging to one of her friends about her afternoon at Ivy's.

He resisted the urge to suggest she start writing her paper. He was sure it wasn't due the next day. Let her gloat . . . she'd earned it. Yolanda had lost her mother at a critical time, during her first year in high school. It made him happy to see his daughter so enthusiastic about what could have been a disaster. Issuing a money order for an incorrect amount had worked out pretty well for him, and not just where Yolanda was concerned.

He'd been startled when Ivy asked him for a rain check for dinner. From what little he knew of her, she wasn't the type who tossed out insincere remarks just for the sake of flirting. She really wanted to go out with him.

Dealing with the conflicting emotions of his attraction to her along with the fear of being rejected made for a congenial but remote conversation. He suspected she was being wined and dined by that scoundrel Mitch Crews, but her obvious ease and comfort when relating to Yolanda and Maya tugged at his heartstrings. He'd been warned by his buddy Rodney that most women would resent his having custody of his children and the responsibilities parenthood entailed, but it didn't seem to bother Ivy at all. Of course, he really didn't know her well.

But he intended to.

Chapter 11
A Cure for the Common Kid

"So what happened with you and that handsome Ray Jones after I left last night, Ivy?" Reneé asked.

"We ordered Chinese food and ate dinner. Then they left."

"Gonna see him again?"

"As a matter of fact . . ." Ivy paused as she considered confiding in her bookkeeper. "Reneé, I need your advice."

In what amounted to about a time span of three seconds, Reneé wheeled her chair over to Ivy's desk and sat in it, an expectantly curious expression on her face. "All right. Tell me *everything*," she said with a grin. If they were cartoon characters, her ears would have suddenly enlarged to elephant size.

"I like Ray, Reneé. I had a good time with him when we went to my reunion, and I had a good time with him last night."

"Wait. What about the other guy, that rich dude?"

"Mitch. I haven't had too much time to see him

because of all the functions we've got going on. The best we've been able to do is have lunch during the week, but he has tickets to the opera for Wednesday night. I like Mitch, too . . ."

"But?"

"I met his kids on Easter Sunday, and they struck me as . . . well, kind of bratty."

Reneé nodded knowingly. "And we both know Yolanda Jones is definitely not a brat, and that little one seemed precious."

"She is. I know you've had stepchildren. Have any of them been difficult? Did it go away with time, or did your first impression of not liking them pretty much stick?"

"I've been fortunate in that respect. My third husband's kids were grown by the time we got together, and my second husband's kids were very sweet, although in the beginning there was a little bit of hostility, like they perceived me as some kind of competitor for their father's attention. The biggest problem was getting them to mesh with my son. All of them accused me of favoring the others at one time or another. But don't give up on Mitch if you really like him. Try to get to know his kids better. Maybe your perception of them will change. In the meantime, there's no rule that says you can't date both of them, but it might get a little sticky if, uh . . ." she cleared her throat delicately.

"That's the last thing on my mind, Reneé. I barely know either of them. There are other issues at stake here."

"You mean there's more? Don't hold back. Cut the cake."

"Not with Mitch. With Ray. I own and operate Jubilee, and since you keep the books you know how well we're doing. Ray is a postal clerk. Do you see anything wrong with that picture?"

"Do you?"

Ivy sighed in exasperation. "You're not supposed to answer a question with a question."

"I don't mean to be difficult, but I don't see a problem. Do you think he can't afford to take you to a movie or to dinner?"

"No, of course not."

"Well, do you think his table manners might embarrass you, or his speech habits?" She began to giggle. "Remember when you first got your Cruiser and that security guard at that client in Long Island City called out to us, 'What kind of car that is?' I remember saying to myself, 'Your grammar is why you're fifty and working as a security guard, Jack.' "

"We're talking about Ray, remember?" Ivy hoped she didn't sound terse, but Reneé had a way of getting off the topic that could be annoying.

"Sure. As I was saying, does he have a limited vocabulary or not understand words with more than ten letters?"

"No."

"Is he ill at ease in formal wear?"

"No, he appeared very comfortable, he used the right fork, wiped his mouth, didn't belch, and he speaks as well as the next guy."

Reneé shrugged. "So, I repeat, what's the problem? Because I don't see one."

Ivy leaned back in her chair. "I see your point."

"My advice is to go out with both of them. Have fun. See what happens. From where I sit either one of them might turn out to be the man of your dreams. It's way too early to worry about who brings home the bread."

"Are you crazy?" Bethany demanded. She and Ivy were at Bethany's luxurious apartment, where their friends would be gathering for one of their regular chat fests, but no one had arrived yet. "Ivy, what's wrong with you?"

"No, I'm not crazy, and there's not a thing wrong with me. Ray said he would have taken us to eat at a German restaurant if we didn't order Chinese, and I asked if we could do it some other time."

"But what about Mitch?"

"I'm not going to stop seeing Mitch."

"But why see Ray in the first place?"

"Because he's nice and I like him. And because maybe something will come out of it."

"Mitch is perfect for you, Ivy. Why bother seeing another man who isn't? I don't understand it. You have more rules and conditions about dating than anyone I know. You wouldn't even go out with that movie director because he's based in LA. 'What's the use?' you said. 'I'm not relocating, and neither is he.' And even *I* wouldn't go out with anyone who works at the post office, any more than I'd go out with someone who drives for UPS. They might make a decent living without having to get their hands dirty, but those aren't careers; they're jobs."

"I think about Ray all the time, Bethany. I have to see if there's anything to it. I know I've never dated a regular guy before, but that makes it wrong?"

"But why bother when you've got so many strikes against you? He'll resent your success. They all do. Only with him it won't take as long as it usually does."

"Ray might not have a two-million-dollar town house, but he's hardly poverty stricken, Bethany. He told me his lawyers negotiated a very nice settlement for them in the wrongful death suit he filed for his wife."

"Did he say how much?"

"Of course not. That's his business, not mine."

"To someone who works at the post office, a quarter

mil would be 'very nice.' You and I know it isn't, especially when someone's died. Besides, what did he do with it? The man still lives on West Thirty-seventh Street, for heaven's sake.''

"Everybody can't afford a Park Avenue duplex like you, Bethany. Ray invested the award he got for his daughters' future, and I suppose for his own as well. He's probably got more ready cash than Mitch, who's had to cut back since his divorce. His ex didn't answer phones for a living, you know. She easily made as much as he did, but now he's got to pay for his lifestyle all by himself. He mentioned how he made a killing on some dotcom stock a couple of years ago, and I'm sure those profits help. But even with that he had to sell his car, and he rented out the housekeeper's quarters.''

"All right, I agree that many a private home in Manhattan has been sold when the owners divorce. But Mitch has managed to hold on to his. So what if he got rid of his car? He still has his kids in private school, doesn't he? And you said his new housekeeper is just part time, but it's not like he has to dust and vacuum himself. If you ask me he's still head and shoulders above someone who sells stamps for a living.''

"Ray's daughter goes to parochial school. And he might sell stamps, Bethany, but it's not like he can't afford to take me out.''

"Sure, to the movies. Or to some cheap Tenth Avenue luncheonette. Do you honestly think he'll be taking you to the Met to see Tosca? Or to a supper club? Those sixty-dollar cover charges and fifty-dollar minimums would kill him. But maybe if he scrimps and saves he can spring for orchestra seats for a Broadway show . . . once a year.'' She giggled.

"You're not being fair, Bethany.''

Ivy's protest only served to give her friend more fuel. ''And what about vacations? I'll bet his idea of a wonderful trip is a week at the Jersey shore . . . but of course if he's lived in New York all his life he probably can't even drive."

"Bethany, that's enough!" Her voice held a warning, and Bethany finally stopped talking. For a few seconds.

"All I ask, Ivy, is for you to think about it. Especially if you're thinking about dropping Mitch."

"All right, I'll think about it." Anything to get Bethany to stop her tirade. *Where was everybody, anyway?*

But Ivy had already thought about it, and she knew exactly what she was going to do.

A week went by and Ray didn't call, but she was too busy between work and lunching with Mitch to have much time to worry about it.

She and Mitch were getting along so well these days she was glad she hadn't broken it off with him. She genuinely liked Mitch, in spite of feeling that she owed it to herself to explore her intense attraction to Ray.

When Mitch called saying he had to make a last-minute business trip to Boston and would be gone overnight, but his housekeeper was unable to stay with the children, she didn't hesitate to offer to keep them. The arrangement was a simple one. The children would sleep in her guest room, and she would get them to school in the morning. That was it. Mitch's housekeeper would be on duty when the school van brought them home in the afternoon. She actually found herself looking forward to spending time with Casey and Elgin without Mitch, to get to know them, like Reneé suggested.

The housekeeper delivered them to the loft at six o'clock, telling Ivy they had done all their homework and already had dinner. But barely ten minutes later, after she showed them the room where they would be sleeping and the bathroom, Elgin announced, "I'm hungry."

She suspected this might happen and was prepared. "I've got some leftover spaghetti. I just had some, and it was really good."

"Ooh, spaghetti."

She smiled. "I'll heat some up for you. Casey, would you like some?"

"No, thank you. But is it all right if I change the channel on the TV?"

"Sure. The remote should be somewhere on the coffee table." She went to the kitchen and spooned out spaghetti onto a plate to heat in the microwave.

Within seconds the siblings were arguing about what they would watch. Elgin insisted on watching something he called, *Jack,* which turned out to be the old sitcom *Three's Company,* while Casey wanted *The Fresh Prince of Bel Air.* "You have to go eat, so let me watch my show."

Elgin was by Ivy's side in a flash. "Um . . . I'm not really hungry after all."

"I didn't give you a whole lot, Elgin. If you're hungry at all you can eat it."

"But I'm not really hungry. I'd rather watch TV."

"A minute ago you told me you were hungry. I've got a plate of food heating up for you in the microwave. I don't know what you do at home, Elgin, but here our lives don't revolve around what's on television. The TV will still be there when you're finished, believe me."

"But my show will be over!"

She struggled to keep the frustration she felt from creeping into her voice. "Elgin, I want you to sit at the table, and I'll bring you your plate in just a minute."

He stalked off, the familiar sulk on his face.

Ivy rolled her eyes as she poured him a glass of juice. When she brought the glass and his plate to him he was still sitting with his head down and his lip poked out.

"You're welcome," she said pointedly when he did not acknowledge her action.

His "thank you" was so soft that if she had hadn't run a cotton swab in her ear that morning she probably wouldn't have heard it. Casey's loud laughter as she watched *Fresh Prince* didn't help matters, either. Ivy felt sure all the mirth was purposely to provoke Elgin further; Casey had probably seen the episode where Tom Jones sang and danced with Alfonso Rubiero fifty times.

"When you finish eating, Elgin, you can name the program you want to watch." Ivy spoke loudly enough for Casey to hear. Only then did the boy pick up his fork and start twirling the pasta around it.

Elgin finished eating by the time *Fresh Prince* was over. Casey didn't object when he switched to *I Love Lucy*, but when it ended and she pointed out it was now her turn, Elgin began whining again. Ivy solved the problem by sending him to take his bath.

Casey had asked if she could use Ivy's computer, and she was busy playing a game.

Ivy watched her from the kitchen as she cut refrigerated chocolate chip cookie dough into chunks, wryly noting how Casey lost interest in watching television the moment Elgin was out of the room.

The ringing telephone was a welcome diversion. Ivy quickly slipped the cookie sheet into the preheated oven and reached for the kitchen extension, but it had suddenly stopped ringing. Then she heard Casey talking and saw that she held a receiver to her ear. That nosy little witch had answered her phone!

Casey continued to talk, telling Ivy it was Mitch on the line. Thank heavens it hadn't been Ray; Casey was the type to run straight to Mitch and tell him another man was calling her, which of course was none of Mitch's business.

Finally the child turned around. "Miss Smith, it's my daddy. He wants to talk to you."

Ivy picked up the extension and said hello.

Mitch sounded jovial. "How's it going?"

"Oh, fine. Elgin is taking his bath. I'm baking cookies. And Casey"—she couldn't resist a dig—"has apparently appointed herself my receptionist."

"That's just like Casey, to take over people's telephones."

She wasn't surprised that he didn't seem to think there was anything wrong with that. She'd heard her married friends complain about parents who thought it was cute when their little ones did things like not attempting to cover their coughs and sneezes, or belched loudly. Ivy felt that crass behavior was no less such in an eight year old than an eighty year old, but the only way small children could know etiquette rules were being violated was if their parents told them. It was known as home training. She was beginning to think that Casey and Elgin Crews had none.

"I hope they're not driving you crazy," Mitch added.

"Nothing I can't handle. It'll soon be time for them to go to bed, anyway. What time is lights out, nine?"

"About that, yes. Sometimes I let them stay up until nine-thirty, especially on Wednesdays and Thursdays. But no later than that."

"Well, since today's Wednesday, I guess it'll be nine-thirty. It won't take long to walk to school." The private school the children attended was just six blocks south of the loft, on West Twenty-second Street.

"Ivy, I can't tell you how much I appreciate your helping me out like this."

"I'm glad I could help. Oh, there goes the call waiting beep. Can you hold for just a minute?"

"I'll let you go. I need to go over a few things for tomorrow's meeting. I'll call you in the morning."

"All right. Talk to you then." She clicked the receiver. "Hello."

"It's Bethany."

"Hi! How was drinks?"

"Marvelous. It turned into dinner."

"Ooh, tell, tell. Wait a sec—Elgin, did you hang up your towel?"

"Yes."

"All right. Casey, it's your turn to take a bath, or a shower if you prefer. Hurry up, I've got chocolate chip cookies in the oven."

"Chocolate chip, my favorite," Elgin said.

"Don't touch the computer, Elgin. I'm in the middle of a game," Casey said as she headed for the hall.

"I want to watch TV."

Ivy was relieved to see them make the transition without bickering. Then she realized Bethany must have heard the exchange. Ivy could only imagine what her friend was thinking.

"What the hell is going on there?" Bethany asked when Ivy indicated she was back. "It sounds like *Romper Room*."

"I've got Mitch's kids for the night. He had to go to Boston, and his housekeeper goes home at night."

"He couldn't get her to stay over just once?"

"No. She's got a family of her own."

"He probably needs to get an au pair. He'd hardly have to pay her anything, and plane fares from Europe are down. His parents don't live in the city?"

"No, they live upstate someplace, and his in-laws live in Westchester. Of course, if I hadn't been able to take them that's where they'd be, but I'm sure Mitch would rather they not miss a day of school."

"So how are the little rug rats?"

"Oh, just fine," Ivy said brightly.

"I get it. You can't talk. Well, I'll take advantage of that and tell you all about my date. . . ."

Ivy listened as Bethany filled her in on the details of her blind date. The meeting had been suggested by one of the members of their women's group at the recent meeting at Bethany's. The group had no real agenda or purpose; they mostly offered support for problems that arose in the workplace and in their personal lives, like coping with male underlings who resented having a female superior, handling the ever-present racism, and, for the unmarried, the difficulty of finding suitable mates among less financially successful men. When they weren't discussing those matters they gossiped or talked about current events.

Ivy ended the conversation when the timer went off, signaling that the cookies were done. The sweet scent of melted chocolate filled the loft.

Elgin was sitting at the table enjoying his cookies with a cold glass of milk when a pajama-clad Casey came and joined him. Ivy deliberately hadn't told them about the convertible coffee table in the living room. The way they poked and pushed at each other during their frequent disputes, allowing them to sit there would be begging for stained upholstery from spilled foods and liquids.

Satisfied that the children wouldn't erupt into another argument, Ivy went to inspect the bathroom. Her breath caught in her throat. "What the . . . ?"

Water covered the floor. The heavy rubber-backed bath mat was saturated. She moved the shower liner to the outside of the tub while running Elgin's bath water, and apparently Casey hadn't noticed it was out when she took her shower. *I guess she forgot to ask for a mop.* Instead she had taken the towels and spread them on the floor to soak up the excess, with only mild success.

Ivy gathered up the wet towels and mat and headed toward the washing machine. She heard Elgin whining about how he wanted to use the computer and Casey loudly overruling him. Ivy shook her head. Perhaps it would have been best if she had told Mitch she had something to do tonight. She had enjoyed having Ray, Yolanda, and Maya over, enjoyed being with them, and experienced a lingering hollow feeling when they left. But Casey and Elgin made a quiet night in front of the television with a solitary glass of Chianti sound wonderful.

She wished Ray would hurry up and call.

Ivy drew in her breath when her phone began ringing. The book she was reading was a real page turner, but the call might be important. Her parents had driven to North Carolina to scout for a place to live once their house in Lakewood was sold. They wouldn't be likely to call her to report they had arrived safely—that call would go to Stephanie—only if something went wrong and they needed help. But ignoring the phone wouldn't be right. "Hello."

"Hi, Miss Ivy."

She immediately perked up. Only one person called her that. "Yolanda?"

"Yes. How are you?"

"I'm fine. What a nice surprise to hear from you!"

"Well, you did invite me to call if anything came up that you might be able to help me with . . ."

"I sure did, and I meant it. What's come up?"

"The spring dance at my school. This year I'm sixteen, so Daddy says it's okay for me to have a date."

"Is it a formal affair?"

"It's dress-up. I mean, the fellows are just wearing regular suits, not tuxes or anything like Daddy did for your reunion party. I wanted to ask if you would go shopping with me to help me pick out a dress. My grandmother offered to come, but she's so old-fashioned. I'm afraid she'll want me to wear something with those big poufy sleeves, like a bridesmaid, except in white, like a bride."

Ivy laughed. "I've got news for you, Yolanda. Most bridesmaids try to avoid that style of dress, too. And I'd love to go with you, provided it's all right with your father."

"He says it is. When I told him what I think about Grandma's taste, he said he doesn't know about dresses, and he suggested I call you."

Her eyes widened. Ray asked Yolanda to call her?

"He's here, and he wants to talk to you."

Before Ivy realized it she was hearing Ray's cheerful voice. "Hello, Ivy. I hope you don't mind the Jones family asking you for help again."

"Of course not, Ray. The only thing is, I'm pretty booked on the weekends. It's the wedding season. When is Yolanda's dance?"

"Not until the weekend before Memorial Day, so we've got time."

"Can you hold on a minute? I want to check my book. I think I've got a day off coming, but I want to make sure."

"Sure."

Ivy rushed to get her agenda. "Yes, next Saturday my associates are handling all our events. Even during the busy season we can usually work it so everyone gets time off. We can make an afternoon of it, maybe drive out to the malls in New Jersey. Why don't you and Maya come along? I wouldn't want to pick out anything you don't approve of."

"I think we will. That's considerate of you, Ivy. But the more I get to know you, the more I wouldn't expect anything else."

Chapter 12
Shop Till You Drop

Ray glanced at his eldest daughter, who was sitting in the windowsill in his parents' dining area. "I think you can sit in a chair, Yolanda. Ivy will honk when she gets here, and it'll only take a minute for us to get outside."

"I can't wait to see this dress she's going to pick out," his mother said dryly.

"Miss Ivy isn't going to pick out my dress, Nana. *I'm* picking it out. But she'll help."

"And I'll have the final say," Ray added.

"I don't know why you had to get that rich girl involved in the first place. I would've been happy to help you choose something appropriate," his mother said.

Ray caught Yolanda's frantic look his way, the plea for help in her eyes. He chose his words carefully, not wanting to hurt his mother's feelings. "Mom, Yolanda wants something . . . hip."

"I see. And by 'hip' you mean something where she's half naked. I've seen photographs of those singers wearing dresses cut down to the navel and up to the crotch, or merely draped fabric held together with Band-Aids. Then there was that woman who wore a see-through dress to the Academy Awards. They had to shoot her from the neck up for television. Indecent, it is."

"I'm sure you don't think I would allow Yolanda to wear something that outrageous anywhere. Not while she's living under my roof. I don't care if she's forty," Ray said. "And what makes you think Ivy would encourage Yolanda to dress provocatively? It was her idea that I come along, to make sure I approve."

"Yeah, right. A woman living in the fast lane. I can only imagine how she got the money to start that business of hers."

"Mom, I think that's enough." His tone held a warning.

"Yes, Trudy, cut the girl some slack," his father agreed. "It's good that Yolanda has a role model. Not that you haven't done a fine job, but she needs someone closer to her own age now that Dolores is gone. The fact that this girl's done well for herself can't hurt, either."

Ray watched as his mother gave his father a withering look, then continued folding laundry without another word.

"Here she is!" Yolanda said excitedly. "Let's go, Daddy. " 'Bye, Nana. 'Bye Granddad." She grabbed Maya's hand and ran out the door.

"I'm not sure if she's more excited about getting a new party dress or riding in Ivy's car," Ray remarked easily. He had no intention of running outside like he'd been waiting by the window. "She's got one of those retro vehicles, a PT Cruiser." He picked up Maya's car seat. "I'll see you later."

When he got outside, Ivy was standing beside her double-parked vehicle, holding Maya and talking to her.

Yolanda was in the front seat of the Cruiser, running her hand over the dashboard.

Ivy's face lit up when she saw the car seat he was carrying. "Hi! You must have been reading my mind. It just occurred to me that Maya would need a car seat. I was thinking we might have a problem."

"I've had this ever since Maya was an infant. Every summer I rent a car and drive down to the Maryland shore. That's about the only time we use it, but it's here at home if we need it." He opened the rear door and bent to place the chair in the seat. "Yolanda, time for you to stop being nosy and get in the back, but sit behind Ivy. I'll probably have to push the passenger seat back a bit for leg room."

"I thought you might want to drive, Ray," Ivy said.

"Sure. I always carry my license with me. But you'll have to tell me which way to go once we hit Jersey."

"If you're driving I'll need to sit on the other side behind Miss Ivy, Daddy," Yolanda said.

"That's right." He pushed the car seat over so that it was directly behind the driver's seat. Yolanda and Ivy took their seats while he fastened Maya in the car seat, and finally he slid behind the wheel, pushing the seat back for more leg room. Ivy handed him the keys.

"I love this car," Yolanda said when they were riding north on the West Side Highway. "Look how the people are looking at us."

"I used to get a lot of stares when I first got it, but it really isn't a novelty anymore," Ivy said. "I guess these folks just don't have anything else to look at."

"It handles nice," Ray said. He hadn't expected her to give him the choice of driving and was pleased that she had. He knew it was hopelessly old-fashioned and sexist, but he preferred to be the one behind the wheel if he was riding with a woman. Dolores used to tease that he never wanted to give her a chance when they made their annual drive to Maryland.

The uptown traffic was moderately heavy but moved nicely. Before they knew it they were crossing into New Jersey on the George Washington Bridge.

They went to Stern's first. Ray found a chair near the fitting room and sat patiently while Yolanda and Ivy made their way through racks and racks of prom dresses. They each carried an armful into the fitting room, and then Yolanda came out every few minutes, wearing a different dress.

Maya busied herself by burying her face in the soft satin and tulle of the various gowns on the racks. When Yolanda came out wearing an especially pretty strapless black and white gown, Maya looked at her sister, her forehead wrinkled in confusion and said, "But howdya keep it from falling down?"

They all laughed, and Ray scooped her up. "When you get older the way you're shaped is going to change. But you don't have to worry about for a long time. Now you're still my little girl." He studied Yolanda and frowned. "It actually looks very nice on you, but I think it's too sophisticated. What do you think, Ivy?"

"I agree. I told her as much, but she wanted to try it on anyway. She asked me not to say anything to you in case you felt differently."

"Aw, shucks," Yolanda said, clearly disappointed.

"I guess she thinks I'm blind," Ray said to Ivy.

"Yolanda, that dress is more like something I would wear," Ivy said.

Ray inadvertently licked his lips at the thought of Ivy in the sexy shoulder-baring dress, in tight-fitting black from the bosom to the knee and a flowing white skirt extending to her feet. A draped white scarf gave it almost an ethereal appearance.

Ivy didn't see his action, but Maya did. "Are you hungry, Daddy?"

"No. My lips felt a little dry, that's all."

At what seemed like an eternity of trying on dresses at four department stores, Yolanda chose a lime green satin A-line gown with matching shawl at Nordstrom. Ray liked the simple lines and not-too-low-cut square neckline, and Ivy said she hadn't seen it in any of the other stores they'd been to. "You don't want to walk in and see two or three other girls wearing the same dress, but they'll probably all shop at Macy's or Ann Taylor or Bloomingdale's, stores right there in the city."

"All right. That wasn't too bad. It's after five, and I'm sure I'm not the only one who can stand to eat something. What say we get something to eat?" Ray suggested.

"Oh, not yet, Ray. Now we have to get shoes and a purse," Ivy said.

"It'll only take a minute," Yolanda added quickly.

He realized his displeasure must be showing on his face. "All right. Why don't Maya and I take a walk to that toy store we passed in the mall?"

"Yes, Daddy, yes," Maya said, jumping up and down.

"We'll meet you in front of this store within half an hour," Ray said. He placed Maya in the stroller he had rented for her and walked off.

At Ivy's suggestion they went to the Cheesecake Factory in Hackensack, and by the time they finished their food no one had room for cheesecake or any of the other desserts. Instead they got back in the car and headed for home.

"Are you all right to drive?" Ivy asked Ray.

He laughed. "After those crab cakes, maybe I should *walk* home."

"I know what you mean. Those baby back ribs are going to give me very sweet dreams."

The drive home seemed shorter than the drive out, for reasons Ivy never could understand.

"I can't wait to show Grandma and Grandpa my outfit," Yolanda said when Ray guided the Cruiser to a stop parallel to the cars parked in front of their building. She followed Ivy to the rear of the car to remove the packages while Ray unbuckled Maya. Ivy was pleased when the teen gave her a warm hug. "Thank you so much, Miss Ivy."

"I hope you'll take pictures and show them to me when you wear it."

"Maybe you can come over that night, so you can see me yourself."

"I'd like that, if I'm not working that night." She doubted that would be a problem, but she felt she needed to give herself an out, just in case this afternoon was a one-time only deal. Very prominent on her mind was the fact that Ray still hadn't called her about dinner.

Ray and Maya joined them; he was holding the car seat.

"Well, I'm real happy we got Yolanda all squared away," Ivy said. A yawn escaped from her at the end of her statement. "Sorry about that. I'm feeling a little sleepy. I'd better get on home." She was surprised at how much she had enjoyed the day. Shopping for herself was drudgery, but outfitting Yolanda had been fun. She squatted in front of Maya. "Do I get a good-bye kiss, Missy?"

The child obliged.

Ivy put an arm around Yolanda and squeezed her shoulder. "You be good, now. And just call if I can help you with anything else."

"I will. Thanks again, Miss Ivy." The teen gave Ivy a quick hug.

Ivy turned to Ray. "I think we did good, don't you?"

"We sure did. Just a second." He turned to Yolanda. "Here, take this," he said, holding out the car seat. "Your packages will fit on top of it. Maya, follow Yolanda. You guys visit Nana and Granddad for a few minutes until I get back."

"All right. 'Bye, Miss Ivy."

"Good-bye." She turned to Ray. "Can I drop you someplace?"

"I'm bringing you home, Ivy."

"Oh, you don't have to do that. I know it's dark out, but the garage I park in is only two doors from my building."

He shook his head. "None of that. Come on, let's go. This time you drive, since you know exactly where your garage is."

She knew further protest would be useless. Ray was such a gentleman.

"Yolanda is just tickled with her dress," he said as they rode downtown. "She says my mother's taste is too old-fashioned."

"It's hard for a grandmother to keep up with the trends. So much has changed since you and I were her age."

"My mother has always been a little on the proper side. I remember her saying hot pants were vulgar."

"Wasn't that just another name for shorts?"

"Yes, but she didn't like the name. Good thing I never had a sister. Her life would have been miserable."

"Are you an only child?"

"Now I am. My brother died of a sudden illness when we were kids. My mother's been just a little bit sour on life ever since."

"Oh, I'm sorry."

Ivy parked in her assigned spot in the garage. She knew Ray would see her to her door.

"I hope you can come over the night Yolanda goes to the dance so you can see her all done up in her dress," Ray said as they walked into the elevator.

"She suggested that, too. I'd like that. I just hope I don't have to work that night."

"You've got a couple of weeks yet. Maybe you can clear your schedule. I figure you and I can make an evening out of it. After Yolanda leaves I'll take you for some German food. Maya can stay with my parents."

"Sounds good." They were approaching her door now, and her body tingled with anticipation. Was he going to kiss her on the mouth this time?

"After all, I did promise you. And I'd really like to express my appreciation for all you've done for Yolanda."

Was that all? The tingling stopped, and hope left her spirit like the last of bathwater down the drain.

Chapter 13
Ask Me No Questions

Ivy fell asleep, swathed in a down-filled quilt and her disappointment. She felt so strongly drawn to Ray Jones, it was all she could do not to grab the back of his head and kiss him when he brought her to her door, but that would be foolish of her, especially after he stated his reason for wanting to take her out.

She rose early and listlessly dressed. She was overseeing a wedding reception at four P.M., a small affair at an elegant midtown hotel. Ivy was glad she didn't have to travel to Westchester, New Jersey, or the North Shore of Long Island. She had plenty of time to enjoy the day before arriving forty-five minutes before the guests were expected.

Ivy popped the last of her breakfast—ham, egg, and cheese on a pumpernickel bagel—into her mouth, then picked up the ringing phone. She was shocked to hear her brother Otto's voice on the other end of the line.

"I'm in the East Village," he said. "I wanted to come by and talk to you about a couple of things, if you're not busy."

"I'll be leaving here about two-fifteen, and I'll need a good hour to get ready . . ."

"I was about to head home now. I can be there in a few minutes."

"All right. See you soon." As she hung up she wondered what in the world he wanted. She hadn't seen him or talked to him since their parents announced their plans to relocate and he stormed out so angrily, and here he was making like nothing had happened.

Otto arrived within half an hour, casually dressed in a sweater and slacks. "This is really a nice setup you've got here," he said, looking around the large room. "It's been so long since I've been here, I've forgotten how it looked."

"Thanks. Come in and sit down."

She crossed her legs and rested her palms on her knee in an expectant pose, determined not to make it easy for him.

"I guess you're wondering why I asked to come over."

"Yes, Otto, I am."

"Okay. I . . . I acted pretty bad that day Mom and Dad said they're retiring. I'm sorry. It's just that I felt like my home was being sold out from under me. You can understand that, can't you?"

"Not really. I'm in control of my own home. If they didn't renew my lease for whatever reason I'd just find another place."

"All right, I get the message. But I'm working on it. Mom and Dad are going to rent the house, not sell it."

"Are you going to rent it?"

"No. I can't afford to. But the reason they're holding off on selling is to give me a chance to get my stuff together. They already have a tenant lined up, and they're going to offer a two-year lease. By then I should be able to afford to rent it, even if I have to get a roommate to help out. But they're going to be leaving in a couple of weeks, and I've got to get a job."

"I thought you already have a job."

"I'm not at the supermarket anymore."

She rolled her eyes. "I won't ask."

"And I won't tell you," he snapped. He hung his head for a moment and regained his composure. "I'm sorry, Ivy. This is still scary for me, and I don't like being scared. Sometimes I deal with it by lashing out. Anyway, I was hoping I could work out something with you."

She raised an eyebrow. "What'd you have in mind?"

"I'd like to get on your roster of waiters. I could work evenings and weekends, and I'm sure I can find some kind of work during the day. Here in the city I can get around easy without a car. In Lakewood I can't get anywhere on foot except the Wawa."

The Wawa. She always thought that was a dumb name for a convenience store; it sounded like baby talk. "So what you're saying is that you plan to work two jobs."

"Yes."

"And you'll live in the East Village with whomever you stayed with last night?"

He looked embarrassed. "Well . . . no. We don't really know each other that well."

In other words, he just met her last night. What a slob. East Village, my foot. I'll bet the skeezer lives in Alphabet City. "So you're saying you want to stay with me."

"Well, you do have that extra bedroom, and I'll pay you rent."

She waited for him to add, "even though you don't need the money," but to her surprise he didn't.

"Let me think about it." From the look on his face, she knew he was feeling panicked.

"I'm trying, Ivy."

"I realize that, Otto, but I don't think you'll be able to make enough money working banquets or dinner parties to be able to rent Mom and Dad's house in two years. And even if you do, you'll be living in Lakewood. Not only will you have to have a car to get around there, but you'll have to commute to work in the city, and PATH isn't cheap. I have the feeling you're going about this all wrong."

"What do you suggest, that I join the army or something?"

"That's probably not a bad idea, but even though you're still young, you're not *that* young. I'm not sure they take people over thirty. But have you thought about getting financial aid and going to school?"

"College?"

"Not necessarily. Trade school. Learn to do something specialized so you don't have to keep doing these two-bit jobs."

"That takes too long. I don't have forever, Ivy."

"I'm sure Mom and Dad will give you another two years if you need it. But quite frankly, Otto, I don't see you sleeping in my guest room for two years, much less four."

"That's not a problem. I'm sure I'll come up with something before too long. Maybe my friend over on Avenue B."

Alphabet City. I knew it. Ivy wondered if her handsome brother had ever considered becoming a paid escort. If he was going to charm women out of their clothes, he might as well do it with someone who could make it worth his while.

"This is a lot to absorb, Otto, and I've got other concerns right now, like keeping my client happy this afternoon. I can't give you an answer straight out."

"I guess that's only fair." He stood. "I'll check back with you in a couple of days."

It wasn't until after Otto left that Ivy realized he hadn't even asked how she was; he merely came straight to the point, and once he made it he left. No sticking around, not even for a few minutes, just to talk or to exchange ideas, and of course if he didn't want something from her he would have simply gotten on the PATH train to go home without even calling to tell her he was in the city. It was all so typical . . . and it hurt more than she wanted to admit.

At one o'clock she got into the shower. For more formal occasions such as wedding receptions when she was more visible, she skipped her standard "uniform" of blue chambray shirt, navy blazer, and khaki slacks and dressed more like a guest. She knew her ethnicity alone would make her stand out, but at least her attire would blend in. She selected a sheath of beige silk and matching long jacket, along with comfortable tan pumps for all the standing and moving around she would no doubt be doing.

She had showered, partially dressed, and was applying her makeup when the phone rang again. "Hello? Oh, hi!" Her tense muscles relaxed at the sound of Mitch's voice. They had had a pleasant lunch together on Friday, and she hadn't talked to him the day before at all. She'd been prepared to tell the caller she'd have to get back to them later, but she had time for Mitch. "What's up?"

She frowned as he talked. "Mitch, you know I'd love to help, but I'm afraid it's out of the question. I've got too much on my plate to take the kids while you're in Chicago. You know how busy I am with Jubilee. . . . Yes, I know. I was glad I could help you before, but that was only for one night. From tonight through Tuesday night is more than I can handle. I won't even be here tonight; I'm on my way to the Sherry Netherland right now. My clients are entertaining sixty-five people at their reception." She nodded in agreement with his response. "Yes, I guess you'll have to bring them to their grandparents'. You know, Mitch, you're really going to have to get a live-in maid who can stay with Casey and Elgin. If your job is going to insist you travel at the last minute like this, you're going to have problems galore with child care, and the kids will miss a lot of school unless their grandparents come down to your house. What's that? Well, yes, I can see your not wanting your former in-laws to have free reign of your house when you aren't there, but you've got to do something. Yes, all right. I've got to run. Have a good flight, and I'll talk to you later."

She thought about Mitch during the cab ride uptown. She had tried hard to put aside her dislike of his children and pursue their relationship and she enjoyed being in his company, but his request disturbed her. They had discussed her schedule at lunch Friday, and he knew she was working a wedding this afternoon. She couldn't help wondering if he wanted a serious relationship or a baby-sitter.

When she arrived at the hotel she confirmed that the rows of oval-backed chairs were in place for the ceremony, as well as a table with a large vase of lilies that would serve as the altar. The guests would be served cocktails and hors d'oeuvres in a different room after the nuptials while the staff rearranged the setting to that of round tables for dinner.

Then she checked in the kitchen. The chef was putting finishing touches on the hors d'oeuvres, and the wait staff was ready.

She knew from having been informed earlier by the

cake designer that the cake had been delivered, and she stopped to look at it. What a hoot, she thought as she took in the three layered creation with elaborate vanilla frosting with yellow and purple decorated flowers. The bride had been married twice before and the groom three times, and in a whimsical gesture they had requested to have, in addition to the traditional bride and groom figures on the top layer of the elaborately frosted cake, figures representing previous spouses pushed headfirst into the cake at varying levels. The cake designer neatly covered any ruptures with smooth fondant icing. She could imagine the meaningful glances and suppressed chuckles of the guests at a couple with such poor marital records promising to remain wed till death did them part. Still, she had to commend them for being so open about their previous marital failures. Sometimes you just had to know when to call it a day. Was the tension in her own belly ever since Mitch's call a sign of the inevitable?

As she looked at the cake she had an idea that made the discomfort disappear and her lips shape into a smile.

Ivy spotted Bethany at the bar at Mekka and rushed over. "I hope you weren't waiting long."

"Long enough for the men who've approached me to think I'm lying when I said I was meeting someone."

"Sorry."

"What happened? You just miss a train or something?"

"No. A train pulled in just as I got there." Ivy wrinkled her nose at the memory of the rush hour subway ride. Whoever designed subway cars must have been a pervert. Where else can women sit and get close-up views of men's crotches?

"If the train was there, what took you so long to get here?"

"Mitch called, and I talked to him for a few minutes." Ivy smiled at the bartender who approached. "A bay breeze, please."

"Oh, is Mitch back?" Bethany said.

"Yes, he got in yesterday. I asked him to stop by here."

"So I'm going to get to meet your future husband. I'm honored."

"He's not my future husband, Bethany."

"You'd better hold on to a good thing. And you worry too much. His kids will outgrow their brattiness in time."

"Yeah, well, you try taking care of them. They'd have a great time messing up that white carpet in your duplex. You know, he asked me to take care of them again while he was gone."

"You're kidding. Why doesn't he just hire a live-in nanny?"

"He says he's interviewing, but it's hard to find the perfect person."

"What'd he say when you told him no?"

"He was fine with it. He said he knew it was a long shot, but he was desperate. He said he would bring them to his in-laws in Mount Vernon, and they'd just have to miss two days of school."

"If he doesn't hurry up and find a reliable sitter, his kids will end up having to repeat a grade," Bethany remarked. The appetizer she ordered was delivered, and she bit into a catfish strip. "This is good. I haven't been here in a while. I was really ticked off when I was here a few months ago. A man had the nerve to bring me here on our first date."

Ivy lowered her chin to her chest and looked at her friend quizzically. "I don't get it. You love soul food. Why was that a crime?"

"Because the man was Irish. I can't deal with people

who think in stereotypes. That was a short-lived relationship. When he brought me home I didn't think it would work out. It was best to break it off before he could bring me to Brothers Barbecue."

"Funny you should say that. I'm going to break it off with Mitch."

"*What?*"

"It's not going to work, Bethany. There are too many strikes against us. The way I feel about his kids is a major issue, and I don't like the way he's always asking me to watch them when he travels. His whole life is a mess."

"And you're not interested in helping him get on track?"

"It's just not something I feel motivated to do," Ivy confessed.

"Tell the truth, Ivy. Do you want to give Mitch up because you want to explore a relationship with that guy from the post office?"

"Ray has nothing to do with this. It turned out he's not even interested in me. The only reason he wants to take me to dinner is to thank me for helping out his daughter." As she said the words Ivy tried to tell herself she didn't care, but she knew she did. It bothered her as much now, on Wednesday, as it had when he made his parting comment four days earlier. Why couldn't it have been Mitch who was interested in taking her out for all the wrong reasons? Maybe she was crazy. Most women in her position would jump at the chance to meet a man like Mitch, a man who, as Bethany said, "knows a demitasse isn't just half a cup." Instead she was willing to walk away and let some other woman— actually Bethany, though her friend didn't know it yet— benefit from her disinterest. "I'm just not feeling it. I don't know why. I just know that these things can't be forced."

Bethany shrugged. "You're right about that. I think it's scientific."

"And, Bethany . . ."

"What?"

"I meant to tell you. Ray *can* drive."

Chapter 14
I'll Tell You No Lies

"I don't get it, Ivy. What does *that* have to do with the price of tea in China?"

"You said Ray probably couldn't even drive. I just wanted you to know you were wrong."

"All right, I was wrong. He can drive. I'm sure he can even parallel park on the first try." With a frown, Bethany waved away smoke from a nearby patron's cigarette. "You weren't kidding when you said you couldn't stop thinking about him, were you?"

Ivy sighed. "I don't understand it, Bethany. Everything keeps coming back to him. And when he said why he wanted to take me to dinner I felt like a balloon with air escaping from it."

"I wish I knew what to tell you. But you know I'm pulling for you."

"I know. Thanks."

"Oh, look, there's Terry Harris!" Bethany said.

Ivy turned to see a mutual acquaintance being led to

a table by a waiter, followed by a portly man with graying hair.

"That must be her new husband, the judge," Bethany said.

"I haven't seen her in ages. She doesn't come to the meetings anymore."

"I hear they live in Sands Point, but I don't think anyone's heard from her since she got married, not even a thank-you note. Now, you know her mama raised her better than that."

Ivy shook her head. "Carmen Carter did the same thing when she married her second husband. Remember how we were all wondering what happened and talked about how tacky she was not to acknowledge our gifts? Terry was the first to say she'd still join us when we got together, and no one's seen or heard from her since. Do you think we should go by their table to say hello and watch her squirm?"

"Oh, Ivy, you're mean. And how did you know I was about to suggest the same thing?" They laughed. "I don't know. Maybe we should just leave it alone. Terry might have realized she made a mistake and is too embarrassed to let anyone know. I mean, look at that stuffy look on her husband's face. Does he look like he's got his boxer shorts caught in his butt or what?" They muffled their laughter, and then Ivy abruptly straightened up. "Shh . . . Mitch is here."

Bethany looked toward the door, and when she spoke it was out of the side of her mouth, like a prison inmate trying to prevent his lips from being read. "Oh, my, he's gorgeous! Ivy, I can't believe you're giving him up. I honestly think you must have rocks in your head."

"Gee, thanks," Ivy replied dryly. "By the way, I forgot to tell you something."

"What's that?"

"I think it would be great if you and he got together."

* * *

Ivy smiled as she hailed a cab. Her friend Glenda came through right on time. She'd call Glenda when she got home and thank her for helping her out.

Her plan was working fine. Bethany and Mitch were involved in an intelligent discussion about the financial markets when Glenda called on Ivy's cell phone at the prearranged time. Ivy spoke to her briefly, deliberately inserting an urgency in her tone.

"Is everything all right?" Mitch asked when she hung up, as she expected he would.

"Oh, it's one of my clients. She's all up in arms because some people came into town that she just *has* to invite to her dinner party tomorrow night. I'll have to cut the evening short, though, because this needs my immediate attention. The whole thing has to be rearranged. I might need another waiter, and I don't even want to think about what the caterer is going to say."

"Oh, no. I was just going to suggest we order some dinner," Mitch said.

"You two go ahead. Don't let me spoil your evening." She gulped down the last of her drink and left as Mitch and Bethany were moving to a table. Bethany had made a quick recovery from the shocked expression she wore when Mitch approached. Ivy smiled. She knew it had been less than considerate of her to drop that announcement so casually, but she wanted it to sound like a spur-of-the-moment thought, not like something she had all planned out.

She invited Mitch to lunch the next day. "So, how did you and Bethany get along?" she asked after they had placed their orders.

"It was a very pleasant dinner. But you almost sound like you were fixing us up." He looked at her closely. "Wait a minute. That phone call . . . that sudden departure . . . Is this your way of handing me over to your friend?"

Ivy shifted in her seat. She hadn't expected him to be so astute. Suddenly the cozy atmosphere felt awkward. "Um-m-m-m . . ."

Mitch leaned in closer. "Tell me the truth, Ivy," he said gently. "All those times in the last couple of weeks where you couldn't go out with me because you said you were so busy with work . . . were you really?"

"Oh, yes, I was. I wouldn't lie to you about that. I've never tried to avoid you, Mitch. It's just that. . . ." She realized she had to tell him the truth. Nothing else would do, especially since she'd just stressed how honest she was. "There's someone else." She cringed at the line. *It's straight out of a fifties melodrama.* But corny or not, it fit.

"Is it Ray?"

She couldn't stop her face from registering shocked surprise. "Ray?" she repeated.

"The guy who escorted you to the reunion. Nice fellow, but I was getting vibes from him that said 'keep away from my woman,' if you know what I mean."

Ray with a proprietary attitude? Mitch might as well have just told her the sun had turned green. "I . . . didn't realize," she finally said. "But yes, that's who it is. We haven't been actually dating or anything, but I've been helping him out . . ." She couldn't say she was helping with Ray's daughter, not after she'd refused to help Mitch with *his* kids—"with some family problems. I don't know if anything will even come of it, but under the circumstances I don't feel it's fair for me to go on seeing you. But you're such a wonder-

ful man, Mitch, and Bethany's not involved with anyone, so I thought . . .''

"I'll be honest, too, Ivy. I had a feeling this was going
to happen. Something in your voice when I called you
on Sunday. I got the distinct impression that you're not
ready to get involved with a man with children.''

She was grateful he'd forgotten Ray saying at the
reunion that he, too, was a custodial parent, but of
course she knew better. She'd already told one fib, and
to agree with Mitch now would be outright lying. "Well,
I don't know if I'd say *that*—''

"It's all right. Anyway, Bethany and I seemed to hit
it off rather well, but of course I didn't ask for her
number or anything. Now I know better, of course, but
last night as far as I knew, you and I were seeing each
other. We might not have had an exclusive arrangement, but as a friend of yours I considered her off
limits.''

For all his gallantry, she couldn't help remembering
how he'd had no problem wrangling a business card
out of her so he could contact her socially when she
was at the reunion as Ray's date. "I'm glad you like her,
and I'm glad you aren't upset. I'll give you her office
number. I know she'll be happy to hear from you.''

He stared at her, clearly confused. "Did she tell you
that?''

"She *didn't* tell me, and that's the key. If she didn't
like you she would have called last night and told me,
but I haven't heard from her. Her silence speaks for
her.''

Ivy beamed at Yolanda. The sixteen year old looked
lovely in her gown, even if her hair was uncombed and
her face bare.

"Oh, Miss Ivy, I'm so glad you could come early," she said, holding out her arms.

"You know I'll help you out if I can." Ivy hugged her briefly.

"I need help fixing my hair and my face."

"Yes, you do," she said with a laugh. "Let's see what we can do." Ivy stepped into the apartment. Both Ray and Maya came from the living room to greet her. She picked Maya up, as had become her habit, and Ray reached out for her free hand and held it slightly longer than he needed to, not that she objected.

"Thanks for coming," he said.

Yolanda led Ivy to the dining area, where a heated curling iron and a cosmetic bag awaited. "Let's do your hair first," Ivy suggested. She indicated for Yolanda to sit down.

Ivy pinned up the back of Yolanda's short hair, wavy like Ray's, then curled the top and side strands, which were too short to be pinned. "We'll comb it out last," Ivy said. She rummaged in the cosmetic bag and pulled out a pair of tweezers.

"Ouch!" Yolanda squealed when the first eyebrow hair was plucked.

"I'm sorry it stings, but it's the cost of being beautiful."

"I'm changing this channel, Yolanda," Ray said from the tastefully decorated living room, where he sat on a blue-and-maroon plaid couch with Maya on his lap. He held the remote control poised in the direction of the television.

"Daddy, no!"

"I can't stand listening to these nonsinging singers. If this act had been part of amateur night, they would have been booed off the stage."

"The power of a hit record," Ivy remarked.

"Please, Daddy. I really want to see them."

"Oh, all right." He ambled over to the dining table and sat down. "Look at all this stuff," he said, rifling through the contents of the makeup bag.

"I got it with my store discount."

"I think you're too young for eye makeup, Yolanda. Why don't we just work with mascara, lipstick, and a little blush?" Ivy suggested.

"But all the girls from school wear eye makeup, Miss Ivy."

"We're going to abide by Ivy's recommendations, Yolanda," Ray said firmly.

"Oh, all right."

Ivy had shaped Yolanda's eyebrows and was applying blusher when someone knocked on the door.

"I'll get it," Ray said, getting to his feet. "It's probably Nana and Granddad."

"You have nice, smooth skin," Ivy said to Yolanda, hoping casual conversation would help calm Yolanda's nerves. She didn't consider that Ray's parents would be by, but of course with them living in the building next door it was only natural. "When I was your age I had breakouts."

"Your skin's pretty now."

'Thanks. I've long since grown out of it."

"Well, well, if it isn't Miss America."

"Hi, Granddad."

Ivy put down the makeup brush and held out her hand. "You must be Mr. Jones. I'm Ivy Smith."

"Well, hello there," he said as he shook her hand. "I'm glad to finally meet you. Yolanda talks about you all the time."

Ray's mother stepped forward and, ignoring Ivy, tipped Yolanda's chin upward for a better look. "Oh, heavens! Eye makeup? I think that's a bit much, Yolanda."

"But I'm not wearing anything on my eyes, Nana. Daddy said no, and so did Miss Ivy."

"I just shaped Yolanda's eyebrows, Mrs. Jones," Ivy said. "That can sometimes give the illusion of makeup." She was about to introduce herself when Ray intervened.

"This is Ivy Smith, Mom," he said.

Ivy greeted his mother warmly.

"So you're the one I've heard so much about."

"I suppose," Ivy said with a limp shrug. Mrs. Jones welcomed her with the coldness Mrs. Danvers displayed to the second Mrs. de Winter in the movie *Rebecca;* her open assessment, looking Ivy up and down, did nothing to ease the tension.

"Yes, Mom, she's the one." Ray moved behind Ivy and looped his arms around her shoulders, clasping his hands just below her chin.

He had stood close to her when they danced at the reunion, but this sudden action seemed much more intimate, perhaps because it was unexpected, and compounded by his simple statement, "She's the one." Ivy bit on her lower lip and willed herself not to tremble. In that instant she knew precisely what Bethany meant about attraction being scientific. She genuinely liked Mitch, but in spite of her affection for him what they had never could have developed into a romance. On the other hand, she felt drawn to Ray from the first time she saw him that day in the post office. The moment Ray kissed the back of her hand and looked into her eyes the night of the reunion, she was gone. No wonder she hadn't been able to stop thinking about him.

The embrace only lasted a few seconds, but just before he pulled away he squeezed her shoulders with his palms. Ivy interpreted the gesture as a signal not to let his mother get to her. She remembered what he said about the dour effect the death of his brother had had on his mother's personality.

She decided to try to be friendly. "I hope you approve of Yolanda's dress, Mrs. Jones, Mr. Jones."

Ray's father had taken a seat in a navy easy chair and put his feet up on the matching ottoman. "It's just perfect."

Mrs. Jones remained standing. "It's very nice," she said. "I was afraid she might choose something too mature."

"She tried to," Ray said.

"Daddy, I'll bet someone at the dance will have that black and white dress on," Yolanda said.

"Well, that's *her* parents' problem."

Yolanda's date, a gangly young man who looked like his tie was choking him, arrived and duly greeted everyone. Ivy almost felt sorry for him; she was sure he hadn't counted on being presented to so many people. They all left the apartment at the same time, Ray holding Maya, who looked rather comical after insisting on having makeup applied to her face, too. The three-year-old's hair had been brushed back into a ball of curls at the back of her crown, but the strands around her hairline were sticking up from a day of activity, and her cheeks and lips were tinted with color. When they reached the street Mr. and Mrs. Jones bid them good night and disappeared into the attached building with Maya. Mrs. Jones made no effort to lower her voice when she told her husband, "I'll have to scrub Maya's face good to get all that gunk off."

Ivy waited with Ray to make sure the youngsters had no problem getting a cab. Yolanda waved to them as the cab drove off, and Ray turned to Ivy. "Hungry?"

"Just a little."

"The restaurant's up on Forty-eighth. We can get a cab if you'd like."

"No, it's a lovely night for walking."

They strolled up the avenue, reasonably close to each other but not touching. The evening was pleasantly warm, and most restaurants they passed had placed a few tables and chairs on the wide sidewalks for al fresco dining.

Ivy was disappointed to see no outdoor tables at their destination, but Ray requested the hostess to seat them on the terrace, which was in the back of the building.

"Oh, this is lovely," she said when she stopped outdoors. The terrace had been decorated to look like a Bavarian garden. The sound of taped ethnic music from the main dining room drifted outside whenever the door was opened.

Ray asked the waiter for a half carafe of Piesporter while Ivy perused the menu. "I never had German food before, but I think I'd like the Jaeger schnitzel. Fried pork with mushroom, onion, and pepper gravy. Makes my mouth water."

"I promise you won't be disappointed. I'm in the mood for bratwurst and potatoes myself." He flagged down the waiter and gave the order. "I hope you didn't find my mother too difficult," he said when they were alone.

"No, of course not."

"She can be rather blunt."

Ivy chuckled. "Well, I'll admit I didn't think it was necessary for her to tell me not to make Yolanda look like Bozo the Clown when I was putting color on her cheeks."

"I wonder if I'll be that rigid when Maya is in high school. By then I'll be in my fifties and probably a lot older than her classmates' parents."

"I guess we can't help growing older, no matter what our circumstances are."

"Sometimes I feel old now. I remember when my

wife and I were on line to get tickets to see the movie *Titanic* a couple of years ago. I was telling Dolores how someone at work had said that the special effects were so good it gave the audience the genuine feeling of being on a sinking ship. Someone behind me went, 'Oh, man,' and when I turned around a teenage boy there with his date said, 'Thanks a lot for telling us that the ship sinks.' "

She laughed heartily at the anecdote. She didn't even feel uneasy with his mention of his late wife. After all, they had been married a long time; it would be foolish and probably unnatural for him to act like she never existed.

Ivy patted her stomach. "I probably shouldn't have eaten that German chocolate cheesecake. You're going to have to roll me out of here."

"I'm glad you enjoyed it," he said as he helped her up. "Don't worry about it. We'll get a cab home."

She rested her head on his shoulder as they rode downtown, in what seemed like a perfectly natural gesture. She was thrilled when he put his arm around her shoulder.

"There's something I think you should know," he said softly.

She immediately lifted her head so she could look at his handsome profile. "What is it?"

"As much as I appreciate your mentoring Yolanda, that's only part of the reason I asked you to have dinner with me."

She practically squealed in excitement. "It is?"

"Yes. I've been alone for two very long years, Ivy, and while I can't say I haven't been without feminine companionship in all that time, I can truthfully say that with you it's different. I sense you're very special, and I'd like to see you again."

"Really?"

"Really."

"Well, in that case you owe me an apology."

His forehead wrinkled in confusion. "Excuse me?"

"I was so disappointed when you said you wanted to take me to dinner just to thank me for helping out with Yolanda. Quite frankly, I hoped you were attracted to me, because I was attracted to you."

Ray broke into a smile. "In that case, I apologize. I wasn't sure if you'd want to go out with me. I thought your friend at the reunion was more your type."

"Who, Leslie?"

"No, silly, her cousin."

"Oh, Mitch."

"Yeah. You, uh, ever talk to them?"

"Leslie called me the other day." She had actually called to express how disappointed she was to learn Ivy was no longer involved with Mitch, but Ray didn't have to know that. "And Mitch . . . I thought he would be perfect for one of my friends, so I introduced them." At least it was the truth, just not the whole truth.

"You did?"

She nodded and held his gaze. Her breath caught in her throat when he moved toward her, and her lips inadvertently parted. Their mouths came together hungrily, his large hand and outstretched fingers cupping her throat, chin, and jaw, for the dual purpose of holding her face in position and concealing the intimacy of their open mouths from the taxi driver's view. She gripped his muscular upper arm and held on, wanting their kiss to go on and on, and she knew she would savor it long after. She couldn't remember the last time she had kissed and been kissed with such fervor, such naked passion. Mitch's kisses told her he was looking

for a lover who could also sit with his children when
needed; Ray's said he wanted her heart.

When they broke apart she was shocked to see they
were just one block from her loft. Kissing Ray had made
everything come to a standstill in her mind, but now
she saw the world had continued to move around them.

"I've been wanting to do that for a long time," he
said quietly. "You could probably tell."

"And I enjoyed it, as *you* could probably tell." She
managed to sound calm, even though her skin tingled
like she had a mild sunburn. When Ray got out to pay
the driver she realized she had slipped off her shoes,
and she hastily bent to put them back on—but first she
had to straighten her toes, which had reflexively bent
backward while she and Ray kissed. *I guess the toes knows.*

Chapter 15
The Morning After

Ivy watched curiously as the cab drove off. She knew Ray had reasons for letting the cab go other than an intent to stay the night with her, but she couldn't imagine what. It wasn't like him to assume he would be invited inside; he wasn't the presumptuous type.

He patted his stomach. "I'm going to walk home. I could use the exercise, after a meal like that." Then he checked his watch. "Before I know it Yolanda will be getting in."

"And you'll be nervously awaiting her arrival by the door," she teased.

He laughed. "I tell you, this dating thing is enough to age a father ten years. But I do feel better knowing she's at a chaperoned school function than out and about someplace on her own."

They fell into step and entered the building. "Did they ask you to be a chaperone?" Ivy asked.

"They sent a letter home, but I decided I'd feel silly standing around by myself like a security guard. Yolanda would certainly feel uncomfortable, because you know who I'd be looking at the closest."

"Let's see . . . That would be her and her date."

"When I checked with the school they said they had accepted the offers of sufficient sets of parents. That's the key, 'sets.' That type of thing is best left to husbands and wives as a unit, not single parents. They'll have something to do other than stare at all the kids."

The elevator stopped on the third floor, and as they walked down the hall to her door he placed an arm around her shoulder.

"Did you want to come in for a while?" she asked. They stood in front of her door, and he removed his arm and gave her room to unlock the door.

"Not this time. I really want to be there when Yolanda gets home."

"I understand." She pushed the door open and reflexively reached for the light switch, but the lights were already on, and so was the television.

Ray frowned. "Is someone in there?"

Otto pulled himself away from the female companion beside him on the sofa and stood. "Ivy, hi."

Ivy walked toward him, Ray close behind.

"I didn't expect you home so early," Otto said.

"It's after eleven, Otto."

"Is it?" He extended his hand to Ray. "I'm Otto, Ivy's brother."

"Ray Jones."

Otto gestured toward the woman on the couch, whose braids were askew on the right side of her face and whose blouse was unbuttoned at the bottom. "This is Lakeisha. Lakeisha, this is my sister Ivy and her friend Ray."

They exchanged greetings, and Ivy noted that Lakeisha at least had the decency to look embarrassed.

"Excuse us," Ivy said, taking Ray's hand and leading him toward the hall.

She brought him to the exercise room and closed the door behind them. "I'm sorry about this, Ray. My brother asked if he could stay here and join my roster of waiters, since our parents are about to retire to North Carolina. He's only been here a week. I'm afraid I didn't cover the rules of entertaining when we discussed the specifics."

"I suppose it's a little unsettling, your coming home and interrupting a make-out session, but there's no harm done. You have nothing to apologize for."

Ivy's mouth set in a determined line. "I don't see why he had to bring her here in the first place. She's got an apartment."

"Everybody likes a change in scenery every now and then. You might be taking this too hard, Ivy. They were only watching TV in your living room, not making love in the bedroom." He took her hand. "Maybe you should talk to him, lay down some ground rules. If you think he might invite her to spend the night and don't want to bump into her when you go to make your morning coffee, it's probably a good idea to tell him before it actually happens." He glanced at his watch. "I'd better be on my way." He pulled her to him and gazed at her soothingly. "Come on, Ivy, give me a smile. I want to picture you that way in my dreams tonight."

The thought of him dreaming about her made it easy to comply. "Will you call me when Yolanda gets in?"

"If you're sure it won't be too late, I will." He kissed her briefly, and she walked him to the door. "Good night, folks," he called to Otto and Lakeisha before slipping out.

* * *

Ivy awoke to a glorious spring morning. She made a few last-minute calls regarding the lavish children's party she had arranged for that afternoon, then quickly set about doing her housework. She didn't have much time; she had to get to New Jersey by one o'clock. Her chores took longer than they used to now that Otto was staying with her. When she went to transfer her wet clothing from the washing machine to the dryer stacked above it, she was dismayed to find the dryer full of Otto's clothes. He was such a slob.

At least his things were completely dry. She scooped them up and dropped them in a chair in the exercise room. Otto wasn't up yet, and she didn't want his laundry laying around her nice, neat living room until he got to it.

She put on a Diana Krall CD while she did her chores. Those old standard numbers were the best songs. As she sang along to "Let's Fall in Love" she couldn't help seeing a mental picture of Ray and remembering that deep, sensuous kiss in the back of the cab. There would have been another if it hadn't been for Otto and his girlfriend making out on the couch.

Ivy sighed. She wasn't being fair, and she knew it. She couldn't expect her brother to stay cooped up in his room while he was staying here. Years of living alone made it difficult for her to adjust to suddenly having someone else in the loft, and her bitter disappointment over not being able to spend a few quiet moments alone with Ray in the comfort of her living room made her resent Otto's presence more than anything else. But she had to give Otto a chance to do something with his life; as his sister she owed him that much.

She frowned when she saw the dirty plates and glasses in the sink. Otto and Lakeisha had apparently had a snack last night. Well, not taking out her personal frustrations on Otto was one thing, but if he wanted to stay at her place he'd better learn to clean up after himself.

"Great shot," Ray said as the basketball teetered for a few moments before falling through the net.

"Yeah, but they're still gonna lose," his friend Rodney said confidently.

"Here you go, fellows," Rodney's wife Cathy said, placing a tray containing a bowl of pretzel mix and two beer steins down on the coffee table.

"Thanks, Cathy," Ray said.

"You're welcome. What've you been up to lately, Ray?"

"Oh, I'm keeping busy."

"That's code for, 'I'd rather you weren't in my business, Cathy,' " Rodney told his wife with a laugh. To Ray he said, "She wants to fix you up with one of her man-hungry girlfriends."

"Celeste isn't man hungry, Ray," Cathy protested. "She's a very nice girl."

Ray had heard this before. Sometimes he suspected Cathy was keeping a calendar; her first offer to set him up "with a very nice girl" came right after the first anniversary of Dolores's accident, and subsequent offers usually began with her pointing out how much time had passed. "It's been thirteen months . . ." "It's been fifteen months . . ." "It's been eighteen months . . ."

"Actually, Cathy, I'm seeing someone," he said.

"You are!"

Even Rodney looked startled. "Hey, you didn't tell me that. You holdin' out on me, man?"

Cathy took a seat opposite them and leaned forward expectantly. "Tell us about her, Ray."

He didn't like being put on the spot this way, but Rodney and Cathy were good friends, and refusing to elaborate wouldn't be right. "Her name's Ivy Smith. I met her at the post office, when I made a mistake on a money order she bought. She gave it back to me, and from then on we would talk whenever she came in for stamps. It was only a matter of time before we moved it outside."

"Does she live in the city, or just work here?" Cathy asked.

"Both."

"How old is she?"

"Cathy!" Rodney said. "What does that have to do with anything?" He turned to Ray, uncertainty in his eyes. "She ain't twenty-three, is she?"

"No. She's in her late thirties."

"What kind of work does she do?" Rodney asked.

"She owns her own business, Jubilee, Incorporated. They do all sorts of things involving entertaining. Consulting, even planning, training waiters and waitresses. They work with a lot of wealthy folks and celebrities." He saw both the Townsends' expressions change from smiling to worried looking. "What's wrong with you two all of a sudden?"

"It sounds like she's rolling in Benjamins, Ray," Rodney said. "That doesn't scare you?"

"Should it?"

"It sure as hell would scare *me*, some woman making a whole lot more than I did. A couple of thou more I could live with, but she must be pullin' in what? A half mil a year?"

"I'm sure her company grosses in the millions, but I doubt she gets to keep that much after expenses. She has three or four people working for her, for one thing."

"Tell us about her place," Cathy said.

"She rents a loft on Twenty-eighth Street."

Cathy frowned. "What's that, the Grammercy area?"

"No, Chelsea."

"My uptown girl," Rodney said affectionately. "Doesn't know anything south of Thirty-fourth Street."

"She's got a nice setup," Ray continued.

"How many bedrooms?" Cathy asked.

"Three, I think."

"Baths?"

"I don't know, Cathy. One in the hall, a powder room by the door . . . I don't remember if there's one in her bedroom. There probably is."

"Is there a doorman?"

"Damn, Cathy, give the man a break," Rodney said. "You're firing off questions quicker than a tommy gun."

"No doorman. It's a mixed use building. Some are apartments, some are offices, others are both."

"Still, a setup like that must go for fifty or sixty bills a month," Rodney said.

"Does she have a car?" Cathy asked.

"Yes. The company also has two vans. She parks them in a garage a few doors down from her building."

"Oh, man, forget it," Rodney said. "If she can afford to park three vehicles in a garage in New York she might as well be Oprah."

"Have you been seeing each other long?" Cathy asked.

"No, only for a few weeks." He hoped he would be forgiven for the fib. Technically, they'd only gone on one date just last night, two if he counted the reunion, but that wasn't really a date. Maybe it was too soon to be telling his friends about her.

A loud noise from the bedroom where Maya was playing with the Townsends' sons had Cathy up and running in to check on the children. Rodney asked, "Where do you take a woman like that? She's probably used to the best restaurants, orchestra seats. . . . She sounds pretty high maintenance to me."

"We go out to dinner, and not to Fifty-Seven Fifty-

Seven or Lespinasse," Ray said, naming two pricey midtown bistros. "Just ordinary places on the West Side."

"And she's okay with that?"

"She's fine with it."

Rodney shook his head. "I don't know. Sounds like you're begging to have your heart broken. Sooner or later she's going to meet some investment banker, and you'll be as obsolete as Windows 95."

"I guess I'll cross that bridge when I get to it. In the meantime, we're missing the game."

Ray thought about the conversation when he and Maya left the Townsends' Columbus Avenue high rise after the game and caught the downtown local. He knew his friends meant well, but they were getting involved where they really shouldn't. They didn't even know Ivy, and they had her labeled as the shallow type who only cared about what a man had. Maybe a lot of women did feel that way, but when you got right down to it, Ray felt it really shouldn't matter. He and Dolores had been a team, like any good partnership. Closer than close, their friends used to call them. If he should ever get lucky enough to experience that again, he wouldn't let the matter of a discrepancy in income get in the way, not even one as wide as the Hudson River.

Ray had two locks on his apartment door. After he unlocked the top one he heard Yolanda unlocking the remaining one from the inside.

"Thanks," he said. "You home already?"

"I just got in a few minutes ago. There wasn't a big crowd at four, so for once they closed my register on time."

"Good."

"Daddy, Miss Ivy just called. She invited us to her place for brunch tomorrow."

"What'd you tell her?"

"I said I was sure we could come, but that I'd ask you to call and let her know for sure."

"Miss Ivy, Miss Ivy," Maya sang.

"We can go, can't we, Daddy?" Yolanda asked.

"Sure. I'll call her in a few minutes. I'm thirsty."

"She left her cell phone number. She's working. A player for the New Jersey Nets is having a real fancy birthday party for his five-year-old son. Ivy barely had time to talk. She's got some kind of walkie-talkie where she communicates with the staff, and I heard her telling someone to get to the door and offer arriving guests champagne."

"The adults, I suppose."

'Of course, Daddy. They had people dressed up like Winnie the Pooh and Yogi Bear to offer the kids punch. Isn't that neat? I'll bet Maya would have a great time there."

"I'm sure she would, but we don't know any millionaire basketball players." Ray went into the kitchen and poured himself some ice water, which he downed in one gulp and let out an "aah" of satisfaction. How considerate of Ivy to include the girls in her invitation.

He took the number Yolanda wrote down for him before he went to his bedroom, making a mental note to add it to the business card Ivy had scribbled her home number on that day at the post office. Funny. He hadn't called Ivy enough to know her home number by heart, but after just one kiss he had memorized the planes of her face, the hollows on the side of her throat, the curve of her jaw, the raised mole in front of her ear, and most of all, the sweetness of her mouth.

Chapter 16
He's Not Who You Think He Is

Ivy stuck one end of several small pieces of tape on the back of her hand to have available as she needed them. During her college years she had done gift wrapping at a department store over the Christmas season, and after all these years she still tried to make the tape as inconspicuous as possible.

She folded the paper around the box and taped it into place, then squared the upper and lower edges on both sides. She had tied it with ribbon, which she was curling with scissors when the phone rang.

"Hello."

"Well, you sound abrupt."

"Hi, Bethany. I don't mean to sound rushed, but Ray and the girls will be here for brunch any minute, I've got to get to Glenda's baby shower this afternoon in Westchester, and Stephanie just called. Otto spent the night with our parents in Lakewood last night, and the movers are coming tomorrow. They're all going to drive up early this afternoon to say hello and bring Otto back, so that'll give me a chance to say good-bye to my parents before they leave."

"I can't believe how quickly your parents have gotten this move together."

"Once they decided to rent their house instead of selling it and got a tenant, there was nothing holding them back. My father is a foreman at a plant, and my mother does private duty nursing. Neither of them had to give months of notice."

"I suppose you're cooking for Ray and his kids."

"Actually, I'm wrapping the shower gift. I've got pancakes, bacon, sausage, and home fries warm in the oven. I'll do the eggs and biscuits when they get here. What's up?" She waited for Bethany's response, and when her friend didn't say anything right away Ivy drew in her breath. "Oh, I'm so sorry. I've been so busy I completely forgot you went out with Mitch last night. How was it?"

"We had a lot of fun. We went to a party up in Greenwich. One of his coworkers at Morgan Stanley." She yawned. "It was kind of a late night."

"I trust Mitch had no child care difficulties."

"The college girl next door, but he finally hired a live-in housekeeper who'll start work in about two weeks. His town house looks gorgeous from the outside, by the way. Even the burglar bars on the ground level are pretty."

"Burglar bars are never pretty. And how did you happen to see his house, anyway? Connecticut is north of New York, and he lives south of you."

"We took my car, and I offered to pick him up. He brought me home when we got back and took a taxi back to his place."

"I'm sure he was impressed with Park Avenue."

"Well, he didn't see much beyond the lobby, the elevator, and the hall. It's not like I invited him in. But I can't remember the last time I felt confident enough to allow a man to come to the building. Even executives get intimidated by my place."

"Bethany, you have a nine-room duplex in a prewar condo in a city where thousands of families have to squeeze five and six people into four-room apartments. If the uniformed doorman doesn't intimidate men, the curved staircase, library, maid's room, twelve-foot ceilings, and wood-burning fireplace will."

"At least Mitch didn't seem panicky when he saw the building. It make me feel hopeful. Listen, I won't hold you; I know you've got a lot to do. I'll talk to you later."

"All right. 'Bye."

Ivy finished tying the ribbons and placed a bow on the gift. Glenda Arnold was about the only friend of hers who hadn't vanished after getting married. But Glenda wasn't part of Ivy and Bethany's social group. She met Glenda several years earlier when they were dating men who were friends, and their friendship continued long after both affairs petered out.

She had just finished with the gift when the Joneses arrived shortly after eleven.

"Miss Ivy, I'm hungry," Maya said as Ivy picked her up.

"I'll bet you are. And I've got some pancakes all ready for you."

"How'd you know I like pancakes?"

"Oh, just a hunch." Ivy and Ray shared amused glances as he and Yolanda came inside.

"Sorry about that," he said. "We haven't yet covered the importance of being tactful."

"That's all right. She's perfect." She gently lowered Maya into a dining chair upon which she'd placed two telephone books for added height. Ray made sure Maya was evenly balanced, then presented Ivy with a paper-wrapped bouquet of spring flowers.

"Oh, thank you."

"You're welcome." He shocked her by leaning and kissing her square on the mouth.

Ivy quickly turned her attention to Yolanda, curious to see the teenager's reaction to Ray's display of affection. But Yolanda merely smiled. "Miss Ivy, can I help you with anything?"

Ivy put Yolanda to work breaking eggs into a bowl and mixing them with a wire whisk while she placed her flowers in a water-filled vase and then heated a plate of pancakes and bacon for Maya.

Ray sat at the table eating a pink grapefruit with a serrated spoon. "I can't remember the last time I had fresh grapefruit. I usually eat cheese danish for breakfast."

"Well, that's healthy," Ivy said, the twinkle in her eye saying she really didn't mean it.

"The eggs are ready, Miss Ivy," Yolanda said.

"All right. Just have a seat, or get some pancakes and meat if you'd like. I'll cook the eggs to coincide with the biscuits coming out." Ivy took Maya's plate out of the microwave, brought it to the table, and began cutting the pancakes.

Ray hastily wiped his hands on a napkin. "Ivy, let me do that."

"I'm fine. Keep eating." She finished cutting and poured a small amount of syrup over the pancakes and then handed Maya a spoon. "Enjoy them."

"Thanks, Miss Ivy."

Within minutes Ivy had cooked the eggs, and all four of them sat around the table, the only sound the clanging of stainless steel utensils against stoneware and an occasional, "Mmm," or "This is good."

"I guess we were all really hungry," Ray said as he pushed his chair back. He got up and brought his and Maya's plates to the kitchen.

"Just put them in the dishwasher, Ray," Ivy said.

"I wish we had a dishwasher," Yolanda said.

"We do. You," Ray answered, laughing at his little joke. He wandered to the foyer and picked up the beautifully wrapped package from the console table. "Oh, Ivy, you shouldn't have."

She laughed. "Don't worry, I didn't. As I'm sure you can tell from the wrapping paper, it's for a baby shower I'm going to this afternoon."

"Hey, where's your brother? Still sleeping?"

"No, he stayed at my parents' place last night. They're leaving for North Carolina tomorrow. My whole family will be here this afternoon. My sister and brother-in-law are bringing Otto back, and their kids and my parents are coming along for the ride. This way I'll get to see my parents before they leave."

"You've got a full afternoon. What time is the baby shower?"

"Four o'clock, up in Westchester."

Ray checked his watch. It's almost noon already, Ivy. What time is your family coming?"

"My sister said it would be about one or one-thirty. They went to brunch first."

"You won't have much time for a visit."

She shrugged. "Time enough. I don't have to leave for the shower until three or so."

Ivy and Yolanda joined Ray and Maya in the living room when they finished in the kitchen. Maya had been sitting close to Ray on the sofa, but when Yolanda sat on the love seat the toddler jumped down and went to snuggle with her big sister.

"I guess nobody wants to sit with dear old dad," Ray said with mock hurt.

"It's not that, Daddy," Yolanda said soothingly. "It's just that Maya loves me, too."

"I'll sit with you Ray," Ivy said. She sat at what she felt was a respectable distance, but Ray pulled her so close to him she was practically sitting on his lap and she had no other choice but to place her right hand on his thigh. She turned her face so he could see it but the girls couldn't and mouthed the word "no" as she gestured their way by cocking her head. He ignored her and pressed her head against his chest.

The angle made it impossible for her to see the girls' reactions, so she merely gave in to the urge to enjoy his nearness. She was so close to him she could feel the vibration of his beating heart.

They watched part of an old Eddie Murphy movie, and then Ray said, "It's past twelve-thirty, girls. We need to get ready to go."

"Aw, we just got here, Daddy," Yolanda protested.

"We were invited for brunch, not to hang around all day. Miss Ivy's got company coming."

"All right. I'm just going to use the bathroom before we go."

"Me, too!" Maya echoed.

Ivy sat up as the girls disappeared into the hall. "Do you think we should be so demonstrative in front of the girls?" A quick kiss was one thing, but sitting this close was something else.

"Why not? You're special to me, Ivy. I don't think that's something that has to be hidden."

"They might not like the idea, especially with their memories—"

"Maya has no memories of Dolores. And Yolanda has loved having you to talk to. That doesn't mean she doesn't miss her mother or respect her memory. If anything, she's probably happy to see you and I are getting to know each other."

"Have you thought of talking to her about it?"

His voice was unnaturally hard. "No. I don't need my sixteen-year-old daughter's permission or approval to date anyone." He glanced toward the hall. "Come on, the girls'll be back in a minute. I've been wanting to do this ever since Friday night." His face moved in close to hers, but Ivy's uneasiness at knowing Yolanda and Maya could walk in on them any minute kept her from enjoying the kiss the way she normally would have.

The sound of a key turning in the lock made both of them freeze. "It can't be," Ivy said. "Stephanie said they wouldn't be here before one at the earliest, and it's not even twenty of."

"Could it be one of your employees? Don't they all have keys?"

"Only to the bottom lock. Besides, no one would come in on a Sunday. It has to be Otto." As Ivy walked toward the door it occurred to her that maybe the timing wasn't so bad after all. It couldn't hurt for her parents and Stephanie to see Ray and the girls here instead of her being alone, as they undoubtedly expected to find her.

She heard Otto fumbling with the locks; he was still unaccustomed to the New York necessity of multiple locks on doors. Finally he flung the door open and her parents stepped inside, followed by the rest of the group.

Ivy greeted them all with hugs and kisses, even Stephanie. "Everyone, this is Ray Jones," she said with a wave in his direction. She watched proudly as he shook hands with her father and nodded with a slight bow to her mother. Yolanda and Maya returned and stood close to Ray, who presented them as he introduced himself to Stephanie and Jerome.

Stephanie soon determined that Yolanda was only one year older than her eldest daughter, Cheri. All five children soon headed to the exercise room.

"But we're leaving in a few minutes," Ray called to his daughters.

Ivy was glad he decided to stay a little longer. She led the adults to the living room. "Your place looks wonderful, Ivy," her mother said. "I can't remember the last time I was here."

"I think it was last Mother's Day, so it's been about a year." Ivy tried to sound casual, but her smile felt forced.

"Well, Otto tells us he's very comfortable here. He's looking forward to beginning work this week, aren't you, Otto?"

"Sure, Mom."

Ray spoke up. "Mrs. Smith, I detect an accent I can't quite identify. May I ask where you're from?"

"We're from South America. Guyana."

He looked thoughtful. "I've heard of Guyana, but I can't remember what."

Everyone but Ivy spoke simultaneously. "Jonestown."

Ivy's heart went out to Ray. He looked so embarrassed to have been reminded of the tragic deaths of hundreds of members of the People's Temple who had been ordered to drink cyanide-spiked Kool-Aid some twenty-five years ago. Her family's tone suggested they resented the notoriety the mass murder/suicide had brought to their homeland. "But we had been in New Jersey for several years by then," she said.

"Remember how the kids at school teased us and said we talked funny?" Stephanie said.

"And I remember Daddy telling us to say, 'I speak English. *You* speak American,' " Ivy replied.

"You girls still remember that?" their father said, sounding pleased.

Ivy relaxed. The awkward moment passed, and as they continued to talk she was relieved that the conversation stayed on general topics.

Ray called for the girls at a little past one. "Time to go." He wished her parents a happy retirement, told Stephanie and Jerome he enjoyed meeting them, and told Otto he'd probably see him next weekend. Yolanda and Maya kissed Ivy good-bye and uttered shy good-byes to the others.

Ivy felt everyone's eyes on her back as she walked them to the door and Ray kissed her good-bye after the girls headed for the elevator.

"Your young man seems very nice, Ivy," her mother said. "And so handsome."

"You didn't mention he had kids," Stephanie said, almost accusingly.

Ivy didn't bother to point out that she hadn't told them about Ray at all. *But leave it to her to try to make me look like I'm hiding something.*

"Obviously you get along well with them, and that's what's important," her father said. "I hear the traditional family is no longer the majority. And besides, having money means you can afford to do extraordinary things for your children."

Ivy frowned. *Money? What's he talking about?*

"I agree with your father, dear. His being a financial executive will solve just about any problem. He's divorced, I presume," her mother said.

Oh, no. They think he's Mitch! Now she remembered telling them about Mitch after church on Easter Sunday.

"There's an awfully big age difference between those girls. Do they have the same mother?" Stephanie asked, in a tone that suggested no decent man would have children by more than one woman.

"Can I get a word in, please?" Ivy said, exasperated. "I'm glad you like Ray, but I have to clear up a few misperceptions you have. He's not divorced, he was widowed two years ago. And he's not the VP in finance, he works at the post office."

"What is he, a postmaster or something?" Jerome asked.

She knew he didn't mean anything by it; he just wouldn't place her with a clerk. "No. He works a window

most of the time. Other times he sorts mail." She antici-
pated the silence she knew would follow.

"But I don't understand," her mother said. "On Easter you told us—"

"I was seeing a man with that position, but it wasn't
working. Ray and I are much better suited for each
other."

"How can that be?" Stephanie said. "You make so
much more money than he does."

"It hasn't been a problem so far."

Stephanie looked doubtful. "I'm glad, but it sounds
so uneven." She smiled at her husband. "But at least I
know Jerome loves me just for me."

Ivy's eyes narrowed in anger, but Jerome intervened
before she could say anything.

"That's not a nice implication, Stephanie," he
chided.

Stephanie merely shrugged, a hint of a smile on her
lips.

"How did you two meet?" Ivy's father asked, jumping
into the breach.

"Funny. We were talking just the other day, and it
turns out we have the same broker, but we met when
he waited on me at the post office."

"I'm surprised he's even got a broker, with him working at the post office," Otto said. "They pay that well?"

"I don't know anything about how much the post
office pays, but Ray received a very large settlement from
his wife's accidental death, and he's got it all invested."
She turned a cold stare on her sister. "But if it makes
you feel better to tell yourself he's only interested in
me for my money, Stephanie, go right ahead."

Stephanie held firm. "You don't know if he has
money or not. He could just be telling you that to get
next to you."

Ivy merely smiled. "You really are insecure, aren't you?"

"And you really wish you had a strong marriage and great kids like I do, don't you?"

"Stephanie, that's enough," Jerome said.

"You two need to cut it out," Otto said easily.

"Well, I hope you and your young man are able to work it out, Ivy, but I've got to tell you that I wouldn't like it if your mother made more money than I did," her father said. "I wouldn't like it at all. I'd feel like less of a man."

"That's a little archaic in this day and age, Daddy. Fortunately, Ray doesn't feel the same way you do."

"I'm glad to hear that, Ivy," her mother said. "I can't remember the last time I saw you look so happy."

Ivy smiled so brilliantly it blocked out Stephanie's scowl.

Chapter 17
Sweet Success,
Sour Grapes

Ivy half-laughed, half-screamed as another bumper car struck her on the right side. She steered away and was promptly struck again by another car. By now she was laughing so hard she could barely steer.

An evening at Coney Island was just what she needed after another busy but satisfying week. Her parents arrived at their North Carolina apartment safely and had begun house hunting. Stephanie and Jerome had taken over the role as landlords for the people who were renting the Smith house, and Otto had been a waiter at a corporate function on Tuesday plus two weddings, one on Thursday and one on Friday, performing well at each one.

She'd also had a chance to catch up with old friends and make new ones at Glenda's shower. Pregnancy hadn't come easy for Glenda, who was married to Pete Arnold, a chemist at the same manufacturer where Glenda worked as a payroll supervisor, or at least would be working for another few weeks before beginning a new phase of her life as a stay-at-home mother.

The shower was given by Glenda's best friend Vivian, whose own marriage to Zack Warner took place just three weeks before the Arnolds' ceremony. Vivian and Zack had a toddler son, and Vivian was now four months pregnant with her second child. She and Glenda, who knew she was having a boy, joked that if Vivian had a girl this time the pair would probably grow up and get married.

Ivy often felt ill at ease at these type of gatherings, where so many of the women talked about their own experiences with pregnancy and birth and displayed photos of their children, but not this time. This shower had a special gaiety about it because everyone was genuinely thrilled that Glenda was finally having the baby she longed for at age thirty-nine. Ivy also enjoyed meeting Hatch Audsley, whose husband Skye was a good friend of Zack Warner's. Ivy had seen Skye Audsley, a TV journalist, many times on television.

Hatch shared with Ivy how she and Skye had met, and Ivy found the story fascinating. Just a few years before Hatch had been stuck in a dismal, small Midwestern town due to family obligations. She met Skye when he came to do a TV report on the primitive conditions in her hometown. Now she was not only married to him and the mother of toddler twins, but she had the college degree and career she always dreamed of, and she continued to be the guardian of her two much-younger sisters.

Ivy wondered if she and Ray would be able to overcome the odds and triumph over tradition. It was a romantic idea, but their situation was different from that of the Audsleys. It was always different when the man was the one with the income and the woman was poor. Still, Hatch's real-life fairy tale appealed to the romantic in her.

Ivy had welcomed Ray's suggestion for an evening at Coney Island. This was Memorial Day weekend, and most people who could afford to left the city. Mitch and Bethany were at the beach in Delaware ("Separate rooms," Bethany had stressed), but Ivy hadn't thought about making plans until it was too late.

Technically, it wasn't too late. Many times she had left for a weekend on Sunday and returned on Tuesday, avoiding the heavy traffic on Monday evening. As she held on to the chain straps of the Swing ride, she thought about checking availability at bed and breakfasts in her home turf of Ocean County, New Jersey, but approaching Ray with the suggestion had to be handled delicately. Two rooms at an oceanfront inn— Ray would have to sleep separately—wouldn't come cheap, and she didn't want to tread on Ray's pride if he couldn't afford it. He might even be sensitive about her offering to pay for her own room if Yolanda and Maya stayed in it with her. They'd been officially dating for only one week. Had the time come already for their fledgling relationship to be tested?

It was after ten when they emerged from the subway on Thirty-fourth Street. Ray asked Ivy to come home with them so he could take Yolanda's friend home and get Maya in bed before returning her to her loft.

Ivy went to the Jones apartment with Yolanda and Maya while Ray escorted Yolanda's friend to her family's apartment on the next block.

"Maya, Daddy said to go right to bed. You'll have your bath tomorrow," Yolanda said once they were inside. The toddler, who had nodded off on the train and had to be carried home, promptly headed toward her room.

Yolanda turned on a light in the living room. "Make

yourself comfy, Miss Ivy. I'll be right back. I want to turn on the night light for Maya and make sure she goes to the bathroom. She did drink two Sprites."

"Okay." Ivy sank into the comfortable plaid sofa. The cozy furnishings and pine accent tables in Ray's living room were reminiscent of a country inn. If his late wife picked them out she had had excellent taste, taste similar to her own, for the navy and maroon color scheme matched that of her own living room.

Ivy yawned. Her throat felt sore from all the screaming she'd done on the Cyclone, and her back and shoulders were starting to ache. Maybe she should have skipped that repeat go-round on the bumper cars. She'd use this time alone to rest her eyes for a few minutes.

Ray was surprised to see only the hall light on when he opened his apartment door. Maya was probably in bed, but what about Yolanda and Ivy?

Yolanda, wearing a Pooh bear sleep shirt, emerged from her bedroom, a finger to her lips. She spoke in a whisper. "Daddy, I put Maya to bed, but when I came back out Miss Ivy had fallen asleep on the couch. I turned off the lights for her."

Now that his eyes had adjusted he could glimpse a reclining form on one end of the couch. "It's all right," he said to Yolanda. "Why don't you go on to bed. I'll take care of Ivy."

"Okay. Good night, Daddy."

"See you in the morning." He walked toward the couch. Ivy lay with her head leaning back and to the left, her face upturned, like she was waiting to be kissed.

He stood in the dark for a few moments, simply enjoying looking at her, until the impulse became too strong to ignore. He leaned in quickly and planted a light kiss on her lips.

She awoke immediately with a startled jump. He placed a reassuring arm on her shoulder. "It's me, honey. Don't be frightened."

"You just startled me, that's all. I'm okay. Just a little tired."

"Why don't you stay here tonight?"

She shook her head. "Oh, no, I couldn't."

"I don't mean it the way it sounded. You can sleep in my room. I'll stay out here. I sleep on the couch half the time anyway."

She hedged, and he could tell she was weakening.

"I don't know . . ."

"Ivy, you know you don't feel like walking to the corner and flagging down a cab, not after you've already fallen asleep."

"Well, you're right about that."

"Come on." He took her hands and pulled her up.

She followed him down the hall, past the girls' room and around the corner from the bathroom. He flipped the light switch. "It's clean and comfortable, as they say at Motel Six. I've even got something for you to sleep in." He opened one of the closets and pulled out a pinstriped shirt with the eagle insignia of the U.S. Post Office on the sleeve.

"Do you think Uncle Sam would approve of my sleeping in your work shirt?"

"It's none of Uncle Sam's business. Okay, let's see. There are clean towels in the bathroom. Is there anything else you need?"

"No, I'm all set." She frowned as she rubbed the back of her neck.

"Something wrong?"

"Just a little sore, probably from the bumper cars. I think I might feel like I've been in a car accident when I wake up tomorrow."

"Sorry to hear that, but I'm afraid I can't help you.

If I rub your back I'll probably forget my daughters are sleeping in the next room and get carried away.''

With that he left, and now she knew why he hadn't kissed her in this most intimate of settings.

She awoke after a deep sleep, her forehead wrinkling in confusion when she realized she wasn't in her own bed.

Her memory kicked in as she abruptly sat up and focused on the shirt she wore. She was in Ray's bedroom, in his bed; and he was on the couch, just on the other side of the opposite wall.

So near, yet so far away. She stroked the shiny black oval headboard and sank back down. Which of the four pillows did he use?

She couldn't detect his scent on the linens and decided he had just changed them. That led to a startling thought—he'd be inhaling *her* scent that night.

''Okay, let me get this straight,'' Ivy said, counting off on her fingers. ''Your boss's name is Ruben Inocencio, and his wife is Cathy.''

''No, Cathy is married to Rodney Townsend. Elba is Ruben's wife,'' Ray said. ''I can't speak for anyone else who'll be there. But don't worry about mixing up their names. I'm in civil service, not private industry. Nobody can fire me or deny me a promotion because my date called them by the wrong name.''

When they arrived at the Brooklyn home of the postmaster and his family, Ivy was surprised to see how young a man he was, about Ray's age. No wonder they were buddies as well as colleagues.

The girls joined other youngsters in their respective age groups, and Cathy Townsend approached Ivy. ''I'm so glad I had a chance to meet you, Ivy. Ray told us he was seeing someone, and I admit I was curious. As far as I know he hasn't dated anyone since Dolores died."

"And you wanted to see who got him back in the social whirl," Ivy said with a friendly smile.

"Eligible men in our age group are hard to come by. All my single girlfriends were dying to get close to him."

Ivy wasn't sure how to respond to that, so she changed the subject. "This is a nice area, isn't it? I'll bet the house is lovely inside."

Cathy's eyes took in the spacious backyard and the two-story brick house. For a quick moment something in her expression reminded Ivy of Stephanie. "Hmph," she said. "If I was a graphic artist and my husband managed a post office I'd have a nice house in a nice area, too, not a four-room apartment with graffiti in the hallways and a security guard posted in the lobby."

Her vehemence caught Ivy off guard, and she felt it was unfounded. "Well, I suppose no one gave them anything," she said, choosing her words carefully. "Ruben had to test to advance to postmaster, didn't he? And surely a Latina like Elba has had to face as much discrimination as any other minority."

"I suppose. I really don't begrudge them anything, even though I know it sounds like I do. It's just that summer is the most unpleasant time of year in New York. Of course it isn't even summer yet, but soon it'll be so hot and sticky that steam will be rising from the sidewalks. Other people go to the Vineyard, the Hamptons, to Dutchess County or even the Jersey shore on the weekends, and we take the D train to the beach at Coney Island." She sighed. "But I suppose you don't have to worry about that. Ray tells us you're very successful."

Ivy felt her cheekbones go rigid. "Somehow I can't imagine Ray saying that about me." He was too classy to brag about her standing, and too secure to use her success to make himself important.

"You're right. He didn't say that in so many words, but he said you own your own company."

"Yes, I do." Ivy looked away a moment, hoping to see Ray so she could flag him down. She felt uncomfortable being a "have" when Cathy was clearly unhappy about being a "have not," but her days of diminishing the lifestyle her accomplishments afforded her were over. She either had to get someone else to join them or get away altogether.

Finally, Ray came to her side, along with Rodney.

"I can't believe it; a Memorial Day without rain," Rodney said, putting an arm around Cathy's shoulder. "You guys do anything special this weekend besides come out here?"

"We've been pretty busy. We went to Coney Island Saturday with the kids," Ray said. "Last night Ivy and I went to dinner."

"Ray took me to a Spanish restaurant on Ninth Avenue. Best paella I've ever had," Ivy added. "But I'm so happy to have a weekend off I wouldn't have cared if it rained."

"You're the boss lady and you have to work weekends?" Rodney asked.

"All my event managers personally supervise the functions they create. We make up for it by working half days or even taking days off during the week, depending on how busy we are."

"Kind of like you and I taking off a weekday when we work Saturdays," Ray said easily.

Rodney studied Ivy openly, making her conscious of her mother-of-pearl jewelry, her expensive silk knit sweater, and matching plaid Capri pants. "I'm surprised you're even in the city on a holiday weekend. Don't you have a summer house or something, Ivy?" he asked.

"As a matter of fact, I have a cottage in St. Croix, but that's usually rented to vacationers."

"Nice." He poked Cathy in her side. "I guess if these two hook up we'll never be able to keep up with the Joneses, huh?"

"Charming couple," Ivy remarked dryly after the Townsends went to get hamburgers from the grill.

"I'm sorry, Ivy. Rodney can be kind of blunt."

"His wife isn't much better. She has a real complex about finance. And I thought my sister was bad."

"You mean she wants to be rich."

"Well, if she were to be granted one wish, I don't think it would be for health or happiness. What does she do, anyway?"

"She's a nurse's aide. Both of them have always been kind of sensitive about money. Our income was a little higher than theirs because Dolores was a paralegal. They both were amazed that I didn't take my settlement and buy a beach house in East Hampton."

She looked askance at him. "You got *that* much?"

"No. That's precisely my point."

She laughed and reached for his hand. "Let's get some of those burgers before they're all gone."

Chapter 18
Tighten Up on Your Backstroke

"You feeling all right, Ray? You usually eat more of your mother's spaghetti than that."

"I'm fine, Pop."

"Daddy's been working out," Yolanda volunteered.

Ray tried to sound casual. "No point paying for a family membership at the Y if Maya's the only one who uses it."

His mother stared at him knowingly. "Whasamatter, Ray, you worried she'll think you're too fat?"

"Who?" Yolanda asked.

"Your dad's new girlfriend. Ivy."

"Gee, Grandma, you make it sound like her first name's Poison. I think it's tight that Daddy and Miss Ivy go out together. Are we going to the beach, Daddy?"

"No, Yolanda." He knew he sounded a bit abrupt, but he couldn't help it. He didn't like the way this conversation was going. His mother had correctly guessed his motives, and from that self-satisfied smile on her face he could tell she knew it. He had let himself get a bit flabby, and he didn't want Ivy to be turned off by his love handles. He knew he'd never again look the way he did in his prime, but forty-two was too young to let himself go. Already he'd seen some positive results.

He was scanning the weekend section of the Sunday paper after dinner when a name popped out at him. Ivy would love it if he took her there. He'd invite her when he got back to his own apartment.

He lowered the paper. Better yet, he'd surprise her.

"You're going to see Diana Krall at the Regency? I'm so jealous, Bethany."

"Well, you can't have Mitch back."

"It's not that. I'm just feeling a little underprivileged. Ray and I always have a good time together, but we haven't been anywhere special. A movie here, a dinner there, but to tell you the truth, I can't help thinking that I haven't been anywhere really, well, *extraordinary* since I broke it off with Mitch. He might be a little pinched since his divorce, but he knows how to show a girl a good time." When Bethany opened her mouth to say something, Ivy held up a hand palm out. "I know, I can't have him back. But I don't want him back, Bethany. I'm crazy about Ray. It's just that I'd like to go somewhere a little fancier once in a while, like to the show at the Regency. I wonder how he'd take it if I offered to pay for a night on the town."

"Why not just tell him you'd like to see Diana Krall? He has to be getting enough income on his investments to be able to afford a first-class night out once in a while."

"Maybe next time she's in town. Ray's already said he's taking me somewhere special Saturday night as a surprise."

"Maybe he's taking you to see the show."

"No, he's not. He doesn't even know I like Diana Krall. My guess is a Broadway show, not that there's anything wrong with that. You can tell me all about Diana on Sunday."

Ivy gasped when she saw Ray waiting by the cab, wearing a pale yellow blazer, matching shirt, brown cuffed slacks, and paisley tie. "You look fabulous."

"So do you."

She beamed. The red-and-white polka dot dress with pleated skirt wasn't new, but it remained one of her favorites. She'd had her fingernails and toenails painted red as well. She still didn't know where they were going, but her excitement was increasing with each passing minute. She needed a distraction after having had words with Otto earlier, but she refused to let her brother's bad behavior ruin the surprise Ray had planned for her.

Ivy linked her arm in his as they sat in the taxi. "So when are you going to fill me in on the surprise?"

"When we reach our destination."

She made a playful growling sound and squeezed his arm, knowing he meant what he said.

They rode uptown, and when the cab continued north past the theater district Ivy conceded she was wrong in thinking they were going to a show. She was speechless when the cab pulled over in front of the elegant Regency Hotel on Park Avenue. "Ray! We're going to Feinstein's? Diana Krall?"

"I heard you telling Elba she's one of your favorites." He climbed out of the vehicle and helped her out.

Ivy resisted the urge to throw her arms around him and kiss him right there on the street.

* * *

"I enjoyed that so much," Ivy said when they were riding back downtown.

"I'm glad. I thought she was pretty good myself. It was nice seeing Mitch again, and to finally meet Bethany. I've heard so much about her."

"I'll never forget the look on her face when we stopped by their table. She told me she and Mitch were going, and I was envious."

"Why didn't you just tell me you wanted to go?"

Her mind raced. She knew she had to choose her words carefully.

"Well . . . Feinstein's is one of the more costly night-clubs around. The cover charge and minimums have to be a hundred dollars a head or more. You have to admit it's awkward, Ray."

"But if it was Mitch you were dating you wouldn't have hesitated to ask him."

"Ray . . . you're not being fair, bringing up situations that don't exist. I'm not dating Mitch, I'm dating you. So don't be upset with me."

"I'm not upset, Ivy."

She couldn't see his face well enough in the shadows to know whether he was telling the truth. The taxi stopped in front of her building, and after he helped her out she impulsively took his arm. "It's still early. Why don't you let the cab go and come up for a bit, or did you not want to leave the girls too late?"

"They're spending the night with my parents, but what about Otto? Do you think he might be enter-taining?"

"No. Otto's going to be leaving. I told him today. He didn't show for a booking last night."

"Why not?"

"I don't know. Maybe there was a full moon. He's always done pretty much what he wanted to do without much regard for rules. That's why he's as old as he is and doesn't own the proverbial pot. I'm surprised he's lasted this long, and I was willing to give him a chance as long as he stayed with the program, but now he's out."

Ray handed the taxi driver a few bills and opened the building door for her. "How'd he take it?" he asked as they stepped into the waiting elevator.

"He stormed out in a huff, probably to his girlfriend's. Monday I'm changing the locks."

"Do you think his girlfriend will let him stay with her?"

"If not, he can bunk with Stephanie and Jerome, or go to Asheville for all I care. It's not my problem anymore, Ray. I gave him a chance, and he blew it, just like he always does."

He moved behind her and massaged her shoulders. "All right. I can see this episode has you upset. I didn't mean to get you thinking about it again."

"I'm all right."

"Bethany and Mitch looked like they're getting along pretty well," he remarked as they entered the loft and sat in the living room.

"She says she's happy. I hope it works out for them. Bethany's all but given up on ever finding her dream man. She says there's not a man alive who won't feel intimidated by her money."

"She's got bucks, huh?"

"Millions. She can probably buy and sell Mitch a couple of times. But I don't think it bothers him." She paused, realizing she had opened the door to ask the question that couldn't be ignored, not if their friendship was to continue to grow and ignite into the flame of love she already knew she had for him. "Does my money bother you, Ray?"

He'd been sitting next to her, but now he rose and walked a few steps, his back to her, his hands stuffed in his pockets. "Money is an awkward topic. I don't know why I'm so uncomfortable talking about it."

"Most people are, because it's so personal, but I think we need to talk about it. You don't want to delude yourself into pretending it's not an issue."

Finally he turned and faced her. "All I know is that I'm an ordinary guy who works out at the Y and rides the subway. I'm not particularly ambitious, Ivy. When I decided a military career wasn't what I wanted I was grateful to get hired with the post office. I was studying to take the test for an assistant manager when Dolores died, and after that I never got back to it. I've got a respectable bank balance that's grown nicely and gives me a pretty good additional income, but I still can't decide what to do with it.

"But when I look at you I don't see your money, I don't see this loft, I don't see your car. I see a woman of grace and dignity and kindness. I see someone I have fun with, someone my children adore, someone who's on my mind all the time. When I'm with you I'm happy, and when we part right away I start thinking how long I'll have to wait before I can see you again." He held his right hand out to her, and she took it and stood up so that they were face to face.

"You know," Ray said, "my father has always said it's not the man who chooses the woman, it's the woman who chooses the man."

"Tell me something, Ray."

"Anything."

She knew he meant it; there wasn't a thing she couldn't ask him right now that he wouldn't answer. It made her heart swell with happiness. "Are you feeling . . . sleepy?"

She felt him increase the pressure on her hand.

"Not particularly . . . but I'd like very much to go to bed."

She broke into a smile. "You've been chosen, Ray." She took his hands and began to step backward, toward the hall and her bedroom.

Ivy lay on her side and gazed lovingly at Ray. She had never felt such contentment in her life. She was so happy she couldn't sleep.

Ray didn't seem to have a problem in that area, she thought with amusement as she listened to his even breathing. A few more decibels and it could be described as snoring, but he deserved to rest, poor man. They'd had quite a session—incredibly, three of them.

She yawned. It was almost three A.M., about time for her to be getting sleepy. Ray would have to wake her up or she'd sleep the morning away.

He rolled over toward her with a groan, his arm reaching out to pull her close to him. Ivy, lying facing him, slipped her arm through his and rested her hand on his hip, listening as his breathing returned to normal. Surely there could be no better way to sleep.

She had almost drifted off when she heard him speak, so softly she had to strain to hear. Only the tightening of his arm around her convinced her she had heard correctly.

"I love you, Ivy."

She awakened to an empty bed. Only the messiness of the sheets convinced her she hadn't dreamed last night—she never got them this rumpled sleeping alone. She threw on a cotton kimono and plodded out front.

Ray was in the kitchen. "Good morning. I hope you don't mind my helping myself to one of your muffins."

"No, of course not."

"I wish I could stay longer, but I'm going to have to

leave in a few. I'd like to get home before Yolanda and Maya do."

"I understand."

He smiled at her. "You look beautiful in the morning."

She stroked her hair. She'd been so anxious to find Ray she hadn't bothered to see how she looked, but thanks to a satin pillowcase her style seemed to have held reasonably well. "Thank you." She entered the kitchen. "That smells good. I think I'll have one myself." She kissed him before reaching in the refrigerator. "Oh, good, you left me a blueberry."

"Banana is more to my liking."

"I thought you like cheese danish."

"I do, but I can't eat like that every day anymore. What are you doing later?"

"I'm hosting a get-together of my women's group."

"Oh, yes. What do you call yourselves, Bethany and the Billionaires?"

She laughed. "No. We really don't have a name. One of the girls is turning forty, so we're having a little celebration for her."

"Hen party, huh? What do you guys do, sit and dish about men?"

"You men think there's nothing else we women talk about. We talk about our work, or good deals we've found, good books we've read, movies we've seen, things like that. What are your plans?"

"I'm going to do some laundry, and then watch the game. Rodney's supposed to come over."

She made a face. "Mr. Tact. It's just as well I won't be able to join you, especially if he brings his wife with him."

"I'll miss you. So will Maya. Yolanda's working today."

Ivy had heated the muffin for a few seconds in the microwave and was reaching for it when Ray embraced her from behind. He squeezed her middle and buried his face in her shoulder. "You'll be in my thoughts, that's for sure."

She jerked her shoulder. "Ooh, your beard tickles."

He released her, and she began buttering her muffin. Her body stiffened at the sound of the door being unlocked. Just as quickly she became aware of her attire, as well as Ray's. He was shirtless and barefoot, and while his slacks were zipped, the button on top was undone. She hated the idea of Otto knowing she and Ray were sleeping together. Their relationship wasn't clandestine, but it was personal, something she carried close to her heart and wanted to keep to herself. But she couldn't do anything about that now, for here Otto was.

"I was expecting to see my bags packed and outside the door," he said to her, skipping civilities.

"I see no reason why I should pack for you, Otto."

"Yeah, well, I just came to pick up my clothes. I'll be out of here in half an hour." He took in Ray's bare chest with a knowing glance. "Mornin'," he greeted. With a smug smile Ivy's way, he added, "Now I see why big sis wants me out. I'm cramping her style."

"I'm sure your sister's reasons for asking you to leave had nothing to do with me, Otto," Ray replied calmly, popping the last of the banana muffin into his mouth.

"Sure, Ray, and Star Jones really buys her shoes at Payless. A word to the wise, brother. You'd better make sure you stay on her good side. She controls the purse strings. Cross her, and she'll cut you off in a heartbeat."

"Don't you have things to do?" Ivy said sharply.

Otto ambled toward the guest room without further comment.

"He's a real pain in the—" Ivy broke off when she saw the stricken look on Ray's face. He was frowning, with one eyebrow raised in what ordinarily would have been a comical imitation of The Rock, but this was no joke. Could he actually believe there was any truth in Otto's words? "Ray, he said that on purpose, hoping to create friction between you and me."

"Yes, I'm sure he did."

You don't look sure. He was no longer frowning, but he didn't quite look like himself, either. Tension surrounded him like ants around picnic scraps.

Ray gulped down the rest of his orange juice and rubbed his palms together. "It's almost nine-thirty. I'd better get dressed, or else the kids will beat me home."

"Don't worry about the dishes; I'll take care of them."

"All right. Excuse me a minute."

She watched unhappily as he walked down the hall. She sensed an urgency in his movement, like he couldn't wait to get away from her. Her appetite had dissolved like an Alka Seltzer in water, replaced by an uncomfortable contracted sensation in her belly. She covered her buttered muffin with plastic cling wrap and put it in the refrigerator. Right now orange juice was about all she could stomach.

Chapter 19
Keeping Up with the Smiths

Ivy tried to smile, but it felt forced and unnatural. Bethany was finally finished telling the group about Mitch, and now Ray was the topic.

"I told her she was crazy to give up on a great guy like Mitch for somebody who sells stamps at the post office, but I admit I was wrong," Bethany was saying. "Mitch looks like one of those buff models you'd see on a cover of *GC*, but Ray's awfully good-looking, too. He reminds me of Clark Johnson from *Homicide*, except his hair is black. And he's got money, too."

"Bethany!" Ivy didn't feel the rest of her friends needed to know Ray's business.

"It's all right, Ivy. I'm not going to tell them how much."

"You don't *know* how much." Even she didn't know that.

"Yes, that's right. Anyway, his wife was in a terrible accident, and he sued."

The other women were full of questions about Ray.

"Do you have a picture of him?" someone asked.

Ivy hesitated for just a moment. "As a matter of fact, I do." She excused herself and went to her bedroom for the photo they posed for the night of the reunion. She'd gazed at it many a night since.

The photo drew oohs, aahs, and whoops of delight. The girls were especially boisterous this afternoon. Nina Inniss, the milestone birthday girl, had been presented with all kinds of joke gifts, none of which would be of much use to her, including a magnifying glass, support hose, and, most notably, a jar of Porcelana.

Janice Renfrow, still coping with her husband's walking out on her at the start of her legal career, clutched the photo to her chest. "I'm bringing this home with me so I can sleep with him under my pillow."

"Oh, no you don't," Ivy said, holding out a hand. "Hand it over."

"Does he have any friends, Ivy?" Nina asked.

"What do you care? You're married, remember?"

Nina shrieked, then spoke rapidly, like she was afraid she'd forget what she planned to say if she didn't get it out right away. "Speaking of marriage, did I tell you guys about Terry Harris?"

"No!" the others said, followed by, "Tell! Tell!"

"She left her husband and moved back to Brooklyn."

"No, she didn't!"

"It's only been a few months!"

"Ivy and I saw them at Mekka a little while back," Bethany said. "In hindsight, she didn't look particularly happy."

Ivy wandered off to the kitchen and pretended to be busy cleaning while the others discussed possible reasons for the marital breakup. She wasn't in the mood for gossip. She wasn't in the mood for entertaining, either. All she could think about was that look of pure distress on Ray's face after Otto's comment, and the way Ray rushed to leave, emerging from her bedroom fully dressed something like one minute after he went in wearing only his pants, kissing her chastely on the mouth and saying he would call her later. She barely had a chance to tell him good-bye before he disappeared into the stairwell, not even wanting to wait for the elevator.

Her windows faced the front of the building, and she watched him run across the street and then toward Seventh Avenue.

"Looking for somebody?" Otto had innocently asked when he appeared with his suitcase.

"I was just waving to Ray. It's just something we always do when he leaves." She wasn't about to give him the satisfaction of knowing he'd been successful in creating a rift between them. Besides, it wasn't really a rift. Ray really did have to get home. If she wasn't ready to share their intimacy with her brother, how could she fault Ray for not wanting his family to know about it?

She'd call him as soon as the girls left.

Ray half speed-walked, half-jogged uptown. He probably shouldn't have taken time for breakfast, but making love to Ivy left his belly craving food.

He was out of breath by the time he reached his apartment. The moment he opened the door he knew he hadn't run quickly enough, for Maya came running to greet him, followed by his mother, who greeted him with a knowing, "Good morning."

"Good morning, Mom."

"I guess asking if you had a good time would be redundant," she said with a smile.

"Re-dun-dant," Maya echoed.

Yolanda emerged from her room. "Hi, Daddy!"

He was still holding Maya, and Yolanda came to him

and hugged him on his other side. "You girls are showing me a whole lot of love this morning. What's up with
that?"

"I figured you'd be real happy this morning, since
you stayed with Miss Ivy last night," Yolanda said.

"Who says I stayed at Ivy's? I could have just gone
out to get a paper, for all you know."

She pulled back a bit to look at his hands. "But you
don't have a paper, Daddy. Besides, we went in your
room when we got home. Your bed is made. You never
make it this early on a Sunday morning."

Yolanda frequently used the computer in his bedroom and knew his habits well. He silently cursed himself for leaving his bedroom door open when he left
the night before. "Yeah, yeah." He bent to place Maya
down. "Okay, honey, Daddy's home. You go finish your
cereal now before it gets soggy." The child ran off, and
to Yolanda and his mother he said, "I guess I've been
found out."

"Don't be embarrassed, Daddy. I think it's great,"
Yolanda said enthusiastically. "I wouldn't mind if we
moved into Miss Ivy's loft. Her place is so much bigger
than ours."

"I'd suggest you hold off on packing your bags, young
lady," his mother said. "A successful woman like that
isn't going to be interested in your father for long."
She turned to Ray. "You know there's only one thing
you can give her that she can't get on her own, don't
you?"

"Excuse me, both of you," he said abruptly. He went
to his bedroom and slammed the door closed.

Stretching out on his back with his clasped hands
cradling his head, he pondered the insensitive remarks
his daughter and mother just made. Did a larger apartment mean so much to Yolanda that she would push
him into Ivy's arms to get it, even if that wasn't where

he wanted to be? And how could his mother imply that he had nothing to offer Ivy but sex?

He'd been hungry for her, yes. The itch he'd had for weeks had at long last been scratched. But the first time he took her what mattered most to him was her pleasure. He'd deliberately moved slowly, kissing her over and over again as he lay atop her. From the way she repeatedly moaned from deep in her throat he knew he was successful, and when they became one he found himself doing the same.

The second time everything changed. He was less a considerate lover and more a confident man with a basic need who knew his gun was still loaded, but not for one minute did he forget it was Ivy beneath him, on top of him, and next to him. He fell asleep holding her, satiated, and most of all enjoying the incredible realization that he had grown to love her. It was enough to make him believe they could easily triumph over society's view that the man should be the so-called "breadwinner," but the comments he'd heard this morning had given him pause.

While Yolanda's and his mother's remarks were hurtful, Otto's was frightening. He was Ivy's brother and had known her all his life, and he would know better than most people if Ivy felt that her money gave her control over people.

Maybe he was moving their romance too fast. He probably needed to pull back a little and make sure he wasn't making a huge mistake.

"You and Ivy are getting pretty close these days, huh, Ray?" Rodney asked during halftime.

Ray grunted. "I don't know about all that."

"Y'all looked pretty cute driving off together in that

cute car of hers while Cathy, the kids, and I walked to the subway."

"Come on, man. You know we would have given you guys a ride, but you can only fit so many people in a PT Cruiser."

"Yeah, I know. You guys going away for the Fourth to a nice sandy beach someplace?"

"I don't think so. We leave for our cruise less than a week later."

"Ivy goin' with y'all?"

"How could she? We didn't know each other when I booked it. I'm sharing a cabin with the kids, and my parents have their own."

"Need I tell you that Cathy has started planning for us to take a cruise next year with the kids?"

"Where do you suppose she got that idea?" Ray said with a smile. As sweet and helpful as Cathy could be, she had an irksome tendency to want whatever someone else had or to want to go wherever someone else went. When he and Dolores began vacationing at the Maryland shore, Cathy got Rodney to take their family there as well. When he and Dolores bought new furniture for the living and dining rooms, the Townsends followed suit. Now that he was taking the kids on a four-day cruise to the Bahamas, it was no surprise to learn that Cathy was preparing to do the same. Rodney had only been half joking when he referred to "keeping up with the Joneses." Cathy took the saying literally.

Rodney chuckled. "Well, you know how she is. I don't think she's ever going to change." He popped a french fry in his mouth. "So did you see Ivy last night, or did she have some big society party to plan?"

"No, she was free. I took her to a cabaret act at The Regency Hotel. Diana Krall. She's one of Ivy's favorites."

"Oh yeah, I've heard of her. Blond chick, sounds a little like Carmen McRae. Probably on purpose. A nice cozy setting like that sure beats nosebleed seats at Radio City, but it must have cost a pretty penny. I'd better not mention it to Cathy, or else she'll be after me to take her to see Bobby Short at the Carlyle."

"You know, Rodney, maybe you ought to remind her why I'm able to afford the cruise and nightclub performances."

"I'm afraid to, man. She might arrange to have me crushed by a cement mixing truck." Rodney's eyes grew wide and he drew in his breath audibly. "I'm sorry, Ray. That was a real inconsiderate thing to say."

"That's all right. Dolores wasn't the first person in New York to be killed that way, and I'm afraid she won't be the last. It's a hazard of being around tall buildings." He'd come to terms with Dolores's tragic death, and while he had loved her with all his heart he was ready to move on.

He just had to tread carefully. He couldn't handle another heartbreak.

Chapter 20

Smooth Sailing into Rough Seas

Ivy squealed right in the middle of Fifth Avenue, not that anyone paid her any attention. "You're kidding, Bethany!"

"No, I'm not. I thought Mitch's kids were charming."

"Casey didn't interrogate you about your work, or anything else you might have said that piqued her curiosity?"

"She did ask about my job. Of course, she didn't recognize the term 'CEO,' but when I told her I was head honcho she seemed satisfied."

"Did she ask if you're her dad's girlfriend?"

"No, because Elgin did." Bethany paused. "Mitch told them yes."

"Bethany, how wonderful! I'm so happy for you!"

"Well, I'm not registered at Tiffany's yet. But I have to say it's refreshing to have something else to occupy my thoughts besides things like how my investments are doing, and of course work."

Ivy beamed. "I'm so pleased that I had a hand in getting you two together."

"It's funny how things work out, isn't it? I'm with Mitch because your heart told you to be with Ray. Now all we have to do is make it to the part where we all live happily ever after."

Ivy's shoulder blades tightened so abruptly it made her wince. "Yeah," she said softly.

Bethany didn't notice the change in Ivy's demeanor. "Hey, Mitch and the kids are coming with me to Long Island this weekend. I thought you and Ray and his girls might want to come, too. There's plenty of room." Bethany had a four-bedroom summer house in the Hamptons.

"I'll ask Ray, but I don't know. He and the girls are leaving for Florida a week from Wednesday. He booked them on a cruise, one of those four-day jaunts to the Bahamas where they have activities for kids divided by age groups. They'll be back on Monday. It may be too much for him to do in such a short period."

"Mitch's kids are going down to San Juan next week for the rest of the summer. The timing couldn't be better. It'll really give us a chance to spend time together and hopefully get close."

Ivy shook her head in wonder. "I'm still amazed you didn't find Casey and Elgin intolerable. Meeting them was downright traumatic for me."

"Different people react in different ways. Personally, I find it intolerable when delivery people think I'm the maid rather than the owner of my apartment, and if you want to talk traumatic, you should have seen me when I noticed I had a gray pubic hair. I don't think I'd ever put meeting two kids in either category, no matter how bad the little buggers are."

* * *

Ivy remained curled up on the couch after she and Bethany hung up, loosely hugging a square decorative pillow while thinking about Bethany's offer. Ivy had cited Ray's travel plans deliberately to set the stage for him to decline, as she feared he would. She wasn't even sure if inviting him was the right thing to do. Something had changed between them, and she knew exactly when it started. She hadn't had a moment alone with him since that fateful Sunday morning when Otto took his things and left, but not before tossing out the comment that left an indelible mark on her life.

Sure, she'd seen Ray, but not alone. Last weekend he took her and the girls to dinner. The weekend before that they all drove out to Jones Beach, piling in the Cruiser at sunrise and enjoying sun, sand, and surf with a couple of hundred thousand other New Yorkers until about one P.M., when they rolled back into the city far ahead of the returning crowds of the later afternoon.

This weekend her schedule prevented her from seeing him at all. The short summer season was in full swing, with her handling the premiere of a made-for-cable movie in a private room of a midtown nightclub on Thursday, a wedding in Glen Cove on Friday night, and a child's birthday party on Saturday.

She decided to ask Ray about Long Island after all. He and the girls would soon be leaving for their vacation, and she'd miss them more than she realized. Like Bethany said, it was refreshingly different to have something else to think about besides her work. Everyone needed balance.

Ray would probably think twice before turning down a holiday weekend in the Hamptons. Cathy Townsend hadn't lied when she said summer in New York could be unbearable. The presence of the girls would keep with the pattern Ray had established, but surely they'd get to have some time alone. She felt she shouldn't be the one to bring up the cool-down he'd initiated, but perhaps being alone together would help them recapture what they seemed to have lost.

Ivy looked up from her book to watch Ray towel himself off. "This sure beats the wall-to-wall people you see at Jones Beach," he said as he looked at the well-spaced groups of beachgoers. "Here you can actually have more than three square feet of personal space."

"What happened to Yolanda?"

"She made some new friends. They're all still in the water, down that way." He cocked his head to his right, and Ivy spotted Yolanda romping with other teenagers, male and female.

"I've made a decision," Ray said as he stretched out on his stomach on the beach towel adjacent to where she sat in a low-slung beach chair. "I'm going to start looking for a house right after New Year's."

"Why wait till then, if you've made up your mind?"

"Because I don't want to go anywhere until after Yolanda graduates next June. I'm going to leave the city, and possibly the state."

She placed her book in in her lap. *Leave the state?* "Why, Ray?"

"I want to be able to buy a place large enough to accommodate my parents, as well as one that will allow Yolanda and Maya to have their own rooms. Real estate in the metro area is too expensive. The timing will never be better. Yolanda finishes high school next June, and Maya will enter kindergarten next September. And I can always put in for a transfer."

"How do you feel about leaving the city?"

The apprehension on his face was her answer. "It'll be an adjustment, I'm sure, especially if we end up in the boonies somewhere. It's not like I've never lived anywhere else, but I've spent most of my life right there in Hell's Kitchen. I grew up on Tenth Avenue and Forty-fifth Street. But I really need to get the girls out of that apartment, and my father has to stop fixing people's leaky faucets."

"He's the super?"

He nodded. "And my mother mops the hallway floors and cleans the stairs. So much for retirement. But if they live with me they'll do just fine with their pensions."

"I think that's admirable of you, Ray."

"Thanks. I think it's my best move. Maya will grow up with a yard to play in, my parents will be comfortable. . . ."

Ivy leaned forward, eager to hear how the planned move would benefit *him*, but he never finished the thought, for Maya called to him from several yards away.

"Daddy, you said you'd help me with my castle."

"Okay, here I come." Ray got up and went to join her in filling plastic molds with sand, then carefully turning the molds upside down and lifting it off, leaving the castle shape intact.

"Hi, guys!"

Ivy turned to see Bethany and the Crewses approaching, toting towels and beach chairs. "Hi! I was starting to think you weren't coming."

"Elgin didn't clean up like Miss Bethany told him to, and because of that she made us wait an extra half hour before we could come," Casey said.

"I did too clean up," Elgin said. "*You're* the one who didn't make your bed."

"I did too."

"Did not."

"Did too."

"Did not."

"Did too."

"Hey!" Bethany said loudly. "Are you two going to stop, or will we have to go back to the house?"

The children immediately stopped, but not before Ivy noticed Elgin mouthing one final, "Did not," to his sister.

Mitch spread out a clean, faded quilt on the sand, upon which the children promptly dropped their towels, followed by their shorts and T-shirts. "Go ahead," Mitch said to them easily. "But stay close to shore. You know that swimming at the beach is more difficult than swimming in a pool because of the waves."

"I know, but Elgin doesn't," Casey said in a superior voice.

"I do too."

"You do not."

"Do too."

"Do not."

"Do too."

"Will you two go in the water already?" Bethany said wearily.

Casey and Elgin complied, still volleying back and forth. Bethany shook her head at Mitch, who had comfortably settled in a beach chair. "You know, Mitch, you're really not helping them by being so lenient. If anything, it encourages them to behave badly."

"Yeah, I know. I would have told them to stop, but I like seeing how they respond to you. It's like they're privates and you're the drill sergeant."

Bethany playfully rolled her eyes and sighed as she rubbed sunscreen on her chest.

Ivy watched the exchange with a heavy heart. She could tell Bethany was pleased with what Mitch said; she had been unable to hide the smile behind her sigh. Already Bethany and Mitch were interacting like a cou-

ple who'd long since grown comfortable with each
other, while Ivy's conversations with Ray were mostly
limited to impersonal matters when the children were
present. She was surprised he shared his future plans
with her. It was probably his way of preparing her for
his leaving her life when he moved to Delaware or Penn-
sylvania or upstate somewhere. No wonder he said he
loved her when he thought she was sleeping and
couldn't hear him. She'd never hear those words from
him again.

She forced herself to concentrate on her book, but
in the next half hour she only turned a few pages.

When Bethany and Mitch prepared to go in the water,
Bethany offered to take Maya with them, and Maya was
only too happy to get wet again.

"Even Maya said she likes this beach better than the
other beach we went to," Ray said as he returned to his
towel. "It sure was nice of you to invite us."

"That's me, Ray," she said dryly. "Nice to a fault."

The submarine sandwiches and potato chips they'd
eaten after swimming had worn off by six o'clock. Ray
offered to go for pizza, and Mitch quickly said he would
go along. Ray would have liked some time alone, but
he understood Mitch's not wanting to be seen as a dead-
beat, so he didn't object.

They took Ivy's car. "You know, it's nice out here,"
Mitch remarked, "but there's something wrong when
you have to drive two towns over to get a pizza."

The statement surprised Ray. "Haven't you been out
this way before?"

"Not this far out. One year my ex and I rented a
house out on Fire Island, in one of the family sections,
but we were partial to the Delaware shore. We thought
about buying a place there, but we never got around

to it. Just as well; we would have had to sell it in the divorce." He chuckled. "So look at us, two guys involved with women who've done better than we have. Talk about a toss-up. Should we take Bethany's car or Ivy's to pick up dinner?"

"Does it bother you, Mitch, Bethany's making more money than you do?" Ray initially disliked Mitch when they met at the reunion, out of envy for his position as much as for his making a play for Ivy, and the way Mitch's kids greeted Ivy without having to be introduced made him wonder where and under what circumstances they had met before; but he was willing to put those concerns aside to take the opportunity to hear the viewpoint of another man in the same situation. Besides, all that was well before he and Ivy began seeing each other, and Mitch had been nothing but friendly while they all shared the close confines of Bethany's property. Any fool could see he was enchanted with Bethany.

Mitch responded with a noncommittal, "Eh," and then continued. "My ex made as much as I did, and now she makes more," he continued. "But Bethany's got a fortune. She sold a huge chunk of stock in her company when it was at a record high, and the way she lives reflects it. She drives a Jaguar. She has a four-bedroom summer house right on the bay. By the end of the month the pool and tennis court will be finished. And you should see her apartment. It's on Park Avenue, you know."

"I've seen the outside of your house, Mitch. You're not exactly living in a ghetto."

"It might not be the smartest address in town, but I can't complain. I manage all right. My ex helps with the kids' tuition and with the other household expenses while I have custody. I've had to make a few changes. But in the back of my mind I know Bethany will never know the meaning of the word 'pinch.' I'm only human,

Ray. I guess it does bother me a little. I feel like I'm dating Oprah."

Ray recalled Rodney making a similar comparison about Ivy. "Well, Oprah's got a boyfriend, doesn't she? Just because a woman is wealthy doesn't mean she should be alone."

"You're saying it's not an issue for you? I've gotta tell you, Ray, I find that hard to believe. Ivy and her people are putting together parties for movie actors, pro athletes, wealthy businesspeople, and big conglomerates, meeting the movers and shakers, the so-called Beautiful People; while you work at the post office, hardly the most exciting work there is, and it doesn't bother you?"

"Her success alone doesn't bother me. I just find myself occasionally wondering if her money will ever come between us. It's already made things awkward a few times, to be perfectly honest."

"What would you do if she asked you to sign a prenup?"

"I'd sign, but I'd insist on being involved in the drafting of it. She's entitled to protect her assets, just as I'm entitled to protect mine. But I think you're jumping the gun. Nobody's thinking about getting married."

Ray skipped up the stairs leading to the deck. No point in missing the sumptuous midnight buffet; the shrimp were fabulous. Yolanda was down at the teen disco, and Maya was fast asleep after a morning of supervised activities for three to five year olds and an afternoon shore excursion to Nassau. His parents were asleep, too, in the cabin next door, but he knew Maya would be all right for the few minutes it took for him to go up on deck for a plate.

He wondered what Ivy was doing this Friday night. He'd been thinking of her ever since they parted after last weekend. They left Sag Harbor and drove back into the city early Monday afternoon, and because it was daytime he couldn't object when she dropped them off first. "I've got another busy week," she said in parting as he leaned to kiss her good-bye. "But you guys have a wonderful time on the cruise. Send me a postcard if you get a chance."

The exchange bothered him. All weekend she'd been sweet and sparkling, her usual self, but something was different, something he couldn't quite identify. Her parting remarks were almost *too* breezy, like they were casual friends and nothing had ever happened between them.

In his heart he knew he had no right to complain. He was the one who used his own children as buffers to prevent them from getting too close too fast. How could he object to her following his lead and pulling back as well? But he didn't like it. His gut instinct told him he'd been terribly wrong. He'd hurt himself by not being with her, and more important, he'd hurt Ivy. He tried to get her alone to tell her so, but she was always busy doing something: playing with Maya, swimming with Yolanda, or behind closed doors in the master suite she was sharing with Bethany. Privacy was difficult to come by when eight people were staying under one roof.

They pulled out of Nassau Harbor at three A.M. and would be at sea all day Saturday before docking at Port Canaveral Sunday morning. As with the two previous days, the children went their own ways, and Ray saw them only at mealtimes.

"This has been so much fun," Yolanda said wistfully at dinner. "I wish we were going to be on board longer."

"The trip's been lovely," Ray's mother said, "but

Yolanda, sometimes you have to appreciate what you have instead of always wanting more."

"I know, Nana. I do appreciate it. It's just that I'm having so much fun. Everybody is. Even the waiters look happy, dancing in the aisles."

Ray's father grunted. "I'd look happy too, if all the passengers I'd served were handing me big fat tips. I think the shipping line expects the passengers to pay their employees' salaries. The minute you get on board they hand you a paper recommending how much to tip."

"I can't wait to tell Miss Ivy all about it," Yolanda said. "Wouldn't it have been nice if she could have come with us?"

Ray looked at his mother expectantly, as did his father, causing her to halt raising the key lime pie to her mouth and say, "What?"

"Trudy, we've become so accustomed to you saying something negative about Ivy," his father said, "we figured you'd make a comment."

"All right, I admit it. I was concerned. I didn't know anything about her, what kind of woman she was, and what type of influence she would have on Yolanda. Her being rich made me a little nervous. You don't meet someone like her every day. I've never met anyone like her."

She didn't say she felt she'd been pushed aside in favor of a stranger, but Ray suspected that had a lot to do with her multiple criticisms of Ivy.

"I don't get it, Nana," Yolanda said. "Do you mean that you won't think it's good if I meet a rich man?"

"No, dear. It's different when the girl is poor."

"Excuse me?" Ray said.

"It's the truth, Ray," his mother said. "When a poor girl marries a rich man that's seen as fine, unless of course she's twenty-two and he's sixty. But when a poor man marries a rich girl he's seen as being after her money. I didn't make that judgment, Ray. It's society who dictates that the man should have his own. But now that I've met Ivy and from what Yolanda tells me, she's all right. I can't object to Yolanda wanting someone who's more 'with it,' as they say, than her old Nana.''

Ray shared a surprised glance with his father and elder daughter. He picked up the bottle of wine he'd ordered with dinner and refilled his mother's glass. ''Mom, I'll have to bring you on a cruise every year. You're positively mellow.''

Chapter 21
The Chosen

"Ivy Smith, please," Ray said confidently into the receiver. His assurance turned to surprise when the man who answered the call on the Jubilee line replied, "I'm sorry, Ivy's on vacation this week. She'll be back in the office Monday."

Monday? Ray hastily declined the offer to leave a message or speak with anyone else. He hung up, stunned. Ivy hadn't mentioned plans to go out of town.

That meant the rift between them was wider than he thought.

He wondered if he should tell Yolanda to forget about her party. No, he decided. Even if Ivy was through with him, he simply couldn't make himself believe she would cancel the party and disappoint Yolanda on such short notice.

Ivy let herself into her cottage. Wobbly legs carried her to the bedroom, where she deliberately fell backward on the king-size bed, her arms outstretched. Good thing she'd rode with Rita. One turn and she'd likely forget she was supposed to drive on the left.

She was enjoying a lively social life since arriving in St. Croix on Saturday. Her friends Rita and Kenneth John had a party the same night she arrived, on Monday she took the seaplane to St. Thomas, and that evening she dined with Rita at Rumrunners. Maybe she should have skipped that second frozen banana daiquiri; not only did her legs feel unsteady, her head felt uncharacteristically heavy on her neck.

She partially sat up, supporting her upper body on her elbows. She'd like nothing better than to fall asleep right there, but she had a rule to never go to bed with makeup on. She didn't even need anything other than lipstick, for the Cruzan sun had bronzed her skin nicely, but since she'd put it on she now had to take it off.

After resting briefly, Ivy worked up the energy to go get the cold cream. All this activity was too much. The next day she would just lounge around. Being on vacation shouldn't mean she had be active every day, or else she'd be worn out when she got back to New York. She hadn't even planned to make this trip, but when the airline offered a special promotional fare and she learned her cottage wasn't rented that week, she threw some shorts, shirts, and dresses into a suitcase and left the city behind. The getaway couldn't have come at a better time, right after Ray and the girls left for their cruise, leaving a bigger hole in her life than she expected it to. Better to be a little tipsy here in St. Croix than pining for Ray in New York.

Besides, she had to accept the inevitable. Ray was looking for a way to break it off with her gently. There could be no other reason for his bringing the girls along whenever they went out. He actually believed Otto's accusation. This angered her almost as much as it pained her, for she'd never done anything to make him believe Otto's claim could be true.

It was just like Bethany said. When it came to women making more money, men allowed themselves to be swayed by the doubts of their families and friends.

Ivy splashed water on her face and lathered it before rinsing. She'd had such high hopes for a future with Ray, but here she was, facing the same sadness she had every time a new bond broke. *I have to start thinking like Bethany.* Men were wonderful, but she'd better forget about finding a special one to settle down with.

If she had one wish about the brief interlude, it would be for it to have lasted longer, but she had no regrets. She loved Ray. She *chose* Ray, but that didn't make her immune from the same intimidation factor that killed her other relationships. Surely her feelings for him would fade with time.

She'd go back to her old habit of utilizing Jubilee's postage supply for her personal use so she wouldn't have to endure the discomfiture of seeing him at the post office. She found herself dreading Yolanda's upcoming birthday party, but maybe Ray would arrange to have the food delivered, and send his mother to help supervise instead of coming himself. Mrs. Jones was hardly Ivy's favorite person, but it would be so much easier for she and Ray if they let their liaison end with memories of a pleasant weekend in Sag Harbor.

She patted her face dry. Her head felt lighter now, but she still felt like she could sleep for a week. She pulled her dress over her head as she semistaggered back to her bed, carelessly tossing it on the floor. She knew she'd fall asleep right away; the sound of the ocean rushing to meet the shore always had that effect on her.

But her memories wouldn't let her rest. Closing her eyes brought a picture of Ray holding her as he slept.

With each crashing wave she heard him whispering, "I love you, Ivy."

She laid on her back, her open eyes staring at the rotating ceiling fan above her bed. Getting him out of her thoughts was going to take some time.

Ray waited until Tuesday to try to contact Ivy again. If she was due back in the office on Monday she would have arrived home over the weekend, but he reasoned she'd be busy catching up on Jubilee business after being gone all week.

Yolanda was busy cleaning the kitchen, and Maya was enjoying some prebath TV time. He dialed Ivy's home number on his bedroom extension. By now her office staff would have gone home and her living room undergone the conversion from a place of business back to a home.

"Hello," she said breathlessly.

For a moment he couldn't speak; it had been so long since he heard her voice. "Ivy, it's Ray. Are you all right? You sound out of breath."

"Hi! I just went out to pick up some dinner and heard the phone ringing as I was unlocking the door. I haven't been to the store since I've been home. I was going to call you later. How was the cruise?"

They spoke a few minutes about his vacation.

"I got out of town myself, at the last minute," Ivy said. "The airline offered a special and I had no renters, so I spent a week at my place in St. Croix."

"How was it?"

"Exhausting, but fun."

"I guess you don't feel like you've been away."

"It felt good to have a change of scenery, but I don't ever feel like I have to get away because I'm working so hard. I enjoy what I do so much it doesn't feel like work to me."

"You're lucky. Ivy, I called to discuss Yolanda. Her birthday's less than a month away. It was real nice of you to offer your place for her to have a party, but I thought you might want an out."

"Really? And why would I want an out?"

His shoulders jerked. The voice that radiated characteristic warmth just moments ago now sounded like it could freeze the Hudson River.

"I don't know what's happening with you and me, Ray, but I'm very fond of Yolanda," she continued in that same frosty tone.

Her coldness couldn't disguise that fact she was hurting. He couldn't stand it anymore. "Ivy. I want to see you. Can I come over?"

He waited as she hesitated, not prompting her for an answer even when the silence became uncomfortable. "All right," she finally said. "Come on over."

Ray passed the duty of bathing Maya over to Yolanda. He covered most of the nine blocks with brisk steps, but broke into a trot at Thirtieth Street, arriving at Ivy's building in exactly twelve minutes.

When she opened the door for him he pulled her into his arms and kissed her long and hard, pushing the door shut behind him with his back. Her muffled squeals expressed her surprise, and he noted unhappily that she wasn't kissing him back. She broke away from him, her pretty face contorted in a scowl.

"What was *that* all about, Ray?"

"It's about me missing you. It's about me knowing I made a mistake."

"I don't know what's going on, but I think we should sit down," she said.

He followed her to the seating area. The remnants of a Greek souvlaki sandwich sat on the raised coffee table, and the scent of pork and onions remained discernible. He felt guilty for barely giving her enough time to have her dinner.

"It's all right; I'm done," she said, reading his thoughts as she rolled the foil wrappings into a ball and pushed it to the far edge of the table. "Tell me what's on your mind."

She sat in a corner of the couch, and he took a seat on the opposite end. "I'm sure you've noticed we haven't been as close in the last couple of weeks as we were before that," he said.

"Why don't we skip the condiments and get to the meat, Ray. Our relationship hasn't been the same since Otto warned you to watch out for me. You obviously believed him, since we haven't had a moment alone since. Bottom line. The end."

"I don't want this to be the end, Ivy. I was wrong to let Otto and Rodney influence me."

She raised an eyebrow. "Rodney, too? Why am I not surprised? I guess Cathy did her part as well."

"Rodney made a few comments here and there. He thought he was helping, and he didn't want me to be hurt. Combine his good intentions and my apprehension and you've got the makings of a major wrong move."

"You were apprehensive about me?"

"From the beginning. It's what kept me from asking you out that first day when we had pizza; when you told me what you did I figured you wouldn't be interested in going out with a working stiff like me. But I want you in my life. I need you in my life."

Her expression didn't change, and her posture remained stiff and unyielding. "And what will happen the next time someone makes a comment that makes you doubt me, Ray?"

"I'm through with listening to what people have to say. If something concerns me I'll speak with you about it directly. No more pulling back or hiding behind my kids. I made a mistake. I admit it, and I regret it more than you know. There's no instruction sheet for our situation, Ivy, and we both know it's not exactly typical."

"I understand that, but you can't keep sending me all these mixed messages, Ray." She started speaking in a falsely bright tone, like a doll who spoke when her cord was pulled. " 'Be with me, Ivy.' 'Keep your distance, Ivy.' " In a flat voice she added, "I'm not Howdy Doody."

Ray leaned forward earnestly. "What else can I say to you, Ivy?"

She leaned all the way back, her head against the cushions, and looked up at the top of the opposite wall. "You know, I thought you were coming over to break it off. I was prepared for that."

"And now that you know that's not the case?"

She sighed before turning her head to look at him. "I don't know. I make a lot of money, Ray. I'm considered to be wealthy. I'm not going to apologize for it, not that you're asking me to. I worked my butt off to get to where I am. The way I see it, either you can cope with it or you can't. I want you in my life, too, but I can't live with the stress of never knowing when someone might put an idea in your head that'll make you turn away from me. If my achievements somehow make you feel like less of a man, it just won't work."

He slid over until he was right next to her, putting an arm around her shoulder and gently tilting her neck so her head rested against his chest. "When I see you I never forget I'm a man," he whispered.

He gently stroked her collarbone, her throat, the

curve of her jaw. When at last he felt her completely relax against him he simply held her for a few moments, quietly content to be this close to her after what seemed like years. But eventually that was no longer enough. He shifted so he could face her, cupped both sides of her lovely face and simply gazed at her with all the love in his heart unmasked for her to see. It was easy to determine the moment of recognition in Ivy's always expressive face. Her lips parted and her eyes sparkled with joy as the significance of his gesture hit her full force.

She threw her arms around his neck, holding on like he was a lifeline. Ray buried his face in the curve between her neck and shoulder. "I love you, Ivy; I do," he whispered.

"It's ten o'clock," Ray said.

"I know. You have to go," Ivy said sadly.

By now the darkness outside had darkened Ivy's apartment. Their tender embrace in the living room had given way to a lust so strong and immediate, it overpowered them both. They began pulling each other's clothes off and made love right there, stopping only long enough for Ray to apply protection. "I can't believe we did that," Ivy said afterward. "We acted like a couple of horny college kids."

"We might not be in our twenties, but we're hardly senior citizens," he said. "We've got a lot of good years yet."

They eventually moved to the comfort of the bedroom, where they watched a crime drama on cable, cuddling like they'd been together for years.

Ivy slipped into an oversized V-necked T-shirt while Ray dressed and called home to check on the girls. They walked to the door with their arms around each other, and after kissing her good-bye he told her he'd call when he got home. She leaned out into the hall and waved good-bye as he stepped into the elevator. Life was funny sometimes. Here she was thinking it was over, and it was just beginning. She stood poised on what might well be the sweetest phase she'd ever known.

"This music is giving me a headache," Ivy hissed to Ray.

"I know, but the kids love it."

"After this song is over why don't we put on something slow and dreamy, something you and I can dance to?"

"I don't think the time is right. They seem to be enjoying these fast jams."

"Maybe we can at least make it a little softer," Stephanie suggested. She and Jerome had driven up because Yolanda invited their daughter Cheri. The four adults sat in the seating area closest to the window. The teens kept away from them like they were quarantined, preferring to sit in the other seating area or gather by the dining table. The large foyer area was reserved for dancing.

"There's an idea," Ivy said. "Oops, there's the door." She craned her neck as she looked through the crowd. "Does anyone see Yolanda?"

"There she is. She's answering it," Ray said. "Hey Jerome, your daughter is getting quite a bit of attention from the fellows."

"That's all right. They all know her daddy is sitting right here," Jerome said.

"Cheri's a new face to all of them," Stephanie added.

"Is she seventeen yet?" Ray asked.

"She just turned sixteen a few weeks ago," Stephanie said. "She'll be a junior in high school this year."

"Time to start looking at colleges," Ivy remarked. "Cheri will do well. She can be anything she wants to be."

"She wants to get into broadcast journalism," Jerome said with pride.

"Yes, but I don't know about that," Stephanie said. "I want her to do well, but it might be a mistake for her to do too well. I want her to settle down one day, marry, and have kids. That won't happen if she prices herself out of the marriage market."

"That's a little old-fashioned, don't you think?" Ray said. "There are plenty of up-and-coming young black men out there these days. And even if Cheri makes it as big as Katie Couric from the *Today* show, I doubt she'll marry someone who works in a factory. But chances are she'll make more money than her husband. Very few people get sixty-million-dollar contracts. But if the man who loves her is worth his salt he'll realize it's not who makes what, but how well their family can live because of it. That's what marriage is all about, the husband and wife working as a team to make things as good as they can for their own."

Stephanie made a face. "That sounds real sweet, Ray, but I don't think most men will see it that way," she said. "I always felt that was why Bill Clinton cheated on Hillary, because she made more in private practice than he did as a public servant."

"That's ridiculous," Ivy said. "Bill cheated on Hillary because it's his nature to chase tail, not because she made more money than he did." Stephanie's statement made about as much sense as mannequins with nipples.

"Well, if men don't feel threatened by a successful woman, why haven't *you* ever gotten married, Ivy?" Stephanie asked.

Ivy put her hands on her hips and glared at her sister, but Jerome held out a hand palm out before she could respond. "All right, that's enough. Let's stop this now, before it gets out of hand," he said, adding, "I love my daughter. I want her to be the best she can be, and no one will be prouder than me if she reaches the top of her field. I don't want her to feel she has to give up on her dream because it might not sit well with some man."

"I agree," Ray said. "I think I would be doing a terrible disservice to Yolanda and Maya if I tell them that if they become too successful in their careers they might not ever find husbands. Having difficulty finding someone to share your life with isn't exclusive to women making six figures. There are plenty of secretaries and nurses out there looking."

"Stephanie, even if Cheri becomes the next Oprah, I'm confident she'll find a man secure enough in his own skin for it not to bother him," Ivy said. She felt bolstered by Ray's and Jerome's backing of her position. "Like Ray. But of course he's taken." She squeezed his hand, and he leaned over and kissed her.

The adults kept a low profile until it was time to cut the cake and sing the birthday song. Ivy inserted seventeen candles into the butter-cream frosting, and Ray lit them. When the party ended Ivy stood alongside Ray and Yolanda as they thanked the guests for coming.

The Overtons were the last to leave. Stephanie helped Ivy put away the leftover food Ray had gotten from a local deli. "I noticed you and Ray shared hosting duties," Stephanie said to Ivy as they worked. "I'm curious, how did you explain who you were?"

"Just as a friend of the family."

Jerome yawned. "Steph, you about ready?"

"Yes, I guess so."

Cheri hugged Yolanda. " 'Bye, Yogi. Thanks for inviting me. I had a good time."

"Yogi?" Ivy repeated.

"That's what my friends call me," Yolanda explained. "To family I've always been Yolanda."

"Maybe you can have another party here at Aunt Ivy's next year," Cheri said.

"Actually, I don't think I'll be here in a year," Ivy said. "My rent's going up, and I think it's time to make a change."

"Do you think you'll find anything this nice at a cheaper cost?" Jerome asked.

"That's just it. I need to stop making my landlord rich and buy a place."

"You're going to commute?" Stephanie said, her tone suggesting there was no worse fate.

"No, Stephanie," Ivy replied patiently. "I want to stay right here in Manhattan. Most of my work is here. I know I can get more value in Brooklyn, but that's kind of far if I have to get up to Westchester or Northern Jersey. Besides, that would mean another bridge to cross, and I hate bridges."

Jerome nodded. "I'm sure you'll find a nice place. Hey Ray, can we drop you and Yolanda at home?"

"If you're sure it's not out of your way, I'd appreciate it." He turned to Ivy and rested his palms around her upper arms. "Now, I don't want you staying up all night trying to finish cleaning up. The girls and I will be back in the morning, and we'll help you get everything back in shape."

"All right." Ivy watched curiously as Yolanda pulled Ray aside and whispered something to him. He rubbed her shoulder and shook his head with a quick frown, and then they rejoined the others at the door.

Ray called when he and Yolanda got home. "You're not cleaning up, are you?"

"No. You asked me not to, remember? How's Maya?"

"I'm sure she's in dreamland at this hour. I decided it was best to let her sleep at my parents'. I'll go over first thing in the morning and get her."

"I'd say the party was a big success, wouldn't you?"

"Absolutely. Yolanda couldn't be happier. You know, just before we left your place she told me Jerome and Stephanie could drop her off so I could stay the night with you."

"Oh, my."

"I was surprised, too. She said she may only be seventeen years old and was quick to point out she has no firsthand knowledge, which made me feel a whole lot better, but she said she knows the, um, facts of life."

"What did you say?"

"I can't say I wasn't tempted to take her up on her offer, but it wouldn't be right. She's only seventeen, and I'm responsible for her. As much as I wanted to be with you, I couldn't send her home alone for the night. You do understand, don't you?"

"Of course. It's enough for me that you were tempted."

Chapter 22
He's the One

Ivy rose early Saturday morning. Yolanda and Maya were still sleeping soundly in the other bed in her parents' guest room, and when she softly opened the door to the sewing room to look in on Ray, sleeping on an opened twin sofabed, he didn't move.

It had been a long, all-day ride from New York to her parents' home in Asheville. They would only be there two days before heading back on Monday.

It was Ray's idea to make the trip. He knew she wasn't particularly close to her family, but said it would be a good idea to spend a little time with them, since their only previous meeting had been that quick visit at the loft just before her parents relocated.

Ray was so old-fashioned, she thought with affection. Because the two of them had been practically inseparable for the last two months he felt he needed to give her parents a chance to get to know him. Never mind that she was almost thirty-nine years old and had long been in charge of her own life. She found the gesture rather cute.

Now that she'd had a chance to rest she had to admit it felt good to be there. Stephanie and her family visited as soon as her parents got into their house, helping them get settled. They were planning to make another trip next month for Thanksgiving.

"Good morning," Ivy said as she entered the kitchen. Her parents were up and finishing their breakfast.

"Come sit and join us, dear," her mother said. "I made some bacon, eggs, and home fries. You'll have to heat it up, of course."

Ivy poured herself a cup of coffee. "I know it's soon, but I have to ask," she said as she sat down. "What do you think of Ray?"

"I think he's a fine man," her father said.

"And his daughters are darling," her mother added. "But I was talking to Stephanie. She thinks you might be in for a heartbreak if he can't cope with your having money, and I do, too. Maybe you shouldn't expect too much from him. Neither of us would want to see you hurt."

"I think Stephanie would be secretly thrilled if I got my heart broken. She's been rubbing it in my face for years that she's married and has a family and I have nothing but money. What she doesn't want is to see me acquire both."

"We know you two have never been close, but I'm sure Stephanie only wants the best for you, Ivy," her father said.

She made a face. "And so does Otto, I'm sure."

"Did Stephanie tell you he's working with the cable company?" her mother said.

"No. I've avoided the subject since his girlfriend threw him out and he took up residence on Stephanie's couch. She called me, ranting about how it's all my fault they're so crowded, and then she hung up before I could tell her how dumb that was.''

Her parents exchanged glances, and her father said, ''Well, it probably wasn't fair of her to say that. But she and Jerome pointed out to Otto that he's running out of options and that he'll have to make a go of it. He has to take two buses to get to work, but he's been working for four weeks. He just rented a room so he can get to work easier.''

''Well, I'm sure that's made Stephanie happy.''

''You have to consider that she and Jerome don't have all the advantages you have, Ivy,'' her mother said. ''When Otto stayed with you he didn't have to sleep on your living room couch because you have an extra bedroom.''

''I really don't want to get into a conversation about Stephanie and Otto, Mom.''

''That's right, we were talking about Ray,'' her father said. ''I understand you and he have gotten very close lately.''

''I love him, Daddy.''

Again her parents looked at each other.

''But don't worry, I'll be fine,'' she added. ''A lot of people feel the same way you do, that we don't stand a chance because of the gap in our incomes. We almost let their opinions break us up, but never again. I'm glad you like him. That means a lot to me.''

''But you're doing so well,'' her mother said. ''Stephanie tells us you're looking to buy a house in New York.''

''Yes, I am, but that's a business decision. It has nothing to do with Ray.''

''You don't think he'll feel odd—'' her father began.

''I'm sorry to interrupt, Daddy,'' Ivy said, ''but I can't bear to hear any more. You might not be able to understand, but my success doesn't intimidate Ray. It makes him proud. And that makes *me* proud."

That afternoon they drove downtown to have lunch. They strolled down Haywood Avenue to work off their meal, enjoying the crisp autumn mountain air and munching on fresh-baked chocolate chip cookies from a bakery they passed. Yolanda, always fashion conscious, paused in front of a boutique to look at the clothing on display. "Hey, that's a pretty dress," Ray said, pointing to a tea-length beige lace number.

"It's all right," Ivy replied. She was trying to be polite. The dress reminded her of something a bride would wear for an informal ceremony.

"Daddy, can I try on that sweater?" Yolanda asked, her index finger jabbing the glass as she pointed.

"Sure. Let's go in." Ray held the door open for them.

Yolanda found the sweater she admired with the help of a saleswoman, who offered assistance to Ivy after Yolanda went to the fitting room, Maya close behind.

"No, thanks," Ivy replied. "We're just waiting."

"Actually, there was a dress in the window she'd like to see," Ray said. "That long beige dress."

"Oh, yes." The saleswoman quickly gave Ivy a once-over. "You're a size eight?"

"Yes."

"I'll get it for you."

Ivy turned to Ray after the woman left. "You're determined to see me try on that dress, aren't you?"

"I think you'd look beautiful in it."

"But Ray, it looks like a wedding dress."

"Are you saying you don't want to marry me?"

She stared at him, mouth open, not certain if she'd heard correctly. "Marry you?"

He reached into his pocket and pulled out a diamond

ring. "I'm not sure if this is the right size or not. I know this probably isn't the most romantic setting, but when I saw that dress, well . . ."

"I don't know what to say. Ray . . . You don't think it's too soon?"

"I'm going to be forty-three years old in a few weeks. I never expected to get a second chance to spend my life with a woman I love, but I have it, and I don't want to wait. Maybe you don't realize it, but we've become closer than close, Ivy. You're the one."

She rushed into his arms and flung her arms around his neck. "Yes, yes, yes!"

The saleswoman was startled to find them kissing when she brought the dress to Ivy, as were Yolanda and Maya upon their emergence from the fitting room. Ray announced they were getting married. The saleswoman offered good wishes and quickly retreated. Yolanda was thrilled, muffling a scream with her hands and then hugging both her father and Ivy, but Maya was too young to really understand. Ivy's eyes moistened when Yolanda tried to explain, saying "This means you're going to have a mommy again."

"Wait, I almost forgot," Ray said. He took Ivy's left hand and slipped the ring on her finger.

Ivy caught her breath as she waited to see if the simple but lovely round solitaire would fit. When it rested at the bottom of her finger she let her hand hang normally. The ring didn't move.

"Perfect fit!" Yolanda exclaimed, clapping her hands.

"Yes, perfect," Ray said. He raised Ivy's left hand and kissed it.

* * *

"Ray! Is this really necessary?" Ivy said when Ray clamped his palm over her eyes.

"I don't want you to see where we're going."

"But I feel silly."

"Just be glad I didn't blindfold you."

"I can probably tell which way the cab is going. I know he turned north."

"That could mean almost anything."

He was right. Even if they were to turn east or west, she wouldn't be able to discern what street they were on. All she knew from the stop-and-go movement of the taxi was that they were traveling in local traffic.

She heard the cabbie say, "Here we are."

"Where are we?" she asked.

"Wait a second, Ivy. Let me pay the man," Ray said.

To her annoyance he kept her eyes covered while she moved to get out of the cab, his other hand guiding her waist as he instructed her to step down. But logistics wouldn't allow them to both get out at the same time, so he had no choice but to let go.

Ivy opened her eyes to find herself on a residential block of brownstones. The street sign at the corner said Fifty-first Street and Tenth Avenue. They were still in Hell's Kitchen, even if it was one of the better-looking blocks in the large neighborhood. "I don't get it. Where are we?"

He took her hand and led her to an attractive four-story Gothic Revival brownstone. "Home, I hope."

Ivy's breath was heavy with excitement. The house was perfect. The current owners, husband-and-wife interior designers, were retiring to Delaware. Their offices on the ground floor were plenty large enough to house Jubilee. The third and fourth floors boasted plenty of living space, hardwood floors, and a kitchen and baths updated for the twenty-first century in a house built in 1896. A separate two-bedroom apartment took up the entire second floor. It would make a perfect home for Ray's parents.

"I put a deposit on it last week before we went to North Carolina," Ray explained. "I suppose I was being presumptuous, since I didn't know if you would accept my proposal, but if you did I felt it was perfect for us. My parents can live in the apartment downstairs, if that's all right with you."

"I was thinking the same thing."

"Their asking price is reasonable. This isn't exactly the Upper East Side, you know. We'll have to talk about the carrying charges and how much we want to put down. We can always deposit more to keep the mortgage payment lower. I know my folks will pay us something in rent, but it's not like we can ask them for full market rental."

"Of course not; I agree. Are you sure you want to do this, Ray?"

"Yes. I love the city as much as you do. Except for my time in the army I've lived here my whole life. My parents have always lived here. I don't think they'd be very happy if they had to move out to the sticks. I meant it when I said it's time I started investing in something other than stocks and mutual funds. And I'm male enough for it to be important for me to have a financial stake in it as well. I want it to be *our* house, not your house that me, my children, and my parents live in. We probably need to sit down and lay our financial cards on the table so we know where we stand, but I'm sure we can afford this house."

She squeezed his arm. "Let's go talk deal."

Epilogue
Happily Ever After

"I want double time for this," Reneé said, sinking into the couch.

"Oh, stop complaining," Ivy said. "You know we had it all worked out. The movers moved everything from the loft on Friday and everything from Ray's and his parents' apartments on Saturday. Diane helped me set up the office yesterday, and today it's your turn. It's simple."

"Yeah, but today's Sunday."

"I'm giving you two extra days off for your trip to Florida next week, remember?"

"Oh, all right." Reneé looked around at the large room. White paint and fluorescent lighting helped keep it bright, for the only windows were in the front. A series of built-in white cubes would provide a home for some of Jubilee's massive files, as well as office supplies. "This is really going to be gorgeous when we're finished. I know we'll be able to put in a full day's work tomorrow, but do you really think you're giving yourself enough time to plan a grand opening party for the clients?"

"The first Friday in February is plenty of time. This is our slow time, and you know how things pick up after Valentine's Day. I'm kind of anxious to entertain. I didn't have the open house this year because we wanted to get married New Year's Day. Don't worry. By the time you get back the office will be a lot more than merely workable, so you enjoy yourself in Sarasota."

"Venus."

"Venus? I never even heard of that. I thought you were going to Sarasota."

"That's where the airport is, but my friends live in Venus. V-E-N-I-C-E."

"V-E-N . . . Wait a minute. That spells Venice, like in Italy, not Venus, like the planet."

"Venice? Really? My mistake. Anyway, it's supposed to be a real nice area. I think Burt Reynolds had a dinner theater there at one time."

Ivy choked on her bottled water. "That's Jupiter, Reneé. It's on the Atlantic side of Florida, near West Palm Beach. Sarasota is on the Gulf."

She shrugged. "Venus, Jupiter, whatever."

"You know, Reneé, by the time you get to be seventy you're going to be dangerous."

The next afternoon Bethany stopped by the office after an appointment in midtown. Ivy brought her upstairs to the living quarters of the house. "It's going to take some getting used to, living separately from my office, even if it is in the same building."

"How about being married?"

"Oh, I'm used to that already." She knocked on the senior Joneses' apartment door, and they both greeted Mrs. Jones, who opened the door. "Hello, Missy," Ivy said, holding her arms open wide as Maya came running to her.

"Hi, Mommy."

Ivy closed her eyes as she hugged her new daughter. That was one name she never expected to be called, and after three weeks it still gave her a thrill. The first time she took Maya to the Y for her swimming lesson Ivy had to blink to hold back tears when Maya introduced her to the other children as "my new mommy."

She put the child down. "We're going upstairs now, Mrs. Jones," she said to her mother-in-law. "See you later. If I don't see you before you leave, you and Mr. Jones have fun in Atlantic City tomorrow." Maya now stayed with her grandparents only two days a week; the other days the four year old attended preschool.

"Thanks, Ivy."

"Good-bye, Mrs. Jones," Bethany called.

Ivy noted the smile on her mother-in-law's face as she said good-bye to them and closed the door. Even Ray had said he'd never seen his mother happier. Ivy sympathized with Mrs. Jones for the pain she suffered in her life; the loss of her little boy, the loss of her daughter-in-law, and the hard work she and her husband had been forced to do in their later years to supplement their retirement income. Ivy had feared Mrs. Jones's dislike of her might cause problems between her and Ray—after all, she was his mother—but the older woman's attitude softened the previous summer. They now enjoyed a warm relationship and had even done their holiday shopping together.

"I forgot to tell you, Bethany"—Ivy said as they climbed the stairs behind Maya—"we got our wedding video today."

"Oh, I want to see it!"

Ivy unlocked the door to their duplex apartment and

pushed it open. The late afternoon sun flooded the living room. She popped the tape into the VCR and hit the play button.

Within seconds the television screen changed to an opening title saying 'Ivy Smith and Ray Jones, January first," followed by the year. The screen lightened to scan their family and close friends socializing at the Club Room of the Water Club, waiting for the ceremony to begin. Ivy smiled as her loved ones were caught by the lens. Funny how people's personalities could come across when they didn't realize they were being watched, or in this case, filmed. Her parents and Ray's looked happy. Stephanie was fingering the oak mantel, a wistful look on her face. A bored Otto was checking his watch. Bethany and Mitch gazed at each other with the giddy look of a couple in love ... or maybe they were just happy because Casey and Elgin wouldn't be back from Puerto Rico, where they had spent the holidays, until the next day. Rodney looked laid-back, while Cathy appeared dejected, as if she were thinking she would never be able to top this. Glenda and Pete Arnold had the look of contented young—or perhaps young middle-aged—marrieds, as did Ruben and Elba Inocencio. Ivy's staffers John and Randy both concentrated on their surroundings with the sharp eyes of top-notch event planners, much to the annoyance of John's wife, who tugged at his sleeve and could be seen mouthing the words, "Will you stop?" Randy's date had apparently accepted the peril of attending a function with a professional planner and left his side to talk with Diane and Reneé. Ivy wished she knew what they were talking about, for Reneé had a bewildered look on her face. Sometimes Ivy thought her book keeper didn't understand much of the world beyond numbers.

"I didn't understand something, Ivy," Bethany said.

"What did Reneé mean when she yelled out, 'Cut the mustard!' when you and Ray were cutting your cake?"

Ivy chuckled. "She's always saying 'cut the cake,' when she means to say 'cut the mustard,' so this time she just reversed it." She smiled dreamily as she watched herself enter the room behind Maya and Yolanda. She had chosen to make her entrance alone rather than on her father's arm. Bethany, who had served as maid of honor, didn't take her place by the altar opposite Rodney, the best man, until just before the ceremony began.

Ivy fast forwarded through the ceremony, stopping when she got to the point where guests were offering congratulations. She would never forget her parents telling her how happy they were for her, and her father's acknowledging that now she truly had everything.

Yolanda arrived home just as the tape was ending with a shot of Ivy and Ray standing on the outdoor terrace, she in the lace dress he had chosen for her in North Carolina and he in his tux, both of them trying not to shiver in the January cold. At the photographer's instructions they first faced each other, holding hands, then embraced with their backs to the camera against the backdrop of the East Side skyline before the screen faded to black with the titles, "And they lived happily ever after."

"Hi, Ivy," Yolanda said. Ivy had suggested her older daughter, who was old enough to retain memories of her mother, drop the more formal title of "Miss" and simply call her Ivy. She felt secure that Yolanda's respect for her would remain, even with them being on a first-name basis. "Kelly's here. We're going to study together. Is that okay?"

"Sure. Check on Maya when you go up, will you? Hello, Kelly."

"Hi, Mrs. Jones."

The two girls proceeded to ungracefully climb the

gently curved staircase to the bedroom that Yolanda now had all to herself.

Ivy grimaced. "They sound like a herd of wild horses." She turned to Bethany and was surprised to see her friend wiping her eyes. "Hey, what's wrong? Are you crying?"

"Oh, I'm all right. I'm just so happy for you, Ivy. I mean, just a year ago you were feeling down about not having anyone to bring to your reunion, and now you and Ray have had this wonderful whirlwind romance, you're married now, you've got this beautiful house, you're a mother, with your kids' friends calling you 'Mrs. Jones' . . . it just doesn't get any better."

"We were very lucky to find this house. Since we're not quite on the Upper West Side, Ray jokes that he's moved from Hell's Kitchen to Hell's Living Room. And remember that when it comes to work I'm still 'Ms. Smith.' Changing my name for business will only confuse my clients. Maybe one day you and Mitch will take this same step. You've certainly got those kids of his under control. If you can deal with them you won't have any other serious problems."

"Maybe. We definitely won't move as quickly as you guys did, though. It would be awfully complicated."

"You're thinking of your respective holdings. Ray and I spent an entire weekend laying out what we have and making a plan. I guess you'd insist Mitch sign a prenup."

"Hell, yeah," Bethany said, all sentiment gone now that they were talking about money. "I'm worth twenty million dollars. Some things simply have to be spelled out, love or no love."

"Just make sure you stay together. It's nice for Ray and I to have another couple whose company we both enjoy to go out with. Going anyplace with Rodney and Cathy Townsend is unbearable. Rodney's all right, but all Cathy talks about is how nice it must be to be able to afford to go to such nice places every week and how lucky we are. I didn't win a lottery, and neither did Ray. Luck has nothing to do with it."

"Well, I wouldn't dream of breaking up with Mitch and depriving you and Ray of dinner partners." She glanced at her watch. "Oh my, it's after four. I'd better be going so you can start dinner. Ray will be home soon, won't he?"

"Not until six. I'll have dinner ready by then. After we eat we'll go down to the office and do a little work. Ray's been working on the Jubilee Web site. He said it would make it easier if clients could see possible sites for their functions in the comfort of their homes and offices, so he's scanning photographs."

"Sounds like he's really getting involved in the business."

"I think he should. It would be awful if anything were to happen to me and he didn't know anything about what I left him."

Bethany slipped into her coat. "I've got to get to the store. They're expecting snow tonight, you know."

"Yes, I heard."

After Bethany left Ivy sat at the baby grand piano she and Ray purchased for the living room and tapped out a tune with one finger. Then she wandered over to one of the three windows. The strong afternoon sunlight was gone now, the sky darkening with sunset. Ivy conceded she was probably the only adult New Yorker hoping for snow. She and Ray liked to watch in the evenings as the hansom cabs passed on their way to their stables after a long day in Central Park. The clickety-clop of their hooves on the pavement would be even more picturesque if there were snow on the ground, like an old Currier and Ives imprint.

Bethany was right: Life didn't get any better. Not only was Ivy married to a man she loved, she had a four year old she would raise, a teenager who valued her opinion, and a friendly relationship with her in-laws. It was a good time for other people in her life as well. Her own parents were happy in their retirement, her brother had managed to hold a job for several months, and Bethany and Mitch's romance was thriving.

And Stephanie, well, if she could stop being so jealous all the time, maybe she'd realize how blessed she was.

Ivy had finished making dinner and was sitting in the living room watching the news when she heard Ray's key in the lock. She jumped up to meet him. The sight of his handsome face smiling at her still took her breath away.

"Hi," he said, pulling her into his arms to kiss her hello. "My name's Jones."

"That's funny," she replied. "So's mine."

About the Author

Bettye Griffin is a native of Yonkers, New York, and presently lives in Jacksonville, Florida, with her husband. When not writing, Bettye works as a freelance medical transcriptionist. *Closer Than Close* is her sixth Arabesque title, the others being *At Long Last Love, A Love of Her Own, Love Affair, Prelude to a Kiss,* and *From This Day Forward.*

P.O. Box 20354
Jacksonville, Florida 32225-0354

bundie@directvinternet.com